The Ghost Circus

Diandra Archer

The Ghost Circus

ISBN 978-1-947814-22-6

DISCLAIMER:

This book is a work of fiction. And while some real locations, historical events, company names, and easily recognizable public figures have been used, the story is strictly the product of the authors' imaginations. Beyond that, any names and/or resemblance to actual persons, living or dead—especially dead—is purely coincidental.

The only thing worse than squandering your life because you did not realize how quickly it would pass, is to have been warned and then squander it anyway.

Consider yourself warned.

Dedicated to
The Duffer Brothers

Prologue

Ten days before Christmas, 1939, Ulrich Schröder put his plan into action. He would poison his wife, Onyx, so he could be with his lover, Claudia Spilatro. It took a lot more poison and a lot longer than he imagined it would.

Finally, on Christmas morning, Ulrich went to check on Onyx and found her motionless. He touched her skin and it felt cold and lifeless. He poked her, and there was no response. He was pretty sure she was dead.

Exhausted from the ordeal, Ulrich made his way to the spare bedroom and climbed under the covers. He'd check on his wife one last time to make sure she was truly dead, then call the authorities to report the horrible news.

Twelve hours later, Ulrich woke in complete darkness, having slept the entire day. He got dressed and crept down the hall in his bare feet, wondering why he was trying so hard to be quiet. Onyx was dead, it didn't matter.

Ulrich opened the door to Onyx's room. It was dark. The candle he left burning was now a dry pool of wax. He opened the door further, allowing slivers of light to enter from the hallway behind him.

"Onyx?" Ulrich whispered.

No response.

He approached the edge of the bed. It appeared Onyx was on her side, covers pulled up over her head, unmoving.

"Onyx, darling?" Ulrich said. Still no response.

Ulrich reached out, pushing her slightly. Nothing.

A slight smile formed on Ulrich's lips, and he let out a sigh of relief. It had finally happened.

Onyx was gone.

"Merry Christmas, Ulrich," Onyx said from behind him. Ulrich started to turn, but before he could, Onyx slammed a metal oil can into the back of his head.

Ulrich staggered forward and turned around just in time to see the second blow coming his way. He tried to lift his arms but wasn't fast enough—the can struck the left side of his face. He fell backward onto the bed, then tried to lift himself into an upright position, reaching his hand toward Onyx in a state of bewilderment.

Onyx swung the can toward him for a third and final time. The sharp edge caught Ulrich on the temple, right above his left eye, knocking him back with such force that it ripped a portion of the German's face from his skull.

Onyx waited for Ulrich to get up again.

He didn't.

Onyx went to the bathroom down the hall and retrieved a brass canister she'd filled with kerosene earlier in the day while Ulrich was sleeping and carried it to the bedroom.

Onyx felt the best way to cover her tracks was to set fire to the cottage. After all, Ulrich was known to have one last cigarette in bed before turning in for the night. She lifted the heavy can, tipped it over, and poured a liberal amount of the thick black liquid directly onto Ulrich. Then, for good measure, she poured the balance of the kerosene on the wooden floor around the bed.

Onyx grabbed Ulrich's cigarettes and a box of matches from the nightstand. She removed a cigarette from the pack, put it in her mouth, and lit it. She inhaled, watching the tip glow red, and blew a long stream of smoke in the air. Then she tossed the cigarette on the bed, which burst into flames.

To Onyx's shock and horror, Ulrich's eyes snapped open, and he sat upright. Engulfed in flames, Ulrich rose from the bed and stumbled across the room, collapsing in her arms.

Onyx felt a searing heat on the right side of her face and down her right arm and pushed him away. Ulrich released an ear-piercing scream and stumbled toward the door and collapsed again.

Onyx slapped at the flames on her arm and face but only made it worse. She needed to get out of the house. If she didn't, perhaps Ulrich would have succeeded in killing her after all.

*   *   *

The following morning, Onyx woke in immense pain, her right arm bandaged from her shoulder to the tips of her fingers. An IV tube ran from her other arm to a bag filled with saline solution hanging from a metal rod near the bed. The right side of her face was covered in bandages as well.

Even so, Onyx was alert enough to hear every word two men were saying in the hallway outside her hospital room door.

The first of the two was Sheriff "Hell" Daniels. The second man was the district attorney, and it was clear what they were talking about. They were talking about her. They had come to the only conclusion they could: Onyx had murdered her husband.

For the next two days, Onyx drifted in and out of consciousness. By the third day, she'd gotten her wits about her, and she knew what she needed to do. She needed to escape.

The biggest challenge Onyx faced was getting past the nurses who'd been assigned to watch her around the clock, working in eight-hour shifts. Fortunately, the nurses pretty much ignored her. Which was what Onyx was counting on.

Onyx was being given a plethora of pills for a variety of purposes; pills to make her sleep and pills to relieve her pain. The problem was, that she didn't know which pill was which, so she decided to skip them altogether, shoving the pills deep into a mound of untouched mashed potatoes.

On the third evening, the night nurse brought Onyx her dinner as usual and returned for the tray an hour later. Five minutes later, Onyx made her move. No one expected a severely burned and highly medicated woman to attempt an escape.

After slinking her way down a corridor, she hurried through the main door of the hospital and soon found herself walking barefoot through the woods in a complete state of utter delirium. Onyx followed the sound of the ocean waves to keep herself heading west and used the light from the full moon to guide the way.

How far could it be from the hospital to the lighthouse? Onyx wondered. She had no idea. Her mind was incapable of producing answers.

Onyx could see her breath in the night air as she stumbled forward and realized that in her desperation to get back to the lighthouse, she'd failed to consider how cold it was outside. She'd also forgotten to put on her shoes.

Eventually—what must have been hours—Onyx emerged from the woods and stopped dead in her tracks when she saw police standing guard at the lighthouse door. Her eyes moved to the left and saw the half-burned-out cottage she and Ulrich had lived in was being guarded as well. With nowhere else to go, Onyx staggered back into the woods. Exhausted and deflated, she lowered herself to the ground and collapsed against a tall pine.

From where she was sitting, Onyx could see out over the cove, the full moon hanging in the sky like a giant white Christmas ornament. She was tired, racked with pain, and delirious from the lack of energy. Then Onyx heard the howling of wolves, somewhere off in the distance.

It wasn't long for the first wolf to arrive, followed by a second wolf moments later. They didn't attack, just stood there, eying Onyx on the ground, propped up against the base of the tree. Maybe they would decide to leave her alone, Onyx thought.

Moments later, three more wolves emerged from the woods. Five wolves in all, now. They weren't leaving her alone. They were waiting for the rest of the pack to arrive.

Minutes after that, it was over.

Once the wolves had completed their mission, any pain Onyx had been in, was gone. All that remained now was an indescribable sense of lightness and calm as Onyx found herself floating through the air—an observer in the dark of night, detached—watching as the wolves below had their way with what was left of her earthly body.

Then darkness.

The darkness was a black *so* black it felt as if everything in the universe had folded in upon itself, leaving Onyx floating in a void where neither space nor time existed.

"You don't have to go," said a voice from the blackness. Onyx knew immediately it was not the voice of God. It was her mother.

"Momma?" Onyx said.

"You do not have to go," her mother repeated. "The choice is yours, Onyx. You can decide to stay if you wish."

Onyx looked down at the wolves who were busy in their voracious feast and suddenly they stopped as if they could sense her thoughts. One by one, the wolves slowly backed away, then turned and ran, disappearing into the pines.

It was only Onyx now, standing over what remained of her earthly body, her limbs torn and scattered on the blood-soaked ground. And then the reality of the situation finally hit her. Her mother hadn't said she could remain alive, only that she could stay.

Onyx had managed to stay in the living plane, but she wasn't alive. She was dead.

She was a ghost.

Self-Portrait, 1941
Pencil on Paper

Chapter One

Walbruga Oesterreich scribbled furiously in the large black ledger on the center of the desk, wishing the numbers were different—not just different, but bigger. This was not how retirement was supposed to be. She'd died peacefully in her sleep in 1961. Fifteen years later, she started the circus, a decision she was coming to regret.

To calm her nerves, she lit a cigarette and took a long drag, then blew a billowing cloud of blue smoke that filled the entire circus trailer. The cigarettes were expensive, and even though the circus was struggling financially, she had no intention of smoking anything else. She'd been smoking Sorbaines since the 1930s after discovering them on a trip to Europe.

The taste of the tobacco wasn't important anymore, it was the message they sent. They were black with gold-tipped filters that looked elegant in her hand and told others she was powerful, sophisticated, and not to be trifled with. She also wore a long black dress, even in the most casual of situations, with a matching black hat. No one had ever seen her in anything else.

She insisted every member of the circus call her by her nickname, Dolly. Dolly was short, easy to pronounce, and suggested she was friendly and approachable. She was neither. Dolly barked at people incessantly and swore up a storm when angered. Everyone was scared of her. She was a woman in a man's world with a circus to run, and she needed every edge she could get.

A knock on the trailer door snapped Dolly out of her trance, and she reluctantly stubbed her cigarette out. "Come," she barked.

The door to the trailer swung open and Dolly saw Antoinette standing there, in her full trapeze costume. Next to her stood Willy Burks, who was unquestionably one of the most attractive men Dolly had ever laid eyes on—so profoundly and breathtakingly handsome that women's hearts would flutter at the very sight of him. This was one of the good things about being dead since ghosts always came back as flawless, perfect versions of themselves.

The irony was that when he was alive, Willy had been a circus sideshow star, billed as *The Man with Three Eyes and Two Noses*. He'd been born with frontonasal dysplasia, a rare condition where the two halves of his face failed to fuse before childbirth. The result was a face that featured a deep-cleft upper lip, garishly open palate, and a distractingly large space between the two halves of his face where his nose should have been.

Seven years after Willy Burks died, he found himself wandering down a dirt road in rural North Carolina with no idea how he'd gotten there. Fortunately for him, Dolly's circus just happened to be passing by. Some people believed Willy appeared where and when he did because he was drawn to the circus. It might well have been. No one knew for sure how the ghost thing worked since everyone's experience was different.

"Whatever it is, it'd better be important," Dolly snapped. "I'm in the middle of doing the books."

"It is," Antoinette said.

"The Indian dropped her again," Willy offered.

"That's right!" Antoinette said, almost shouting.

"Dolly can hear you just fine," Willy said. "Just tell her what happened."

"Well, I think we just did," Antoinette said.

"Are you injured?" Dolly asked, knowing full well the trapeze artist wasn't. Ghosts could not be injured, not seriously at least. And whatever damage did occur healed itself in seconds. "You look no worse for wear to me."

"That's not the point!" Antoinette said, raising her voice again. "What does it say about me if this happens in a live show?

I was a Flying Concello, for Christ's sake. Am I the only professional around here who cares about their reputation?"

"Toni has a point," Willy said. "This is your circus, Dolly, it does have your name on it."

The Indian in question was Joseph Brandt, a full-blooded Mohawk who went by the nickname Mohawk Joe. Admittedly, the Mohawk wasn't an experienced trapeze artist. He *had* worked as a day laborer during the construction of the Empire State Building back in 1930, often suspended a thousand feet up in the air, held by nothing but a leather harness. This did not make him qualified to be Antoinette's trapeze partner, of course, but trapeze artists were hard to come by. Dead or alive.

"I'll see what I can do," Dolly said.

* * *

The idea that two of her employees had just questioned Dolly's ability to protect the reputation of the circus riled her up more than it should have. Still, she wished she could bring herself to close the damn thing down. What kept her going was a sense of obligation she had to the members of the circus community. What would they do if she abandoned them? Where would they go? They were like family.

The truth was that Dolly didn't care about anyone but herself. She wanted to be needed—*needed to be needed*—especially when it came to men.

As a young woman, she attracted the attention of wealthy factory owner, Fred Oesterreich. Fred made his fortune manufacturing women's clothing, which is where Dolly first became aware of the importance image played in the world. And, as with clothes, the image she and Fred presented to the world was that of the perfect marriage. Carefully hidden behind the walls of their splendid home, however, Fred drank heavily and became physically abusive.

The abuse didn't bother Dolly as much as the long periods where Fred simply ignored her. So, she solved the problem in the only way she knew—by having an affair. And not just any affair. It was with a handsome 17-year-old named Otto Sanhuber, who worked as a sewing machine repairman in her husband's factory.

Otto was taller than Fred, thinner than Fred, and twice as handsome as Fred on Fred's best day. But how to get him alone? Dolly pretended to have a problem with her sewing machine and asked if Otto could come to take a look.

Dolly wasted no time seducing him, greeting him at the door in a sexy silk robe and fishnet stockings. Within weeks, Otto had been transformed from a sewing machine repairman to Dolly's personal sex slave.

One day, Dolly made an odd proposal. She suggested Otto move into the attic of the house. This way, she could have him anytime she wanted day or night, without anyone knowing. Otto, totally smitten with the German woman, readily agreed. Otto's secret desire was to quit his job and write pulp fiction novels. He could hide upstairs in their secret love nest and write, with Dolly bringing him meals and asking for sexual favors anytime she wished.

"As long as you're quiet, Fred will never know," Dolly insisted. She was right.

The arrangement was perfect until Dolly decided she no longer wanted to fulfill her role as a housewife. "What are you saying?" Otto asked when Dolly informed him about the new household duties.

"I'm saying this is the list of household chores I expect you to do in exchange for room and board," Dolly explained.

Otto looked at the list and laughed. "You can't be serious." She was. From that moment on it was Otto's job to cook, clean, wash the dishes, and make the beds once Fred had left for work.

Oh, and to screw her whenever she wanted him to. For whatever reason, Otto agreed.

One evening, Dolly and Fred got into a massive argument, so loud that Otto could hear the entire thing from his attic hideaway. Fearing that Fred was going to kill Dolly in a fit of rage, Otto raced downstairs and put three bullets into Fred's chest with the gun she'd hidden in the attic for such an occasion.

"Oh, Jesus. Oh, God, what did I do," Otto stammered. "Oh God..."

Dolly grabbed Otto by the shoulders and said, "There was a break-in, someone tried to rob the house, that's the story we're going to tell, understand?"

"But... but... how do we explain my being here?" Otto asked, still in shock.

"We don't," Dolly said. "You weren't here at all, Otto. The *robbers* broke in and killed Fred."

"They might think you did it," Otto said.

"Well, what if you lock me in the closet?"

It was genius.

"Grab Fred's watch, and the money from his pocketbook," Dolly directed. "It has to look like a real robbery."

Otto removed the diamond-encrusted watch from Fred's wrist, locked Dolly in the hall closet, then scurried up the stairs to his attic hideaway. And it worked, at least for a time.

A few years passed with the police unable to tie Dolly to the murder. Eventually, it came to light that Dolly still had Fred's watch, and the game was up. Dolly was arrested and put in jail, and Otto fled the country. The trial ended in a hung jury. Dolly found a new lover, this time allowing him to live downstairs with her like a normal couple.

More than any of the men she'd been with, Dolly missed Otto most. He was young. He was vibrant. Full of life. At least until she got her hooks in him. Until she owned him. The truth was that Dolly didn't want to be wanted by a man as much as she wanted to own one. It had been so long since she had her thumb on a man.

Now, Dolly had her sights on Willy Burks.

Dolly lit her third Sorbaines in less than twenty minutes and smoked it in the darkness of the circus trailer. Dying of cancer was off the table, so why not? After she'd smoked it down to the filter, she crushed it out in the ashtray and stood up.

There was nothing she could do about the perilous financial situation the circus was in for the rest of the night, nor was there anything she could do about Antoinette's inept Mohawk Indian trapeze partner.

Dolly looked down and examined her hand, which looked gray in the dim light of the trailer. *Too gray.* She walked to the trailer door and looked out. The sun was low, flashing a last line of crimson across the Northern California sky. In another hour it would be dark, and she could head off to the city.

If Dolly's plan to seduce Willy Burks was to be successful, she'd need to care more about her looks. Fortunately, Eureka was a big enough city to find what she was looking for.

Chapter Two

Before autism was described as a condition, there was a piano prodigy named "Blind Tom" Wiggins. Blind Tom's first public performance took place during the Civil War, at the age of three, and his abilities were extraordinary. And a bit eccentric.

After hearing a song, Tom would walk around, stand on one foot, pull at his hair, bang his head against the wall—and then play the song exactly as written. Any song, by any composer, from any era. Mozart. Beethoven. Didn't matter, Tom could play it.

Skeptics challenged Tom to listen to a new composition, something no one had ever heard before, which could not *possibly* have been practiced in advance. Not only would he immediately play the song perfectly, note for note, but he could also play with his hands behind his back and crossed one over the other.

150 years later, another autistic savant would come along. His name was Newt Drystad.

The middle child in a middle-class family, Newt suffered from SPMD—Selective Paralytic Mutism Disorder—a rare condition that placed the young boy in periodic states of suspended animation, where he would not speak or move unless led by the hand. His condition was so rare that doctors gave it its name—Drystad's Daiquiri—likening Newt's "cocktail" of conditions to the popular frozen drink.

Early on, when Newt slipped into one of his frozen states, he could be stimulated by mathematical games and puzzles. Like the day Newt's father came home from the university with a Rubik's Cube. "Look at this, Newt. It's a game."

As was often the case, Newt glanced up but was otherwise non-responsive. Newt's father waved the colored cube in front of Newt, then gave it several twists before placing it in his son's hand. "Can you get it back to where it started?"

Immediately, Newt began twisting the cube—*twist, twist, twist, twist, twist, twist, twist, twist, twist, twist, twist, twist*—then let it drop to the floor, each side the same solid color again.

Once again, Newt's father mixed up the cube and handed it back to his son. This time, however, he glanced at his watch. The standard-size Rubik's Cube had forty-three quintillion possible combinations. The current world record for solving the puzzle was one minute, nineteen seconds. Sixteen seconds later, Newt dropped the cube to the floor. He was five years old at the time.

For whatever reason, a year later Newt stopped communicating altogether. For the next two years, nothing anyone tried could reach him. The doctors ran out of ideas. The family feared their young son was lost to them forever.

Then, one day, Newt's father decided to go to a Saturday matinee called, *The January Man*. "Do you think it's a good idea to take an eight-year-old to an R-rated movie about serial killers?" Newt's mother asked.

"I don't think it matters," Newt's father said. "For all we know, Newt doesn't even know he's in a theater, let alone what the movie is about." But he was wrong. In the middle of the movie, Newt turned to his father and announced, "All the dates are prime numbers."

It was the first time Newt had spoken in almost three years. "What?" his father stammered in shocked disbelief.

Newt put his finger to his lips. "Shush, Dad, keep watching."

Moments later, the FBI agent on-screen explained that the victims were all killed on dates with prime numbers. Newt tapped his father on the shoulder and whispered, "He doesn't know about the buildings yet."

"The buildings? What buildings?" Newt's father managed.

"Each building marks a position on a map, a constellation," Newt whispered. "Each murder is like a star in the sky, like part of a constellation."

Again, Newt was right. The buildings where the victims were murdered formed the constellation Virgo when connected on the map.

Unfortunately, when the movie was over, so was the conversation; Newt didn't speak another word once the closing credits began rolling.

On the way home, Newt's father stopped at a video store and rented every serial killer movie they had. When he got home, he gathered the entire family in the living room and inserted *Manhunter* into the Betamax player.

Newt's mother was not amused. "What are you doing? We can't watch this with the girls in the room."

"It's okay. Just watch."

Ten minutes into the film, Newt started talking and continued talking non-stop for the next two hours, while his sisters danced around the living room and his parents held each other and wept.

For reasons beyond anyone's understanding, Newt Drystad was fascinated with serial killers, and this had somehow unlocked his mind and his body. Why? How? The Drystads didn't know. All they knew was they'd found a way to reach their son.

*   *   *

To his parent's delight, Newt Drystad's fascination with serial killers did not fade, it only increased. Which kept him active, alert, and quite involved with various killings being reported by the media. In every case, Newt developed a profile of who the police should be searching for.

Concerned that authorities weren't making fast enough progress, Newt began writing letters to the Federal Bureau of Investigation. One of those letters not only changed Newt's life but also altered the FBI's Violent Criminal Apprehension Program. Known as ViCAP, for short, the program had been specifically created to link serial homicides with killer profiles and behavior patterns.

Newt's letter read:

Dear FBI:

I have been following The Dallas Ripper case and believe your agents are on the wrong track. Based on currently available information, it is clear that:

1) The killer is a male with an overprotective mother, perhaps a schoolteacher or nurse, probably from the Amarillo area.

2) He killed small animals, but probably kept them. Have your agents cross-reference all taxidermy schools in a 500-mile radius of the last killing.

3) You should also check arrest reports between 1945–1955, as he most likely was arrested for petty crimes as a teen (maybe even assault).

4) The killer is not stupid like the papers think. Probably the opposite, pre-med perhaps? Check for dropouts at medical schools in Texas and Oklahoma, 1948-1955. In any case, he will have falsified a college/medical degree to impress people.

5) Married, divorced; twice possibly.

6) Gunshots to back of head suggest inability to look victims in the eye due to low self-esteem.

Please reply. I am available to assist.

Sincerely,

Newton Drystad, Tusseyville, PA 16828

P.S. I believe the label "Dallas Ripper" misses the point. The killer isn't a "ripper" he's a collector. I'm thinking he takes their eyes.

P.P.S. Please don't let the fact that I am 10 years old be an issue. I'm sure I am right.

As it so happened, the FBI had just arrested Charles Frederick Albright for the murder of a prostitute. They also believed the man had killed two other women before that. In all three cases, the killer had removed the victim's eyes and taken them—a fact that had *not* been released to the media.

Newt had been correct on almost every detail—right down to the falsified medical degree the FBI found hanging on Albright's apartment wall.

The FBI thought someone was playing a joke. But when they checked, they found the letter had been postmarked ten days before they had even identified the suspect.

Over the next week, the FBI pulled every letter they'd ever received from the ten-year-old and were shocked to find that in 71% of the cases, Newt's profiles were right on point. What's more, he'd done it only with the information available to the public.

The next thing Newt knew, he was invited to visit Langley, Virginia, by Special Agent Pipi Esperanza, the individual who had been assigned to review and dispose of letters from "helpful citizens" (aka, nut jobs) claiming to have information. Newt may have been a nut job, per se, but he wasn't a nut.

In one fell swoop, Newt Drystad became the youngest employee in the history of the bureau, and Pipi Esperanza was on the fast track to becoming its first female director.

Chapter Three

Crimson Cove was a sleepy little tourist town nestled a mile from a set of cliffs that dropped straight down to the ocean below. With a population of 2,900 in the winter, the town grew exponentially larger during the warm months of summer. To the locals, the town was a quiet hideaway from the hustle and bustle of urban Portland, one-hundred miles to the east. To others, it was known as the home of Onyx Webb, a 120-year-old ghost who lived in a lighthouse and—as legend had it—killed people by sucking the life energy from them. Which was exactly the way Abigale Dietz wanted it.

Most others did not.

The twenty-two members of the Crimson Cove Merchant's Association prided themselves on the cove's reputation as a clean and safe place to raise a family, despite the number of unexplained deaths in the area. And if Onyx Webb really *did* exist and *was* responsible for the killings, everyone turned a blind eye since the only people dying were homeless transients, the elderly with terminal illnesses, and those who were otherwise evil and dangerous.

But Abigale thought the deaths, as well as the urban legend surrounding Onyx Webb, was something that should be capitalized on.

"The town needs a killer moniker—oh, that's funny, did I say killer?" Abigale cackled. It was her turn to present ideas to the members of the merchants association, who sat gathered together in the first few rows of the Dietz theater.

"A moniker? What in the hell are you talking about?" the owner of the town's only hardware store asked.

"She means a marketing tagline," Abigale's twin brother, Aaron, interjected. "You know, like *What Happens in Vegas*

Stays in Vegas, or *New York, New York: The City that Never Sleeps.*"

"What's wrong with the slogan we have now?" the realtor asked.

"Seriously? You think, *Where the Ocean Meets the Forest* is attracting anyone to the cove?" Abigale shot back. "No, we need something with punch, something sexy, something like—"

"Crimson Cove: The Ghost Capital of the Pacific Northwest," Aaron said, cutting Abigale off mid-sentence. The look on Abigale's face displayed her annoyance—not because of the slogan, but because she wanted to be the one who introduced it and take the credit.

A murmur of displeasure rose from the group. Two of the merchants stood up. "The idea of turning Crimson Cove into some *Ripley's Believe It or Not!* freakshow is out of the question," said the bakery owner as she gathered her things and walked out.

"I say we take a vote," Abigale said. "All in favor?" Abigale and Aaron both raised their hands. The only merchant to join them was the old woman who ran the psychic and tarot card reading business on the city's main drag. The measure was voted down 17-3. Abigale never even had the opportunity to show the artist's rendition of the statue of Onyx Webb she hoped to erect on Main Street.

This isn't over, Abigale thought as the room emptied. Not by a long shot. There was no way she would let the Merchant's Association kill her idea of turning Crimson Cove into a tourist destination. She needed another way, another angle. But what?

A few days later Abigale had an idea, a way to kill two birds with one stone. She would go on TV. If she could get the public excited about her plan, then the Merchant's Association would have to go along.

*   *   *

Abigale shifted nervously in her chair as Channel 9's TV show host, Sherice Browne, put on a broad smile, looked into the camera, and launched the segment. "So, what do you do when a ghost shows up at your house? Well, most people hope it's Halloween! But our next guest, Abigale Dietz, owner of the Dietz Theater in Crimson Cove, wants ghosts to show up *every day of the year.*"

It was not the start Abigale had hoped for.

"Laugh if you want, Sherice, but in my neck of the woods we've learned to take ghosts quite seriously," Abigale began.

"Come on, Abigale, just between us girls," Sherice said placing her hand on Abigale's shoulder for effect, "This plan of yours is designed to boost tourism, right?"

"Well, it would be nice if tourists included Crimson Cove in their travel plans, but the main reason for the statue is to honor Onyx Webb."

"Ah, yes, let's talk about this ever-elusive ghost of yours. If I've got the story right, she's some kind of vampire?"

"A vampire? No, Onyx Webb is a *ghost*," Abigale said firmly. The last thing she wanted was to compete with Forks, Washington, 300 miles to the north, famous as the setting for the *Twilight* series. Forks owned vampires. Abigale wanted to own *ghosts*.

Suddenly, Sherice threw Abigale a curve she had not expected. "Well, no one knows more than our next guests, Paul and Ingrid Luckner, considered to be two of the world's foremost experts on ghosts. Welcome!"

An elderly man and woman appeared on one of the studio's TV monitors. "Thank you, Sherice," Paul said. "Yes, great to be here," Ingrid added.

"If my production notes are correct, your late son, Dane, was killed being hit by a train?" Sherice said with faux sympathy.

"Yes, that's correct," Ingrid said, as both she and her husband looked down as if the memory was causing them great pain.

Oh, they're *good,* Abigale thought.

"Now, you say you talk to Dane from the beyond, correct?"

The Luckners looked up at the camera and their faces brightened. "Yes," Paul said.

"How often do you talk?" Sherice prompted.

"Virtually every day," Ingrid said.

Abigale felt the rage welling up inside her. She was supposed to be the center of attention, but now she was being upstaged.

"Is it possible to have Dane join us?" Sherice asked.

"No," Ingrid said. "Dane prefers to remain on the other side."

"But some ghosts *do* come over to *this* side, right?"

"To the living plane, yes," Paul said.

"Tell us how it works for ghosts," Sherice said.

The segment was mesmerizing. Abigale forgot how pissed off she was and became absorbed by what the Luckners were saying. Even if it was bullshit, it was helping her cause to promote ghosts as real.

"When a person dies, they enter a ghost state," Paul began. "They can enter and leave the living plane, using mirrors as portals."

"But when they arrive, they have minimal energy and appear transparent, in a vapor state," Ingrid added.

"When you talk to your son, do you see him or hear him?" Sherice asked.

"Mostly we hear him," Paul said, "but he does appear to us in his ghostly form now and then."

"This is a little awkward, and I apologize for asking, but when you see him, how does he look?" Sherice asked. "Being hit by a train, I think our viewers may be wondering if—"

"When ghosts enter the living plane, they appear as the most perfect version of themselves at the time of passing," Ingrid said. "Scars, age lines, crows-feet, and other skin blemishes disappear. Even severed limbs reappear. They have extraordinary hearing, perfect eyesight, even in the dark, and immune to all forms of disease and illness."

"Wow, no colds, no glasses, and no wrinkles! Almost makes me want to get hit by a train myself," Sherice said. If the Luckners were offended, they didn't show it.

"My other guest here in the studio claims ghosts suck the life out of people," Sherice said. "This is a story made up to scare people, right?"

Paul Luckner shook his head. "No, your guest is quite correct. To stay in the living plane, ghosts must take energy from the living. The more energy they take, the more alive they appear, and the longer they can stay."

"I think I speak for most of our viewers when I say the idea ghosts are running around killing people is nonsense," Sherice declared.

"An ostrich can look up to see what's around it, or hide its head in the sand," Ingrid said. "But the danger exists either way. You can choose to ignore reality, but you can't ignore the *consequences*."

Oh, my God! Abigale thought. Things were working out better than she could have hoped.

"We've only got a minute left," Sherice prompted. "Anything else you think our viewers might find interesting about ghosts?"

"You want to see ghosts, come to Crimson Cove!" Abigale interjected. Sherice ignored her and nodded to the Luckners to continue.

"Yes," Ingrid said. "Ghosts do not feel physical pain, but they do feel emotional pain. They can't *feel* joy and happiness—they only *remember* it. But they *do* feel emotions of regret, anger, despair, and loss."

"And they don't eat or drink," Paul added. "Swallowing food and liquids can make them quite ill. And they never sleep."

"Fascinating!" Sherice said. "Now, if someone comes in contact with an entity they suspect may be a ghost, is there a way to tell?"

"They're cold to the touch," Paul said. "No matter how much energy they take from humans, they'll never be warm like you and me."

Sherice reached out and placed her hand on Abigale's cheek. "Hmmm, okay, let's check—well, you're alive! Next up, why do dogs insist on sniffing other dogs' butts? Right after a word from our sponsors."

Chapter Four

Dolly had taken a position inside the entrance to the circus tent where she could watch her eclectic collection of circus performers—acrobat, clown, sword swallower, tightrope walker, horseback rider, archery expert, and more—preparing and practicing for that evening's show. Dolly was especially proud that she also had two of the most dangerous acts ever performed beneath a circus tent: a knife thrower, and a lion tamer. For a time, she even had a human cannonball act, but one day the cannon exploded. The performer was okay, but the cannon was a total loss.

The fact that the circus was reduced to a single tent, rather than the three rings she'd operated with a decade earlier, was a matter of economics. It was getting harder and harder to attract an audience, in the era of smartphones and Netflix, so the more diverse the circus acts were, the better. And animals were critical. This was something Dolly had learned the hard way when she'd gotten rid of the elephants because of the transportation expense and soaring food costs. Within a month, attendance was off forty percent and she was forced to go buy the damn elephants back.

Dolly saw Willy Burks and his girlfriend, Antoinette, walking toward the ladder that led up to the wooden trapeze platform thirty-five feet overhead. As she expected, Antoinette ignored her, probably still angry over the fact that her trapeze partner, Mohawk Joe, kept dropping her.

"You're looking great today, Dolly," Willy said. "Nice color."

Dolly had gone out the night before and taken the healthiest person she could find late on a Sunday night in a city with a population of under 28,000. She always headed straight to a gym. Before fitness centers were a thing, Dolly looked for a boxing ring or meat packing plant. Both required intense physical activity and were, therefore, populated by an abundance of big muscular men. Once she tried looking for victims at the racetrack, only to discover the men were either old and fat, or tiny, underweight jockeys. Yes, boxers and weightlifters were perfect.

The man Dolly took was big, but with more muscle than fat. She killed him in the parking lot on his way into the fitness center, before he had exhausted his energy.

"Excuse me, can you help me?" Dolly asked, stepping directly in front of him. In 47 years, she'd never had a man say, no. It was little things like this, learned through trial and error, which made a big difference to a ghost's survival.

"Sure, what can I—?"

A second later, she was on him, wrapping a hand behind his head and placing her mouth over his. In a state of shocked confusion, the man did not push her away. As the life drained from his body and into Dolly's, it was like watching colored water being poured from one pitcher to another. Dolly's skin tone immediately began to turn from the color of ash to light cream, the man's skin doing the exact opposite.

Seconds later, it was over, and Dolly let the man drop limply to the ground.

"Come on, Willy," Antoinette snapped, grabbing him by the elbow. Willy shrugged and smiled sheepishly as if to say: *She's possessive, what can I do?* Dolly winked back. Willy had no idea the lengths a woman would go to control a man.

But he soon would.

A minute later, a commotion drew Dolly's attention from her thoughts about Willy to the center of the tent where Antoinette lay like a twisted pretzel of arms and legs. Mohawk Joe, Antoinette's trapeze partner, had dropped her again. The girl was right—maybe it *was* time to find a more skilled replacement.

It was a tall order. Not only would the person have to be a skilled trapeze artist they'd have to fit in with the rest of the crew. They'd have to be hard working. They'd have to be willing to follow the rules. Oh, and they'd have to be dead.

Chapter Five

Pipi Esperanza found herself in a pickle.

It was a funny idiom, Pipi thought—*in a pickle*. She spun in her chair and typed in: *"origin of in a pickle"* and pressed enter. From the Dutch word, *pekel,* which refers to a spicy sauce or brine. Pipi imagined drowning in a large pool of spicy sauce *would* be rather unpleasant.

When Pipi decided to seek a career with the FBI years earlier, all she knew about the bureau was what she'd seen in movies, like *Silence of the Lambs.* She imagined herself being Clarice, interviewing serial killers, and saving the day. She imagined it to be very glamorous. It wasn't. Well, five percent of it *was* glamorous, but the other ninety-five percent? It was an endless sea of siege-swallowing bullshit.

As Director, Pipi oversaw 35,000 employees, 300 satellite offices, and managed a budget north of ten billion dollars. The FBI had the broadest authority of all federal law enforcement agencies, which was spelled out in the FBI's list of Agency Priorities, which included:

- Protecting the U.S. from terrorist attacks.
- Protecting the U.S. against espionage.
- Combating cybercriminal activity.
- Combating public corruption.
- Protecting civil rights.
- Combating criminal enterprises.
- Combating white-collar crime.
- Combating violent crime.
- Combating human trafficking.
- Protecting and combating.

And all of the above, 24/7/365.

It was a good thing Pipi never slept.

If all that wasn't enough, many FBI investigations had to be coordinated with other law enforcement agencies. Getting anything done was like herding cats. This was a saying she didn't need to look up, its meaning was self-explanatory.

Now, Pipi was faced with protecting the nation from the biggest threat of all: a previously unknown and previously unseen threat.

Because now she had to deal with killer ghosts.

Pipi had known about the existence of ghosts for a long time. She was also aware that ghosts killed people to take their energy. She'd been quietly collecting data that proved this for over a decade. To date, Pipi had identified fifty-eight active situations, each involving a large number of deaths by natural causes, far too many to be random occurrences.

Others in the bureau had suggested the possibility of ghost murders in the past, but the previous director refused to entertain the theory. He felt embracing the notion would make the FBI look ridiculous and made it clear that anyone pursuing it would not move up in the bureau. As a result, anyone who believed in ghosts kept it to themselves, and anyone who dared to go public was put in a dead-end job filing paperwork in the basement.

The old regime was gone now, and there was a new sheriff in town. Her.

The difference between the previous director and Pipi was she knew for a fact that ghosts were real, and that they were responsible for thousands of human deaths. Like her predecessor, she needed to keep such information hidden, at least from the public. It's the main reason that she created the cover-up of the true origins of the ghost attack at the Mulvaney mansion outside Charleston the year before.

Until recently most of the victims were homeless vagrants, drug addicts, the terminally ill, and in some cases, wanted criminals. In many ways, these deaths had a positive impact on the communities in which they were happening. No one cared.

But things had changed. The victims had become younger. And healthier. And wealthier. The public was starting to notice. Suddenly, they cared. Something would need to be done.

Pipi knew the FBI needed to form a Ghost Division, and there was only one person for the job.

Newt Drystad.

*   *   *

When Pipi approached him with the idea, Newt said exactly what she thought he would.

"No."

"Yes," Pipi said.

"I can't," Newt said, shaking his head. "I'm up to my ass in serial killers. You know that."

"Yes, I do know that, but I still need you. Figure it out."

Pipi turned and headed for the door. She was in no mood for an argument. It was not a suggestion. It was an order.

A command.

"What if I turn it over to Maggie?" Newt said.

Pipi didn't answer. How he got it done didn't matter, she wanted it handled.

Classic Pipi.

*   *   *

Pipi remained at the office, catching up on the endless amount of paperwork that comprised the bulk of her job until darkness enveloped the capital. Soon it would be time for a late-night stroll.

At 10:30 p.m., Pipi took the private elevator down from the 11th floor to the lobby, exited the building and walked three hundred feet to the parking structure next door, and unlocked her car. As the Director she was entitled to have a car pick her up and drop her off each day, but she opted to drive herself. Having her car available at night in D.C. provided flexibility, and she wasn't worried about anyone trying to kill her.

After a glance around to make sure she was alone, as expected at that time of night, she popped the trunk and tossed her briefcase inside, since it would only get in the way.

The air was cool and crisp, not that she could tell, and the sky was clear with a full moon. As she passed people she lowered her head, not that anyone would recognize her—she wasn't a public figure, like the president or the speaker of the house—but one never knew. Better to be cautious.

Pipi made her way down Pennsylvania Avenue, then headed north on 6th Street NW past St. Mary's Catholic Church, then took a right on H Street. Ten minutes later she was a block from her destination.

Union Station had proven itself to be the best place in D.C. to find unsuspecting prey and those who would not be missed. The homeless. Drunk. Drugged. Doing their best to stay warm next to illegal bonfires or huddled in cardboard boxes beneath a freeway overpass. A sign at the Wells Fargo Bank said the temperature was 52 degrees. Staying warm was not an issue for Pipi; she hadn't even bothered to bring a jacket.

Pipi thought about the lengths the Secret Service went to protect the president, guarding doors and carrying guns. Laughable. Killing the president would be easy for someone like her, but what was the point? Another incompetent asshole would simply take their place.

Half a block short of the entrance to the station, Pipi heard someone groaning in pain coming from the alley on the opposite side of the street. Pure serendipity. She'd looked the word up once. The dictionary said serendipity was the occurrence and/or development of events, by chance, in a happy or beneficial way.

Pipi crossed the street and entered the alley where the man lay on the ground, writhing in pain. It was perfect—a chance to do good by ending someone's pain, ridding the world of the unwanted, and taking care of her needs at the same time.

Seconds after she finished taking the man, Pipi heard voices. Male voices. Two, she thought. Off to Pipi's left, she saw a garbage dumpster and quickly slid behind it. Wait, she said to herself, they'll probably pass by and that will be that.

They didn't.

The two young men, in their early twenties, turned into the alley and headed in Pipi's direction.

"What to hear a good one?" the first guy asked. "A kid goes to his mom and says *Mom, how do you spell scrotum?* And the mom says: *You should have asked me last night when it was on the tip of my tongue.*"

The guys laughed, then stopped and unzipped their pants and started urinating on the wall of the building a few yards from where Pipi crouched in the darkness, wondering: *Should I take them, too?*

"Okay, here's a better one," the second guy said. "What's the difference between a wife and a job?"

"I don't know," the first guy said.

"After five years your job will still suck."

When they'd finished pissing and laughing, they zipped up their pants and started walking back toward the street. The code should have been enough for Pipi to let them go. They weren't killers. They weren't old and sick. They were typical men. On the other hand, she hated jokes that made fun of women, not to mention that urinating in public was against the law.

Chapter Six

It was high tide. Onyx stood in the window at the top of the lighthouse and gazed at the tall gray cliffs standing several hundred feet above the gray ocean, its gray waves crashing on the gray rocks below. Gray clouds floated in the gray sky above. Everything was gray, as it had been every day since the day she died.

She *remembered* color, probably in the same way someone who's gone deaf remembers sound. The more time that passed, however, the less confidence Onyx had that her memories were accurate.

The only time Onyx saw any color was for an hour or so around sunset when long lines of crimson painted the sky. Why she could see red but no other colors, was a mystery. Like, how did she return to the living plane as a ghost when others did not? Who knew? Assumedly God, assuming there was a God. Some days she believed there was an invisible hand controlling things; other days she did not. It didn't matter. There was only one thing that truly mattered.

Staying.

Staying in the living plane.

Life was a difficult thing to let go of, even if you're dead.

Onyx crossed the room and looked out the window that faced to the east, across the clearing to the woods a hundred yards away. To most people, the woods were a calm and peaceful place where one walked and camped and enjoyed nature. To Onyx, they were just another bad memory.

The woods were where she'd died, attacked and torn apart by wolves. Like the colors she could no longer see, the pain of that event was now a distant memory. As with every other unpleasant event that occurred in one's life, the pain passes but the memories remain.

At the edge of the clearing were three graves. The first grave belonged to her father. The second was that of her best friend, Katherine Keane. She'd dug both with her own hands.

The third grave was hers.

Several years earlier, Onyx had asked Noah if he would go into the woods and look for her bones. He did, then gave her a proper burial.

Onyx's grave was the only one of the three that was not marked with a gravestone. The lighthouse was enough of a draw for high school kids looking for a place to hang out and drink beer. The last thing either of them wanted was a pair of horny teens having sex on Onyx's grave. Not that it mattered, because she wasn't really there.

Onyx heard the sound of stones being stacked in the clearing down below and shifted her gaze to the rock wall that surrounded the outer edges of the lighthouse property. Her father had collected the stones himself and built the wall with his own hands. That was long ago when men were men.

Now, sixty years later, the wall stood in disrepair. She'd asked Noah if he was willing to fix the sections which had crumbled, though she knew full well he could never do the quality job her father had done. Whether the wall was repaired correctly was not the point, it was that it was done—and that Noah was willing to do it.

The path that led to Onyx and Noah's marriage was a long one, built on love, pain, and chance.

Not long after her father passed, Onyx was forced to deal with something she'd never had to handle before; namely, finances. Bills. Debt.

Crushing debt.

Prior to that, her first husband, Ulrich, had handled the finances. Unbeknownst to Onyx, both her ex-husband and father had held the budget together with little more than duct tape and hope. Then there was Alistar.

Onyx's third benefactor was Noah's grandfather, Alistar Ashley.

Alistar was a lawyer who represented a billionaire who wanted her evicted so he could buy the property and turn it into a bed-and-breakfast. The audacity of someone with money stealing her home and turning it into a weekend plaything infuriated her.

Then the most amazing thing happened. Alistar Ashley took pity on her and changed teams, becoming Onyx's protector.

First, Ulrich.

Then her father.

Then Alistar.

Three men in a row, each coming to her rescue. It was a miracle, plain and simple. It was also a miracle she resented.

Being rescued over and over made her feel weak, like a Disney princess, waiting for her prince to come. And, as if on cue, he did.

She met Noah.

Most women find men in bars, or at work. Onyx wasn't most women. No. She met Noah at Alistar's funeral.

Noah was considerably younger than Onyx, which filled her with considerable guilt.

One of the worst parts of being a ghost— besides the part about being dead—was that ghosts only experienced negative emotions. Anger, jealousy, resentment, frustration, anxiety, guilt. Onyx felt these things in spades.

Especially guilt.

Onyx existed in a constant state of guilt over what she considered to be stealing the best years of Noah's life. What some would call *robbing the cradle* or being what was currently called a *cougar.*

It was the opposite of the norm, in which men had a tendency to date and marry younger women.

When Onyx brought up the topic, Noah pointed out how it was no longer a big deal for couples to have differences in their age. *"Age is just a number,"* Noah would say, having pointed out the age difference between Demi Moore and Ashton Kutcher. *"She's like 15 years older than he is."*

First, Onyx had absolutely no idea who these people were since she never watched television. And the 15-year age difference paled in comparison to their ages since Onyx was 114 and Noah was still in his 30s.

The thing that made the age difference livable, no pun intended, was that ghosts appeared as the age they were on the day they died and returned as their perfect selves. No scars or blemishes or wrinkles. Even severed limbs reappeared. She may have been 114 years old, but in terms of appearance, Onyx looked 39.

And as a ghost, she would be 39 forever.

Assuming she could get the energy.

Onyx watched as Noah took advantage of the last bit of daylight, shirt off—sweating and swearing when the rocks wouldn't fit together—his skin glistening with sweat and red with color.

Onyx held up her hand and examined it. Unlike Noah's, her skin was gray. Transparent. When she held the hand up to her face, she could see right through it.

Unacceptable.

Tonight, she would go to the hospital and see if there was anyone whose time had come. If there wasn't, she would go into town and look for an addict shooting up in a dark alley—the kind that could be found in all towns, even small ones like Crimson Cove.

She had no problem taking drug addicts. They were killing themselves, anyway. If they wanted to die, she was happy to help them along.

Those who were young and healthy? No. Onyx's code would not allow it. They were off-limits.

And children?

Never.

Onyx walked to the opposite side of the lighthouse and peered out toward the water, seeing thin red lines of red forming as the sun was being slowly swallowed by the ocean.

Soon it would be dark.

It was time.

Chapter Seven

Mohawk Joe was not a man who took public humiliation well. After dropping his trapeze partner, Antoinette, Mohawk Joe returned to his circus trailer and proceeded to go about his ritual of sulking, swearing, and screaming at the top of his lungs.

When alive, Mohawk Joe approached every challenge and defeat in life the same way—by drowning himself in cheap whisky. God how he wished he could drink. Which he couldn't do as a ghost. More accurately, he *could* drink, but the alcohol would not have the intended effect, and the mess created when the fluids made their way quickly through him and drained to the floor was a disaster. He knew this to be true because he'd tried it once. And once was enough.

With the escape route of alcohol no longer an option, all he had left was berating himself for his ineptitude. "What is wrong with you, you worthless piece of shit Indian?" he yelled at his image in the mirror. "Why can't you do even the simplest of things? Why can't you be more like Ulrich?"

Yes, Ulrich. Memories of the handsome strapping German flooded Mohawk Joe's mind—in particular, his memories of the day Ulrich Schröder saved his life decades earlier.

The year was 1931. Mohawk Joe had been working as part of a team hired to work construction on the Empire State Building in New York City, since Mohawk Indians had the reputation for being some of the best ironworkers in the world. But this wasn't just ironwork—it was ironwork at great heights.

A fierce and fearless tribe, the Mohawks accepted any kind of work, usually involving dangerous conditions—bridges, skyscrapers, tunnels, it didn't matter—often at below-average, non-union wages. They'd worked on the construction of the George Washington Bridge. And the United Nations Building after that. Most of New York City's most iconic buildings were raised with the hands of the Mohawks.

One morning, after a few wake-up shots of whisky at the Wigwam Bar on Nevins Street, Mohawk Joe had fallen off an I-beam and found himself dangling at the end of a rope one hundred stories in the air. Too weak to climb up the rope, he had only moments left to live. That's when Ulrich Schröder, a man who'd once worked as a trapeze artist in the circus, risked his own life to save him by swinging out on a metal chain and grabbing him in the nick of time. It was an act of courage the likes of which Mohawk Joe had never witnessed before, or since.

"I wish I had your skill and courage, Ulrich," Mohawk Joe said to his reflection in the mirror. "If I did, perhaps I would not be such a failure."

Suddenly, Mohawk Joe realized the image staring back at him was no longer his—it was Ulrich Schröder's. He leaned closer to the mirror. Yes, it was Ulrich! How was this possible? Then, to his surprise, Ulrich's hand came through the mirror toward him, grabbing him by the collar of his shirt. Mohawk Joe instinctively pulled away, and when he did, he pulled Ulrich through the mirror into the room.

To the degree that Mohawk Joe was surprised, it was nothing compared to the shock and confusion on Ulrich's face. "What... what has happened?" Ulrich stammered. "Where am I?"

"Ulrich, it's me, your friend Joe. Don't you remember me?"

"No, no," Ulrich said. "Wait, wait, yes I do—the Empire State Building."

"Yes!" Mohawk Joe said.

"But how—?"

"I don't know but come here and sit, we'll figure it out together."

*　*　*

It took almost an hour for the two men to hypothesize what had happened. The act of Mohawk Joe thinking of Ulrich while gazing into the mirror had somehow summoned him to that place and time.

"So, I am dead," Ulrich said, coming to grips with the situation.

Mohawk Joe nodded. "Do you remember how you died?"

Ulrich shook his head.

"That bitch of a wife, Onyx, burned you to death in your bed."

Then Ulrich remembered. Getting hit repeatedly with the oil can. The searing pain of the flames on his skin. But he also remembered it all happened because he was in the act of poisoning Onyx to death.

"Be careful with your tongue when you speak of my wife, Injun," Ulrich said.

"But she murdered you!"

"We were *both* killers," Ulrich said. "She was simply better at it."

"I don't understand."

"And you don't need to," Ulrich said. No one needed to know everything about a person's life. No one needed to know everything about a person's death, either.

Ulrich stood and walked across the trailer and looked at himself in the mirror. He appeared gray, almost transparent. He held up his hand and he could see right through it. Ulrich turned and looked at Mohawk Joe, who appeared solid and had color to his skin. "You are dead, too, right?"

Mohawk Joe nodded.

"So why do you look—?"

"Alive?"

"Yes, alive."

"I'll tell you, but I'm not sure you're going to like it."

Ulrich remained silent.

"Well, I look alive because I—"

"Because you what?" Ulrich snapped. "Spit it out."

"Because I kill people."

"You kill people?" Ulrich said.

"Yes," Mohawk Joe said. "All ghosts do. That's how we get to stay here, in the world with the living."

"Is killing people the only way?" Ulrich asked.

"That I know of," Mohawk Joe said.

"I don't understand."

"It has to do with energy," Mohawk Joe said.

Ulrich thought for a moment, then he got it. Life required energy. And you had to get energy from somewhere.

The idea that he would have to murder people wasn't good news, but it wasn't a deal-breaker. Ulrich knew he had killed before, but try as he might, he couldn't remember when. Who had he killed? Remembering felt like peering through a fog— every time he felt he'd captured a memory it would disappear like mist.

"I can't remember things," Ulrich said.

"Don't worry, things will start coming back in a few days," Mohawk Joe replied.

Suddenly, something started coming back to him. Ulrich remembered driving his car and parking behind a clump of spruce trees at the edge of a clearing. He closed his eyes and he could see himself walking toward a tall lighthouse as if watching a movie in his head.

Ulrich saw himself walking up to the lighthouse and knocking on the large wooden door. A moment later, the door swung open and a man appeared.

"What can I do you for?" the man asked, looking Ulrich over. "Are you lost?"

"Are you the caretaker?" Ulrich asked.

"If I ain't, then I'm a stupid old fool for taking care of the place," the caretaker said. "Now, what can I—"

Ulrich stepped forward and—with one quick motion—raised his right hand and struck the elderly man in the middle of the forehead with a metal pipe.

"You remember something?" Mohawk Joe asked.

Ulrich didn't answer. Instead, he walked over to the mirror where he'd emerged from minutes earlier and gazed at the gray reflection staring back at him. "This killing thing," Ulrich said finally, "show me how to do it."

Chapter Eight

So, are you going to tell me why Pipi wanted to see you or not?" Maggie McCord asked as she and Newt rode the elevator to the basement of the FBI building.

"I'd rather show you," Newt said as the elevator doors slid open. "Come on."

Maggie dutifully followed Newt down the concrete hallway until he stopped at a door marked B22. He slid the key Pipi Esperanza had given him earlier that morning and turned it. Newt reached inside and flipped the light switch. The fluorescent lights were probably installed when the building was first built, and they took a few seconds to come to life, exposing racks of metal shelves filled with legal-sized file boxes.

"What is this?" Maggie asked.

"It's a problem I hoped we could avoid."

Maggie crossed the room and looked at the labels on the boxes, numbered between 1-58, and organized in numerical order.

"Go ahead, take a look," Newt said.

Maggie pulled a box off one of the stacks and set it on a table in the center of the room. She removed the lid and looked at the manila file folders inside. Maggie pulled out the first folder and read the label aloud: "Farkas, Jody. DOB: 4/20/1983. DOD: 9/16/2009."

"I'll be back in two hours to see what you think," Newt said, turning and heading to the door.

"What I think about what?" Maggie asked.

"I'll bring back lunch," Newt said.

*　*　*

Maggie was happy when she heard the door to the storage room open behind her, first because she had a lot of questions for Newt, and second because she was hungry. But it wasn't Newt. It was Pipi.

"Madam Director," Maggie said, rising to her feet.

"Sit down, Maggie, we need to talk," Pipi said dropping into a chair on the opposite side of the table. "Newt briefed you?"

"Not really," Maggie responded. "All he did was—"

"How far have you gotten?" Pipi asked, pointing at the files strewn on the table.

"Far enough to see we have a ghost problem on our hands," Maggie said. "A bigger problem than I ever thought. Who all knows about this? Here, in the building, I mean."

"Me, Newt, and now you," Pipi said.

Maggie nodded. "Okay, so why am I being shown this?"

"Because the FBI is forming a Ghost Division. We need to get a full understanding of the situation, and how we can control it."

"If by *control* you mean to stop it from happening, I'm not sure how."

"Me neither," Pipi said.

"Who else is going to be on this?" Maggie asked.

"That's up to you," Pipi said. "You're in charge."

"Me?"

"Yep."

"Why me?"

"Because that's the way Newt wants it," Pipi said.

"What about the serial killer cases I've been working on?" Maggie asked.

"Ghosts *are* serial killers, Special Agent McCord."

Pipi had a point. If the remaining files were anything like what she'd already looked at, ghosts were the most prolific serial killers of all.

* * *

Newt returned twenty minutes later, and to Maggie's dismay, he came back empty-handed.

"I thought you were bringing lunch," Maggie said.

"Did Pipi come by?" Newt asked.

"Yes," Maggie said, realizing the Pipi visit had been planned. "You asked Pipi to come by."

Newt nodded.

"Why didn't you tell me yourself?" Maggie asked.

"Because you'd have fought me," Newt said.

"You're damn right," Maggie shot back. "This should be your project, not mine."

"Probably," Newt said.

Maggie released a long breath. There was no use in arguing, Newt always got what he wanted, at least when it came to the bureau.

"What about lunch?" Maggie asked.

"In a minute," Newt said. "First, we've got to discuss one other thing."

"Can we discuss it over lunch?"

"You're going to need a third person on the team," Newt said. "Someone who can be trusted to stay quiet."

"Like?"

"I'm thinking Chad."

"Chad?" Maggie said in disbelief. "You want me to recruit my ex-fiancé to work on this?"

"Yes."

Maggie shook her head. "No, not Chad. Anyone but Chad."

"Chad is the logical choice, Mag," Newt said. "And face it, there's no one who understands computer modeling better."

Maggie finally understood now why Newt hadn't brought lunch. He knew she was going to lose her appetite.

Chapter Nine

O nce per month, Onyx found herself lurking through the woods, or slinking through the dark alleyways of Crimson Cove, in search of that most precious of things. Energy.

Energy existed in many forms: thermal, chemical, electrical, kinetic, and nuclear. Everything in the universe was made of it. And every human relied on it to stay alive. It was the same with ghosts.

Einstein was famous for observing that energy could be neither created nor destroyed; it only changed form. Boil water and it becomes steam. Burn a log in a fireplace and it becomes ash. Flip a switch on the wall and electricity, flowing through a filament trapped in a glass bulb, became particles of light.

Then there is life energy.

People often speak of life as if it is something intangible. Magical. Mystical. It isn't. Life is made of electric energy. Nothing magical or mystical about it. Just science.

To remain in the living plane, ghosts needed human energy. The more energy, the better; the more alive they appeared. With enough energy, it was almost impossible for people to tell the living from the dead. This made it possible for ghosts to walk among the living, undetected, living normal lives. Holding jobs. Going to concerts and movies. Looking alive. But not.

For most ghosts, the act of taking human life was distasteful. Even disgusting. But necessary. To rationalize her actions, Onyx developed a code that justified her actions. First, she never took energy from the young and healthy. She only took energy from people who were terminally ill or drug-addicted beyond saving. She also had no problem taking heinous criminals: rapists, murderers, or child molesters. To her mind, right or wrong, she felt she was helping make the world a better place.

*   *   *

It was a few minutes before midnight and Onyx found herself moving silently through the woods on her way to the city's edge. Going into town too early was dangerous. Too many people were out and about, too many sets of alert eyes watching.

Though she could not see any color other than red, she—like all ghosts—had exceptional hearing. This allowed Onyx to listen to conversations from blocks away as she worked her way through darkened streets and alleys. Once she heard a man snarl, *"Give me your purse, bitch, or I'll cut you."* Seconds later she was on the man, taking him as she took all humans, with the kiss of death. In this case, her actions had been witnessed by the intended victim, a waitress leaving a restaurant at the end of her shift.

When it was over and Onyx let the man's lifeless body drop to the cement, she took a step toward the woman and asked, "What did you see?"

"I... I... didn't..." the woman sputtered. "Please don't—"

"I asked you, what did you see?" Onyx repeated.

The woman finally understood. "Nothing, I saw nothing."

Onyx nodded, then hurried off. She'd made the mistake of taking someone in plain view that evening, but her code prohibited her from killing the woman. To her knowledge, the woman never told a soul.

On this night, however, there was no one to take. No violent crimes, no muggings, no one near death in an alley with a needle in their arm. Now, there was nothing she could do but try again tomorrow. As she was weaving her way through the tall pines on her way back to the lighthouse, Onyx heard it. The unmistakable sound of screeching tires somewhere off in the distance, followed by the sound of crunching metal and shattering glass. Someone had an accident.

There were two questions in her mind: Was the accident of a life-threatening nature? And, if so, could she get there first?

It took several minutes for Onyx to find the accident. A single car smashed into the side of a massive tree. The cause of the crash was immediately obvious as Onyx came around the car. A large buck lay on the hood, its head and horns through the windshield.

In the front seat sat a boy and a girl. Teenagers. They were both alive, but barely. Their condition suggested neither would make it to the hospital alive.

Onyx entered the car through the shattered glass on the driver's side of the vehicle and took the boy first, as he was the nearest to death. She then turned her attention to the girl. The girl was conscious but fading. As with the woman in the alley, the girl had witnessed what Onyx had done. Unlike the woman in the alley, there was no question the girl would never tell.

"Help... me," the girl said with labored breath. "Please... help... me."

Don't worry, Onyx thought. I will.

It was only after Onyx had finished that she noticed a cardboard sign nailed to the tree directly above the mangled hood of the car. It read, *Attention: Improve Tourism, Help Make Crimson Cove Famous as the Ghost Capital of the Pacific Northwest! Sign the Petition Today at The Dietz Theater, Downtown on Main Street.*

Damn that Abigale Dietz.

Chapter Ten

After taking him out for his first kill as a ghost, Ulrich looked a thousand percent better. "How do you feel?" Mohawk Joe asked. "Fit as a fiddle," Ulrich said. "I feel better than I ever remember, and we didn't even have to sleep."

"Good. If you're ready, I'll take you to Dolly."

"Who's Dolly?"

"She owns the circus," Mohawk Joe said.

"Wait, the circus is owned by a woman?"

"Yeah, women run the world now," Mohawk Joe said. "And don't let the fact that she's a woman fool you. Dolly is as tough as nails, and she doesn't take any crap, so watch yourself."

* * *

Dolly lit a Sorbaines and blew a stream of blue smoke in the air while she looked Ulrich up and down. "So, you've worked the trapeze?" Dolly asked.

"He's the best catcher I've ever seen," Mohawk Joe said effusively.

"I'm asking Ulrich," Dolly said.

"Yes, I can hold my own," Ulrich said.

"No fear of heights?"

"Well, I'm dead already so what's to be afraid of?" Ulrich said.

"Ulrich, it's German?"

"Yes, my family was from Berlin."

"I'm German as well," Dolly said. "My real first name is Walbruga, but everyone calls me Dolly."

Ulrich nodded.

Dolly took one more deep drag off the black cigarette and tossed it to the ground. "Okay, let's get Antoinette and see what you can do."

*   *   *

Ulrich recognized Antoinette the minute she and Willy entered the tent. She was Antoinette King. She had been the star of a competing trapeze act called The Flying Concellos.

Antoinette had gained considerable fame as the first woman to successfully execute an airborne triple somersault. Many people felt she was the greatest woman flyer of all time.

"You are Antoinette King," Ulrich said. "I saw you perform once."

"Really? Where?"

"I don't remember exactly, but you were amazing."

"Of course, I was," Antoinette said.

"In any case, it's a pleasure to meet you," Ulrich replied, holding out his hand, but Antoinette ignored it.

"Now that we know who I am, who are you?" Antoinette asked.

"My name is Ulrich Schröder," Ulrich said. "I was a member of The Soaring Schröders, of Berlin."

"The Soaring Schröders?"

"Yes."

"I seem to remember them, a family act. I don't remember seeing you, though," Antoinette said dismissively.

"I left the troupe in 1912," Ulrich said.

"Couldn't cut it?" Antoinette said.

"Family disagreement. You understand how families are," Ulrich said. "Leaving the circus had nothing to do with my proficiency as an aerialist."

"Can you do a full cutaway?"

"Of course."

"Okay, we'll see."

Antoinette started her climb up one of the two thirty-foot ladders to the platform above as Ulrich chalked his hands, then began his climb up the second ladder. It wasn't until he reached the platform that he noticed there was no net below them.

"I'm waiting," Antoinette called out.

"Ladies first," Ulrich yelled back. "After you."

For the next twenty minutes Antoinette King performed every move she could think of, including the most difficult ones she knew—layouts, bird's nests, straight jumps, cut catches; she even threw in a triple somersault and a double cutaway with a half twist. Ulrich caught them all flawlessly. It was as if Ulrich Schröder had been born with a catch bar in his hands.

Dolly sidled up to Willy as Ulrich and Antoinette climbed down their respective ladders. "They look good together, don't you think? Like a match, made in heaven." Willy did not respond.

"What do you think?" Dolly called out to Antoinette. "He'll do," was all Antoinette said, but her face wore a smile no one in the circus had seen in months.

*   *   *

Antoinette's smile was nowhere to be found the following morning when Dolly showed her the advertising flyer she'd produced.

"What in God's name is *this* supposed to be?" Antoinette asked, her face contorted with anger.

Willy took the flyer from Antoinette's hand and immediately saw the problem. The picture showed Antoinette and Ulrich, standing side by side, her 5-foot frame looking minuscule compared to the 6-foot, 5-inch hulking German. He remained silent. Better to stay out of it.

"What's the problem now, Antoinette?" Dolly asked.

"This picture! That's the problem." Antoinette snapped. "His picture is twice as big as mine. Do I need to remind you who the star of the show is?"

Dolly was tempted to say the star of the circus was the elephants but didn't. "His picture looks bigger because he *is* bigger, Antoinette."

"Maybe you could put Ulrich in the background," Willy ventured.

"Yes!" Antoinette said. "It's called perspective, Dolly."

Dolly unwrapped a fresh pack of Sorbaines, pulled one of the black-tipped cigarettes from the pack, and lit it. "Let's get something straight," Dolly said as she blew a cloud of blue smoke in Antoinette's direction. "See the name at the top of the flyer? That's my name. I own this circus—not you, not Willy, no one else but me. You're an employee, Antoinette, an employee that can be replaced. I pay the bills and keep the lights on, while you prance around like a peacock in heat. How's *that* for perspective?"

* * *

Mohawk Joe was sitting on a small threadbare sofa in his trailer when the door flew open. He looked up and saw the clown standing there.

If there was one person in the circus Mohawk Joe disliked more than any other, it was the circus clown. There was nothing funny about the clown. There was something dark about him, something that sent shivers up Mohawk Joe's spine. It was as if the makeup's purpose was to hide something evil.

"Come on," the clown barked.

"You ever hear of knocking?" Mohawk Joe asked.

"I said, come on," the clown repeated. "Now."

Mohawk Joe exited the trailer and caught up with the clown. "Where are we going?"

"Boss lady wants us to go into town and pass out flyers," the clown said.

"Okay," Mohawk Joe said. Passing out flyers was easy work so there was nothing to complain about, and it was a hell of a lot better than shoveling elephant shit. After that, neither man spoke another word for the entire four-mile walk into Eureka.

When they'd run out of flyers, Mohawk Joe said, "We better be getting back."

"You go," the clown said. "I'm going to hang out here for a bit."

Chapter Eleven

Maggie had heard people say getting to Martha's Vineyard was half the fun. Having refused Chad's offer to send his jet, she now knew this was advertising propaganda created by ferry operators. Yes, you might see a whale or some dolphins on the ferry ride over, but flying by private plane or helicopter was the only way to go. Sadly, the DOJ Ethics Rule 41 CFR 301 made such extravagances out of the question, so the ferry it had to be.

Maggie learned many things about Martha's Vineyard during the year she and Chad were engaged, the first of which was the rich never referred to it by its full name. They called it, "MV."

The second thing Maggie learned was despite the multi-million-dollar mansions that dotted the shores, no one who was truly rich lived there. The rich spent the weekend there. They summered there. They hid out from the paparazzi there. But the rich didn't *live* there. The island was too busy in summer, too cold in winter, and too small if you were the least bit claustrophobic.

The third and most important thing Maggie learned was there were two different kinds of money. In the world of law enforcement, there was legal money and illegal money. Out on MV, there was old money and new money, a lot of which was gained illegally. But the rich get away with it, while poor people don't.

The Chatterton money wasn't *old* old—but it was old enough. Amassed in the early 1900s by Carron Chatterton, the family fortune came from building homes on Euclid Avenue in Cleveland, where many of America's early industrialists clustered. "You know what wine and money have in common, Maggie?" Chad asked once while opening a $1,200 bottle of

1998 Screaming Eagle Cabernet on the deck of the family yacht. "They both get older with age."

The newly rich *thought* they were accepted by the old money types on Martha's Vineyard. They weren't. Behind closed doors, the disdain for the newly rich was so palpable you could cut it with a knife. The only reason those with old money hung with rock stars, athletes, hedge fund managers, and recently minted Silicon Valley billionaires like Mark Zuckerberg was for their celebrity. To be able to say they'd attended a party with Elon; to have their picture taken arm-in-arm with Oprah; to be able to brag about having shared a joint with Snoop; only to snicker at them behind their backs for their lack of pedigree.

Chad wasn't like this. Chad was worse. And it was this constant *"I'm rich and you're not"* bullshit that caused Maggie to leave him.

That, and she met Newt.

*   *   *

After her taxi was buzzed through the front gate by security, she was met at the front door by the estate manager, who—like so many of the rich—went by only one name. Burlington.

"Good to see you, Maggie," Burlington said with a smile. "I trust your trip out was a pleasant one?"

"I'm on a tight schedule. Where is he?" Maggie said.

"I believe he's at the dock, working on the boat," Burlington said. "Let me take—"

"I know the way," Maggie said pushing past the tuxedoed man and striding through the marbled foyer, zig-zagging through the labyrinth of rooms and taking a shortcut through the kitchen and out the rear door of the mansion.

Maggie knew full well Chad's not meeting her at the door was a passive-aggressive, power-play on his part, specifically designed to piss her off. Score one for Chad. She could already feel her heart rate going up as she approached the Byte Me, a 286-foot custom-built sailing schooner Chad had shipped over from Germany while they were dating. It featured a bespoke interior by François Catroux because Chad had read an article in Vanity Fair calling the Frenchman the "Über-Rich's Favorite Interior Designer."

It was obvious why Chad wanted to have the conversation on the Byte Me, Maggie realized. The Byte Me was supposed to be *their* boat, part of their planned honeymoon. More games.

Maggie approached the boat and waited for Chad to look in her direction. He didn't. He kept his head down, working. "You can hire people to polish your boat," Maggie said loudly.

Chad didn't look up.

"Chad?"

"Hang on, I'm almost done waxing the non-skids," Chad said.

"Doesn't that defeat the purpose?" Maggie asked. "If the non-skids are supposed to keep you from slipping, why would you wax them?"

Chad finally looked up, set the waxer down, and stood. "If the sun heats the gel coat, it oxidizes and holds dirt. If you don't wax it—"

"Sorry I asked," Maggie said.

Chad walked to the boat's ladder and held out his hand. "Come on board. I'll have the kitchen make us sandwiches and lemonade."

"I'm not staying that long," Maggie said. Getting on the boat was a bad idea, for multiple reasons. "I only came out to ask for your help."

"You want my help?" Chad said. "Doing what?"

"I'd like for you to come back to the bureau," Maggie said. "There's a project I think you'd be really good at, and—"

"No," Chad said, cutting her off.

"I haven't even told you what the project is."

"You've got a lot of nerve, Maggie, you know that?"

"It's important, Chad, if it wasn't I wouldn't be asking."

"Have you and the nerd tied the knot yet?" Chad asked, clearly as a dig he hoped would get to her.

"I'm not going to stand here while you insult the smartest person at the FBI. If your ego can't handle being around people who are smarter than you, well, that's sad."

"I don't mind people being smarter than me," Chad said. "I only mind it when they steal my girlfriend."

Maggie stood there silently, determined to wait him out. It was something she'd learned at the bureau.

"Tell me about the project," Chad said finally.

"No. Be in D.C. on Monday morning and I'll brief you there," Maggie said, then turned and started across the lawn back toward the house.

"What makes you think I'll come?" Chad called out.

Maggie turned around and said, "You'll come because you're the best computer expert the bureau ever had—that, and you're bored stiff."

"You think I'm the best computer expert the FBI ever had?"

"No," Maggie said, "but Newt does."

Chapter Twelve

Y ou look good," Noah said to Onyx, noticing the improved color and glowing complexion of her skin. He thought he had heard her go out the previous night. Now he knew she had.

"Did you know about this?" Onyx said, waving the petition notice in front of Noah's face.

Noah didn't answer. His silence *was* the answer.

"And when were you planning on telling me?"

The real answer was never—not if he didn't have to. Instead, Noah said, "Eventually."

Onyx shook her head, clearly disappointed. They'd had this conversation many times. She wanted to know everything that was happening in Crimson Cove. *Everything.* Noah, on the other hand, wanted her to know nothing. Anything he told Onyx tended to upset her.

Like now.

"I've been putting this off, but I think maybe it's time to pay Abigale Dietz a little visit," Onyx said.

"No, you will not, Onyx!" Noah said. "It's out of the question."

"Are you telling me I'm not allowed to confront Abigale if I want to?" Onyx asked in a tone that communicated her displeasure. This was *also* something they had discussed many times. Onyx's previous husband was responsible for killing her body. She refused to let Noah kill her spirit.

"No, I'm simply trying to make you understand—"

Noah didn't bother finishing the sentence. Onyx had already left the room. Living with any woman could be trying, especially women who were ghosts.

*   *   *

Noah walked to the garage and pulled the canvas tarp off his motorcycle. The bike was a lava-red Harley-Davidson Fat Boy, with a fuel-injected 1550cc Twin Cam engine and silver cast aluminum disc wheels.

It reminded Noah of his two previous careers—the first playing guitar in an unsuccessful rock band, and the second career as a moderately-successful chef—and how the two collided a decade earlier.

It was New Year's Day 2006, and Noah was slicing onions on a cutting board with an eight-inch chef's knife. Then someone turned on the radio. A minute later, a song came on— a hit song by the band he'd been voted out of a year earlier. Overwhelmed by rage, he lost his concentration and sliced off two of his fingertips.

To minimize their liability, the restaurant offered Noah a $30,000 cash settlement. Which he took. After the lawyer took his fee, Noah had $20,000 in his hand—the most money he'd ever had in his life. That's what he used to buy the Harley. Then he opened his restaurant.

Located on Main Street in downtown Crimson Cove, Noah's Grille was an instant hit. In truth, the restaurant's success was due in large part to the restaurant's chef, Carlos. Carlos ran the kitchen and did all the heavy lifting, while Noah ran the front of the house and saw to the service side of things.

A few years later, when Noah decided he wanted out, he sold the place to Carlos for one dollar as a sign of his appreciation for the man's hard work. In return, Carlos kept Noah's name on the building so nothing changed—except Noah's Grille was Noah-less.

Noah guided the bike into an empty spot, turned off the engine, and walked to the front door of the restaurant where he was greeted with a surprise in the form of a for sale sign. How could the restaurant be for sale? Not only that, but the door was locked, and the place was dark.

Noah pulled out his cell phone and dialed the restaurant's number, which started ringing. At least that was working. On the fourth ring, someone answered, but it wasn't Carlos. It was his wife.

"Ellen? It's Noah."

"Oh, hey, are you calling about—?"

"The restaurant? Damn right, I am," Noah snapped. "What in the hell is going on?"

The question was met with silence.

"Ellen?"

"It's Carlos, he lost—he has a gambling problem, Noah," Ellen managed to get out. "He lost a lot of money."

"Shit," Noah said. "I had no idea. How much money did he lose?"

"Everything, Noah. He lost everything, and we owe—"

"How much do you owe?"

"A little over $200,000," Ellen said.

"Jesus. When did he start gambling?"

"On our honeymoon to Vegas," Ellen said. "He lost everything on the first day we were there, that's why we came back early."

"Who did you borrow the money from?" Noah asked.

Silence.

"Ellen? Who did you borrow the—"

"Mickey Spilatro," Ellen said finally.

"Are you telling me Carlos borrowed money from the mob?"

Again, silence.

"Where is Carlos now?"

"He's sleeping."

"Well, tell Carlos to get his ass out of bed and meet me at the restaurant," Noah snapped.

"I don't think he'll—"

Noah hung up the phone before Ellen could finish. He was in no mood for excuses.

* * *

As soon as Noah hung up the cell phone he spotted Abigale Dietz walking in his direction. He hated Abigale almost as much as Onyx did and would have preferred not to have run into her, especially right now.

"Noah, just the person I wanted to see," Abigale said with a big smile. "I was wondering if word got to Onyx about my plans to make her famous?" Abigail asked. "Or are the two of you still putting on the Onyx-is-dead-and-gone charade?"

"Let it go, Abigale," Noah said.

"Let it go, or what?"

"I still have a lot of sway in this town," Noah said. "Trust me, you don't want me as an enemy."

"Oh, I'm shaking," Abigale said. "I think I'll call Clay and tell him you threatened me, for the record."

"Do what you've got to do, Abby."

"By the way, did you hear about the car accident on Route 1? Horrible thing. A young boy and girl cut down in their youth. The coroner said the girl looked a bit—what was it he said—oh, yeah, gray."

"Let it go, Abby," Noah said.

"That's the problem, Noah, isn't it? Onyx runs around killing people at will and what does everyone do? They let it go. People have been *letting it go* for seventy years," Abigale said, making air quotes for extra emphasis. "Maybe it's time to stop."

Abigale didn't bother waiting for Noah to respond and hurried off, leaving him alone on the sidewalk thinking about what she'd said. He knew she was right. People had turned a blind eye to the reality of the situation. And why? Because of self-interest.

People always said *money made the world go round*, but that wasn't true—s*elf-interest* made the world go round—and nowhere was this truer than in Crimson Cove. The truth was that no one wanted drug addicts littering the streets. Vagrants were not only a blight on the city they were also a threat to tourism. People came to the cove to get away from the problems of city life. The last thing they wanted was more of the same. So, yes, the people of Crimson Cove turned a blind eye to the higher than usual number of dead and missing, providing the deaths involved people who were terminally ill, addicted beyond saving, suicidal, or criminals.

Onyx had a code—a code that allowed her to justify her actions—that permitted her to take a human life. Other than a single mistake, years earlier, she never took energy from the young. Or the healthy. Or those with a strong will to live.

The ironic thing was, that Abigale wanted to use Onyx to turn Crimson Cove into the Ghost Capitol of the Pacific Northwest—a place Onyx had already turned into the cleanest and safest city in the Pacific Northwest.

What a pair the two of them made.

* * *

Noah waited patiently on the sidewalk outside the locked front door of the restaurant until Ellen Galvin guided her car into an empty parking spot and turned off the engine. Only she was alone.

"Where's Carlos?" Noah asked the moment Ellen exited the vehicle.

"He's gone," Ellen said.

"Gone? Gone where?"

"I don't know. I went into the bedroom to tell him that you wanted to see him, and the bed was empty. He was gone. He left a note on the pillow."

Ellen stepped forward and handed a piece of paper to Noah. It said: *I'm sorry.*

Chapter Thirteen

Three-hundred and thirty-seven miles directly south of where Onyx Webb left the bodies of the boy and girl involved in the deadly car accident, two detectives in Eureka, California stood in the parking lot of a drive-in theater dealing with a pair of dead teenagers of their own.

"What the frank do you make of this?" Detective #1 said as he peered through the passenger side window into the red Chevrolet Camaro at the two gray, lifeless bodies.

"Hard to tell," Detective #2 said. "They look, I don't know, they look—"

"They look old," Detective #1 said, finishing the sentence. He was tempted to say *old and dead*, but that was obvious.

Standing behind the detectives, the manager of the drive-in asked, "Do you still need me? I'd like to go home and get some breakfast."

"Tell me again, when did you find the car?" Detective #2 said.

"About seven this morning, right before I called you guys," the drive-in manager said.

"What time did the last movie end?" Detective #1 asked.

The drive-in manager scratched his head, thinking. "Around 2 a.m., I guess."

"And you didn't notice the car sitting all alone here for five hours?" Detective #2 asked. "You care to explain that?"

"I was sleeping."

"What do you mean, you were sleeping?" Detective #2 said.

"I mean, I've got a bed in the back and sometimes I catch a few hours of sleep before I make the drive home," the drive-in manager said. "Driving at night is dangerous."

The detectives shot each other a look. "And you didn't see anything between 2:00 and 7:00 a.m.?"

"Nothing but the inside of my eyelids," the drive-in manager said.

"What about these windows?" Detective #1 asked. "You roll these down, or did you find them this way?"

"I already told you, the moment I saw them, I ran straight to the telephone," the drive-in manager said. "I didn't touch the car at all. I've seen enough CSI to know not to touch anything."

Detective #2 leaned forward, peered into the vehicle again, and shook his head. The girl was leaning back in her seat, mouth wide open as if in mid-scream, her skin gray and wrinkled like the hide of an elephant. The boy's skin was equally gray and lifeless. Unlike the girl, it appeared the boy had put up a fight, the knuckles on his right hand were covered in dried blood.

It was then, when the detective looked at the boy's other hand, that he noticed the card.

"You see that?" Detective #1 asked.

"See what?" Detective #2 replied.

"That." Detective #1 pointed at the card in the dead boy's left hand. Detective #2 reached out for the card, but Detective #1 grabbed his arm and stopped him. "You got gloves?"

Detective #2 said, "Yeah, in the car."

"Go grab them," Detective #1 said, "and grab a set for me."

Detective #2 waddled off, leaving Detective #1 and the boy alone. "Listen," Detective #1 said, "just between you and me— what else do you know about this?"

The manager looked away and shifted nervously from one foot to the other. "Nothing. Really, there's nothing."

"Nothing, huh?" Detective #1 said.

"Yeah, really."

Detective #1 looked the boy in the eye and remained silent, waiting. Finally, the manager said, "Well, I knew the girl."

"You knew the girl?"

"Yeah, I know who she is—I mean, I knew who she was."

"How well did you know her?"

"Not well, just from school. We had a few classes together, that's all. She was nice."

"Did you and this girl date?" the detective asked.

"Date, no, nothing like that," the manager said. "I mean, we went out a few times, but—"

"You went out with her a few times? I just asked you if you and the girl dated, and you said no. Now, you're changing your story?"

"No, I—I just don't want to get involved is all," the manager said.

"You found two dead people in a car, son, and you dated one of them," the detective said. "Trust me, you are involved."

Detective #2 returned with the rubber gloves and handed a set to Detective #1, who put them on, reached into the car, and pulled the card from the dead boy's hand.

The card was white, with the words Bingham's Florist printed on one side, along with the florist's address, phone number, and website. Typical stuff. But when he turned the card over, he saw five hand-written letters. The letters were CMIYC.

"You ever shop here, at this Bingham's Florist place?" Detective #1 asked.

"Sure, a few times maybe, but that doesn't mean—"

"Do you know what CMIYC means?" Detective #2 asked, and the manager shook his head.

"Can I go now?" the manager asked.

Detective #1 said, "Yeah, but don't leave town."

Chapter Fourteen

Newt Drystad was in his office, seated in the new chair he'd always wanted. Made by Herman Miller, the Aeron had nice recline function, comfortable arms, good forward seat tilt, 2.5" carpet casters, an iron-clad warranty, and—like the early cars made by Henry Ford—it came in any color you wanted, as long as the color you wanted was black. Technically, graphite gray.

Newt had memorized every detail of the chair reading the specs one time four years ago. The only thing that had changed was the price, which was $1,375, $200 more than when he'd first considered buying one. Some people called this inflation. In Newt's case, it was procrastination.

What tipped the scale in the direction of the Aeron over all other options, was that it came fully assembled. Newt was smart enough to buy the best chair for the price, but also intelligent enough to know he could never assemble it. He was good with his mind, not his hands. Newt purchased a chair from IKEA once, an experience from which he was still recovering. Never again.

In Newt's left hand was a two-page summary of the deaths of two teenagers in Eureka, California. In his right hand was another two-page summary, this one about teenagers on the Oregon Coast, near a place called Crimson Cove. Besides the fact that the deaths were both teenagers, the incidents were eerily similar. The coroners in each case had determined the teens had expired from natural causes. The odds of this were astronomical.

Newt knew the chances of dying from a heart attack are about one in three. Cancer and stroke, approximately one in five. Electrocution, one in 4,906. Accidental gunshot, one in 18,536. The flu, one in 19,000. Drowning in the bath, one in 85,000. Falling off a ladder, one in 145,000. Driving off the road, one in 251,000. Train crash, one in half a million. Snakebite is one in four million; plane crash, lightning strike, radiation from a nuclear power plant, one in ten million. Shark attack, roller coaster, falling coconut, one in three-hundred million. Dying by being hit by an asteroid happened once every 7,236 years, and that was more likely than four healthy teenagers dying of old age on the same evening.

Newt knew two things connected the deaths. One, they were caused by ghosts. The second connection was still up in the air.

The office door swung open, and Maggie stuck her head in. "Guess what?"

"The price of kumquats hit $6.99 a pound," Newt said.

"Besides that," Maggie said.

Newt shrugged and waited.

"Chad's here," Maggie said with a smile. "As I said he would be."

Newt picked up the phone and dialed Pipi Esperanza's extension.

*   *   *

Chad was seated by himself at a small conference table in a room in the basement of the FBI building, surrounded by stacks of sealed file boxes. He was still uncertain why he was there, only that it involved computers. Beyond that, Maggie refused to share a single detail.

The door opened and Chad looked up to see Maggie and Newt come in. "Hello, Chad," Newt said. Chad did not return the greeting. He also didn't stand up, which would have been the polite thing to do. It caught Chad off guard when moments later the FBI Director walked in.

Though he had not been employed by the bureau for over a year, Chad instinctively shot to his feet. "Good morning, madam director," Chad said.

"Nice to see you Chad," Pipi said. "I'm told retirement is serving you well."

"It's fine, ma'am," Chad said.

Pipi waved her hand, and everyone took a seat at the table. "Do you know why you're here, Chad?" Pipi asked.

Chad shook his head. "No idea."

Pipi looked in Maggie's direction.

"We'd like to invite you to join a newly formed division of the FBI," Maggie said.

"Division doing what?"

"Chasing ghosts," Newt said.

Chad smiled. "Chasing ghosts?" he repeated.

Newt nodded. Maggie nodded. Pipi nodded. Chad broke into laughter. No one laughed with him.

"Do you believe in ghosts, Chad?" Newt asked.

"No, Newton, I do not believe in ghosts," Chad replied. "I believe in things I can see with my own eyes, not the irrational, delusional fantasies of gullible people."

"That's what I thought," Newt said. Newt looked in Pipi's direction.

Pipi stood up and held out her hand. Then Maggie reached into her purse, pulled out a knife, and placed it in Pipi's open palm.

The knife was a six-inch, pearl-handled switchblade, the kind that opened with the press of a button. Pipi pressed the button and the blade snapped into place.

"Whoa, what is this?" Chad asked.

"This is the director's way of helping you believe in ghosts," Newt said.

And with that, Chad watched in horror as Pipi Esperanza, who held the highest position in one of the government's most important organizations, pressed the knife to her neck and slit her own throat.

Chapter Fifteen

Abigale Dietz sat at the edge of the bed and pulled on her Spanx. She'd been a fan of Spanx ever since she saw the woman who created it, Sara Blakely, being interviewed on TV. Entrepreneurs were a special breed, like her.

Self-made.

Self-driven.

Women who pulled themselves up by their bootstraps—or, in this case, by their Spanx.

Abigale stood and glanced at her watch. It was a few minutes before 11 a.m. In an hour, she'd open the doors of the Dietz Theater to what she hoped would be a long line of people eager to sign her petition to make Crimson Cove the Ghost Capitol of the Pacific Northwest.

First, Abigale needed to make sure her appearance was perfect. She stepped in front of the full-length mirror in the corner of the bedroom and could immediately tell something was missing. What though?

Ah, a scarf. That would finish the look.

The last time Abigale had gone to Seattle she'd bought an expensive red and black Hermes silk scarf from Nordstrom, which she thought would do the trick. Abigale searched through several drawers before finding it, then returned to the mirror.

Abigale wrapped the scarf around her neck and tied it into a stylish French knot, then took one last look in the mirror. To her shock and horror, the image she saw staring back at her wasn't her own.

It was a younger woman.

Stunningly beautiful.

Flawless skin that looked like porcelain.

Abigale gasped and leaped back, away from the mirror, but there was no escape. Onyx stepped forward through the mirror and shoved Abigale backward and onto the bed.

Before Abigale could get up, Onyx was on top of her, sitting on her chest and wrapping her hand around the woman's neck. Abigale tried to free herself, but it was futile.

"Onyx?" Abigale sputtered.

"You were expecting someone else?" Onyx said, looking down at her. "Maybe you were, you do create a lot of enemies."

"What—what do you want?" Abigale managed, breathing heavily, shocked that she was face-to-face with the legendary ghost.

"You don't know?" Onyx said.

Abigale shook her head violently from side to side.

"This," Onyx said, holding Abigale's petition in front of her face. On the front was a hand-drawn artist depiction of Onyx in a racy black dress and fishnet stockings. "And while we're at it, care to explain the picture?"

"We're going after a younger demographic," Abigale said. "We need to target young males with raging hormones, they're drawn to sexy and slutty—"

Onyx tightened her grip on Abigale's neck. "In what world do you think this was okay?"

"It's, it's—I thought you'd be happy about it," Abigale stuttered.

"Happy? You thought I'd be happy with thousands of people descending on the cove? You thought I'd be happy that scores of teenagers would drive to the cliffs and trespass on my property, trying to catch a glimpse of the sideshow curiosity you're turning me into?"

"No, no, I'm doing it for the good of the cove. Without tourism the town would be dead," Abigale said, immediately regretting her choice of words.

Onyx shook her head. "What's happened to you, Abigale? Your father was a good man, we had an understanding. Did he ever tell you that I saved his life?"

Abigale shook her head.

"It was the weekend of that ridiculous Onyx Webb Film Festival you held when you showed the film of me walking through the woods that night," Onyx said. "I was waiting outside the theater to give your father a piece of my mind. Then Claudia Spilatro showed up."

"You're lying," Abigale blurted. "Claudia was dead when we had the festival."

Onyx remained silent.

"Wait, are you saying—?"

"Yes, Claudia is dead, but she was there," Onyx said.

"That's not possible."

"Really? I'm dead, yet here I am."

Abigale remained silent, trying to take everything in, then she said, "Why was Claudia there?"

"She was there to take your father," Onyx said. "But I stepped in and saved him."

"Why?" Abigale asked, squirming from side to side.

"As I said, your father was a good man," Onyx said.

"Yes, he was," Abigale said.

"The question now is," Onyx said, "are you a good daughter?"

Abigale nodded dutifully, a tear running down the side of her cheek.

"Don't make me come back, Abigale. If you do, it will be the last time you see me, and I promise I won't be quite as understanding." Onyx removed her hands from Abigale's neck, raised herself up, and walked back toward the mirror. "Oh, and one more thing, Abby..."

"What?"

"Your scarf? It doesn't go with that blouse."

Chapter Sixteen

Dolly sat behind the desk in her trailer, finishing a cigarette and pondering what moves she could make to drum up more business. The arrival of Ulrich Schröder was an unexpected plus, shoring up the circus' main act, but not without its side effects. While it made Antoinette happy to have a professional catcher, she hated sharing the spotlight with the handsome German. This was nothing new since drama followed Antoinette like day followed night.

A knock on the door pulled Dolly from her thoughts. "Come," she said loudly.

The door to the trailer swung open and Dolly was delighted to see Willy standing there. "Brought you the paper," Willy said, taking a step forward and laying that day's Times-Standard on the desk.

"Please, sit," Dolly said, lighting up a fresh Sorbaines. "There's something I want to talk to you about."

"Oh," Willy said, lowering himself into a chair.

"Yes, I need your help with something," Dolly continued.

"Sure, whatever you want."

"I'd like you to break up with Antoinette," Dolly said, dropping the statement like a bomb.

"I don't understand. Why would you want—"

"It's for your own good, Willy," Dolly said, blowing smoke toward the ceiling. "She's toxic."

Willy remained silent, apparently unsure how to respond.

"Do you like being part of the circus?" Dolly asked.

"Yes, of course," Willy said.

"Good. Do it today. And there's something else," Dolly said. "I want you to tell her the reason is that you realize she and Ulrich are perfect for each other and you don't want to stand in the way."

"But they're not perfect for each other," Willy said. "Antoinette loathes the man."

"If I've learned nothing else, I've learned that love's a funny thing," Dolly said. "Sometimes it needs a nudge."

Willy shook his head, stood up, and left the trailer.

Dolly smiled, knowing the day was about to get interesting. She stubbed out her cigarette, opened the newspaper, and saw the headline on the front page. She jumped from her chair, opened the trailer door screamed, "Meeting in the main tent, now!"

*   *   *

No one knew what the problem was, but every time Dolly called a meeting the news was never good.

"What is this?" Dolly yelled, waving the newspaper in her hand.

"It looks like a newspaper," Antoinette said flippantly.

Dolly opened the paper and held it up, revealing the headline. It read: *Police Investigate Suspicious Deaths of Two Teens.* "Which one of you is responsible for this?"

Her question was met with silence.

"Who... did... this?"

"What makes you think it was one of us?" the clown asked.

"How many times do we need to have this discussion?" Dolly seethed. "We have a schedule, and the schedule is to be followed. No exceptions. You wait until it's your day to take someone. And no kids, period."

"What makes you think it was one of us?" Mohawk Joe asked.

"Two teens with the life sucked out of them found in a car at the drive-in?" Dolly spat.

"Maybe the movie scared them to death," Antoinette quipped to a bit of laughter.

"You can laugh, but do you know what this means?" Dolly asked. "It means we have to pack up and leave a week early. We are going to have to cancel shows and refund people's money. This is a financial disaster!"

"Where are we going?" Ulrich asked.

It was a good question, Dolly thought. She had no plan for a new destination. All she knew was that it had to be far away from Eureka, and it had to happen fast. "Just pack up," she barked, then stormed from the tent.

Once Dolly was gone, Mohawk Joe looked over and locked eyes with the clown. The clown glared back, the corners of his mouth curling into a slight smile. Dolly may not have known who was responsible, but Mohawk Joe thought he knew the answer.

Chapter Seventeen

S piders.

This is where Newt Drystad believed he'd eventually find the answer to catching serial killers. But not any spiders. Specifically, tangled web weaving spiders. And even more specifically, tangle web spiders on drugs.

Newt had become infatuated with spiders at the age of ten when, on a visit to his father's office at Penn State University, he was exposed to research being done in the field.

The most classic web design, the kind people see most, is called a spiral orb web where the spider starts from the center and works its way out in increasingly larger circles. This was remarkably similar to the kill pattern of serial killers; they start close to home, often killing someone they know, then expanding their kill zone to greater and greater distances.

The next category was called funnel-web spiders. These spiders wove webs in the shape of a funnel, hence the name, they were often found nestled between rocks or in bushes. When a fly, for example, found its way into the web, the spider emerged from the bottom of the funnel and pounced on its prey.

Some serial killers used this approach, as well, drawing their victims to them rather than traveling to find their victims.

Then there was a category called tangle web spiders, whose webs looked like haphazard constructions, like cobwebs. The most well-known of the tangle web weavers were Black Widows. Tangle web spiders interested him most.

After ten years of intense research, Newt concluded that spiders and serial killers had three things in common:

1. First, they're both very smart.

2. Second, when in full control of their faculties, spiders spin near-perfect webs. Likewise, because their intelligence is usually off the charts, most serial killers were highly organized and virtually impossible to catch.

3. And third, when under the influence of a drug, both spiders and serial killers tend to screw up and make mistakes. Lots and lots of mistakes.

And if they were on more serious drugs—marijuana, LSD, Benzedrine, Ketamine, etc.—the mistakes were multiplied tenfold.

The official name of the program Newt had developed was the Predictive Data Algorithm—PDA for short. Around the FBI everyone referred to it as DSP—the Drugged Spider Program.

Even so, no matter how random and distorted the webs appeared, there were predictable patterns embedded in them.

Newt compared the kill patterns of 371 known serial murderers and compared them to six thousand webs spun by spiders under the influence of drugs. And he discovered a pattern. The pattern was subtle, but it was there.

Newt believed that studying spiders spinning webs under the influence could help him predict when a serial killer would take their next victim before they do. In other words, a spider's web was an extension of its subconscious mind. And it was the same for serial killers.

Getting spiders for studying them was not a problem. The problem was getting serial killers to study—in particular, getting a serial killer who was motivated to talk and would tell the truth.

Fortunately, Newt finally had a serial killer to study, one who had been caught by the FBI without anyone knowing. He was the biggest spider ever taken down by the bureau, and they were breaking all the rules by keeping him locked up without a trial or due process.

The man's name was Stan Lee Mungehr.

The media called him The Leg Collector.

Mungehr referred to himself as The Southern Gentleman.

Newt called him The Spider.

The name didn't matter. What mattered was that they finally had the man, and he was all Newt's to study for as long as he pleased.

*   *   *

"Ham and cheese sandwich, chips, and lime Jell-O," the agent said as he placed the tray on the floor inside the door.

"How long do you plan to keep me here?" Stan Lee asked. "I'm fairly certain my rights are being violated."

"It might be a good idea to eat it all this time," the agent said. "You won't be getting anything else to eat until morning."

"I'd like to send a message to—"

"No," the agent said. "Outgoing communications are not allowed."

"Tell Spider Boy I'm ready to talk," Stan Lee said.

The agent said nothing, locked the door and went to the end of the hall, and entered a small side room where Newt Drystad sat studying a case file. "He asked for you like you said he would."

Newt closed the book of crossword puzzles and put his pen in his pocket. "I'll be back tomorrow afternoon. Don't feed him anything else until I tell you it's okay. Understood?"

The agent nodded. "What do I say if he asks for you again?"

"Tell him you delivered the message," Newt said.

"How long are we planning to keep this guy down here?" the agent said in Newt's direction. He didn't get an answer.

* * *

When Newt returned the following day, the agent said, "Mr. Mungehr is not a happy camper."

"What happened?" Newt asked.

"Well, for one thing, he threw one of his prosthetic legs at me when I brought him breakfast," the agent said. "And he's threatening to sue."

"Did he say who he wanted to sue?" Newt asked.

"Everyone," the agent said.

"No, specifically," Newt asked.

"Specifically? Let's see—you, me, the FBI, the federal government, the president."

"He wants to sue me?" Newt asked.

"You, especially," Maggie said. "So, are you going in to see him?"

"Soon," Newt said as he turned and walked to the door. "He threw a prosthetic at you?"

"Sure did."

"Did you take the leg away from him?"

"No. Should I?"

"Yeah. Better yet, take them both."

* * *

Three days later, Newt was sitting behind his desk when Maggie stuck her head in the door. "You've got an agent from St. Elizabeth's, on line one."

Newt nodded and picked up the phone. "This is Special Agent Drystad."

Newt listened, then said: "No, not today. Tell Mr. Mungehr I'll come there tomorrow, but only if he's a good little spider."

Newt hung up the phone and looked over at Maggie and smiled.

"Mungehr's finally cracking?" Maggie asked.

"Like an egg," Newt said.

"You're going over tomorrow?"

"No, I'm going to let him fry until Wednesday."

"Do you want me there?" Maggie asked.

Newt thought for a moment, then said, "No, I want you to keep working with Chad. Get the ghost division up and running and keep Pipi happy. I'll take care of the spider."

Chapter Eighteen

C lay Daniels took his foot off the gas pedal and slowed his cruiser as he approached the road that led to the Crimson Cove lighthouse. The entrance between the trees was so narrow that if you didn't know it was there, it was easily missed. Clay knew where it was but still managed to miss it from time to time.

The road itself was dirt and wove several hundred feet between the trees where he found Noah Ashley working on the stone wall that surrounded the area around the lighthouse. The wall had been built by Onyx's father, Catfish Webb, almost seventy years earlier, back when Clay's great grandfather was the town's sheriff. The wall had survived four generations of Daniels men, each of whom followed the path of working in law enforcement.

Clay pulled the cruiser to a stop and turned off the engine. "Looking good, Noah," Clay said as he exited the vehicle.

Noah did not respond, picking up another stone and stacking it on the wall.

"I said..."

"I heard you, Clay. What do you want?"

"Well, I'm happy to see you, too," Clay said.

"Listen, Clay, you never come out here unless there's a problem of some kind. So, please get to it."

"I got a call from Abigale Dietz this morning," Clay said.

"And?"

"She's not a happy camper."

"Can't remember a time where Abigale *was* happy about anything," Noah said, stopping to wipe sweat from his forehead. "What's her problem now?"

"She claims Onyx came to her and threatened her," Clay said.

"Well, that would be something, considering Onyx is dead and buried right over there," Noah said, pointing to the headstones at the edge of the clearing where the woods began.

"Cut the crap, Noah," Clay snapped. "We both know where Onyx is, she's right where she always is, sitting in her room at the top of the lighthouse. Hell, she's probably listening to everything we're saying."

Noah released a breath. "Assuming Onyx did such a thing—which she didn't—what does Abigale claim this threat was?"

"Something about wanting Abigale to kill her plan to make the cove famous for ghosts."

"Sounds like a good idea, if you ask me," Noah said. "You want a ton of nutcase ghost hunters and tourists traipsing around the town? Sounds like that would make your job a lot harder."

"True enough, but threatening Abigale isn't the way to go about it."

Noah stayed silent.

"I remember a time when we were friends, Noah," Clay said. "I was the best man at your wedding. What happened?"

Noah bent over and picked up another stone. "Thanks for coming by," Noah said.

Clay shook his head and started back toward the cruiser. Then he stopped and looked toward the top of the lighthouse. "Knock it off, Onyx," Clay called out. "I mean it, knock it off."

* * *

"Did you threaten Abigale Dietz?" Noah asked slightly out of breath after climbing the 103 stairs to the top of the lighthouse, finding Onyx exactly where Clay said she was. "I thought we agreed that was a bad idea."

"*You* decided it was a bad idea, Noah," Onyx said, pulling a vinyl record from its album cover and placing it on the old Victrola turntable. "I didn't agree to anything."

"Listen, I'm sorry to have kept you in the dark about Abigale's plan," Noah said. "But, please let me take care of these things, okay?"

Onyx lowered the record player needle. "If you'd taken care of it," she said as the sound of Cab Calloway's voice filled the room, "I wouldn't have had to."

Chapter Nineteen

Dolly Oesterreich knew she needed to quit smoking. Not because she was going to damage her health. Ghosts couldn't get cancer, so the habit came with zero risk. It did come with significant monetary cost, however—$15 per pack once the cost of having them imported from France was factored in—but there was no way she would be caught dead smoking a Kent. Or even worse, Virginia Slims.

She took a long drag and released a billowing cloud of blue smoke in the air that hung overhead like a cloud in the small trailer. Packing up the circus and leaving Eureka prematurely made her furious. It was the third time in a year she had to do so because someone couldn't follow her very simple rules:

First, never take more than one person at a time. It was bad enough when the authorities had to deal with one otherwise healthy person dying of natural causes, let alone two.

Second, never kill a child. Admittedly, kids were tempting due to their high level of energy. Dead old people caused a few tears, but nothing drew the wrath of the police more quickly than a dead child.

And, lastly, follow the damn schedule and wait your damn turn.

Dolly felt the trailer slow, then come to a stop. She glanced at her watch. They were there.

"Are you sure we're outside the city limits?" she asked as she stepped from the trailer into the bright sunlight. She had no intention of filing for permits or jumping through bureaucratic hoops and regulations of fire marshals and building officials.

The biggest concerns for a small operation like Dolly's were wind and fire. The tent had to be secure enough to withstand 50-mile-per-hour winds without suffering damage. Then there was fire.

The worst circus fire in history happened to the Ringling Bros. and Barnum & Bailey Circus in Hartford, Connecticut, in 1944. The fire killed 167 people, and 700 were injured. Dolly wished she could get that many people to the circus, period. Things like wheelchair ramps? Fire-retardant coating? Emergency alarm systems? Cirque Du Soleil might have money and tolerance for such bullshit. She didn't.

"Yes, Dolly," Willy said from the bottom of the trailer steps. "We're about two miles from the edge of town."

"Can we get any closer?"

"No. The map shows nothing but forest from here all the way to the Crimson Cove city limits," Willy said. "We either set up here or try ten miles on the other side of town."

Dolly scanned the horizon and saw what appeared to be twenty acres of flat, open field and realized Willy was probably right. "Fine, we'll set up here. Chop, chop, everybody!"

*   *   *

Setting up the circus required a highly choreographed effort, something Dolly used to oversee herself. Now she had Willy. Erecting the main tent. Staging of equipment. Audience seating. Lighting. Wardrobe, dressing trailers, and animals. Tent master was a big job, one which Willy took to like a fish took to water.

Once everything had been properly staged, it was time for the dramatic moment of raising the big top roof. Two main masts supported the canvas roof, each 32 feet tall, which had been raised with the help of a hand-operated winch system. Even with the help of the winch, the task required the brute force of 20 people, working in unison to raise three separate sections of roof fabric. Then over 30 smaller fabric wall panels had to be secured to complete the sides of the tent.

All told, it was a process that took ten to twelve hours to complete. More importantly, the process took an enormous amount of energy.

Energy.

By the end of the day, Dolly knew every member of the circus would be exhausted. Trips into town, however, were out of the question. Killing your customers was bad for business. As much as some of the performers needed to take someone, it was going to have to wait.

Dolly saw Antoinette and Ulrich walking in her direction and could tell there was a problem. Of course, when it came to Antoinette, there was always a problem.

"When will our rig be up? It's been six hours and they haven't even started!" Antoinette whined. "Ulrich and I would like to practice. We're working on a front-end, back-end straddle whip. It should be a showstopper."

"I don't know," Dolly said. "Ask Willy, he's in charge."

"I'm asking you," Antoinette said with an edge in her voice.

Ulrich stepped forward and attempted to play peacemaker. "Anything you can do would be great, Dolly," he said.

"Fine," Dolly replied. "Send Willy to my trailer and I'll find out what's going on."

* * *

"You wanted to see me?" Willy said as he entered Dolly's trailer.

"Yes, Willy, take a seat," Dolly said.

"Am I in some sort of trouble?" Willy asked. "Everything is on track. We'll be ready to open by—"

"There's no problem, Willy," Dolly said. "I thought it would be nice if you and I spent some quality time together."

"Quality time doing what?"

Dolly held her pack of Sorbaines out. "Smoke?"

Willy shook his head.

"Did you break up with Antoinette, like I asked?"

"I tried," Willy said.

"You tried?" Dolly asked. "You either did or you didn't."

"She said I couldn't break up with her."

"Do you like me, Willy?" Dolly asked.

"Like you? Well, sure," Willy said. "Why wouldn't I like you?"

Dolly made her way over to Willy's chair and lowered herself on his lap. "I'm not asking if you like me, Willy," Dolly said, turning in such a way that her breasts were inches away from his face. "I'm asking if you *like* me?"

Willy began squirming uncomfortably in his seat. "I... I..."

Dolly leaned forward and began kissing Willy's neck with her painted-red lips. "I want you, Willy," Dolly whispered. "The question is, do you want me?"

Chapter Twenty

C had Chatterton was presented with two inescapable facts: First, ghosts were real. And second, FBI Director Pipi Esperanza was one. Even so, he still couldn't stop himself from saying, "I can't believe it," for the tenth time.

"You watched her stab herself in the neck, Chad," Maggie said. "That isn't proof enough for you?"

"No, it is," Chad said. "It's just, I don't know, it's so unbelievable."

"You say it's unbelievable one more time and I swear, I'm going to punch you," Maggie blurted.

Chad sat silently for a few seconds then asked: "Do you know how it happened? How did she die?"

"You remember Oklahoma City?" Maggie asked.

"What, you mean the bombing in '95?" Chad asked. "I was ten years old at the time, but, yeah, I remember it. It's all the news talked about for months."

Maggie stayed silent and let Chad grasp what she was saying.

"Are you telling me Pipi died in the bombing of the Murrah Federal Building?"

Maggie nodded yes.

"And she told you this?"

"No, Newt told me."

"Newt? Why would Pipi tell Newt?"

"She didn't have to tell him," Maggie said. "Newt was there."

"What, wait, Newt is a ghost?"

"No, you idiot. Pipi let Newt stay in the car while she ran inside to visit a friend," Maggie said.

"How old was he?"

"He was ten."

"Ten? And she left him alone in the car?"

"What? You'd rather she had him come in with her and die in the blast?"

"Just finish the story," Chad said.

"There's not much more to tell. Three years after the bombing, Pipi walked into an FBI field office," Maggie said. "The assumption was she'd survived the blast and spent a couple of years moving from homeless shelter to homeless shelter, suffering from amnesia."

"That's not possible. The FBI would have run down every detail and discovered the story wasn't true."

"Normally, yes, but the story about an FBI agent miraculously surviving the bombing was PR gold. The last thing the brass wanted was to dig up something that would poke holes in the story, so they didn't ask questions."

"Figures," Chad snorted.

"You ready to start?" Maggie asked.

Chad turned his gaze to the file boxes stacked along the walls of the office. "Yeah, but where?"

"Doesn't matter," Maggie said. "It's all got to make its way into the computer, otherwise the data is worthless."

"This many files could take a year or more to get them in. We're going to need help."

"I hate to break it to you, Chad, but you *are* the help."

*   *   *

One floor up, on the west end of the building, Newt Drystad studied the details of the two dead teenagers discovered in their car at the drive-in in Eureka, California, a week prior. The police report said *the gray, lifeless bodies had been found sitting in the front bucket seats of the boy's Chevy Camaro by the drive-in night manager.* The report also said *the night manager had been cleared of the murders,* assuming the cause of death was indeed murder.

Two things bothered Newt about the report.

First, while Newt had zero reason to suspect the manager of the killings, there was no way the guy should have been cleared since he had no verifiable alibi, telling the police he'd been asleep alone in the office with no one to vouch for it.

The second thing that bugged Newt about the report was the repeated use of the term *night manager.* What other kind of manager could it have been? It was a drive-in theater. Were there any drive-ins that showed movies during the day?

Unnecessary words aside, the report was thorough but held no clues of any value.

Except one.

Someone, presumably the killer, had left a card in the boy's hand.

It was a standard 2x5 inch business card, white, for a place called Bingham's Florist. Printed on the backside of the card were five hand-written letters: CMIYC.

There was no doubt in Newt's mind about who had placed the card in the boy's hand. It was a serial killer named Doyle Slade.

Slade's first victim was a woman who lived in the building next to his, and it was Doyle himself who discovered the body. The woman had been strangled with her nylons.

Doyle was interviewed and released, and the murder went unsolved. Not long afterward, Doyle moved away and his whereabouts were unknown for the next 16 years. During that time a total of 19 women were murdered, each strangled with a piece of their own clothing, and in each case, a card with the letters CMIYC written on it was found nearby.

The 20th victim survived the attack and was able to provide police with a detailed description of the assailant, which was widely shown on TV. Someone recognized the man and called the FBI. It was then that Doyle Slade was arrested and agreed to a plea deal: life in prison without parole in exchange for taking the death penalty off the table.

It was a well-known fact among FBI profilers that virtually every serial killer in history left a calling card of some sort. The Night Stalker, Richard Ramirez, drew pentagrams on the wall, often using the victim's lipstick. Keith Hunter Jesperson, who killed 8 women over 5 years, left smiley-face drawings. The Zodiac left notes written in complex code. BTK left notes taunting the police, daring them to catch him.

It was the rare serial killer who didn't leave one.

In Doyle Slade's case, the calling card was a literal business card with five letters written on it.

C.M.I.Y.C.

Catch Me If You Can.

That Slade was the killer of the two teenagers in Eureka seemed impossible since Slade had died in prison of liver cancer in 1997. But the evidence before him led him to only one conclusion: that Doyle Slade was back. Which was the last thing Newt needed right then. He wanted to focus his attention on Stan Lee Mungehr, the serial killer he had secretly locked up in the basement at St. Elizabeth's. Digging into the possibility that Doyle Slade was back—as a ghost, no less—was a complication he wanted to avoid. There was only one solution.

Newt needed to let Maggie and Chad deal with Doyle Slade.

* * *

Chad and Maggie sat at the desk across from Newt and Chad wasted no time getting to the reason for the meeting. "We need more help."

"Help? Help to do what?" Newt asked.

"Getting the information from the files into the computer system," Maggie said. "With just the two of us, it could literally take years."

"We're thinking interns," Chad said.

Newt leaned back in his new Herman Miller chair and closed his eyes and wondered if interns were a good idea. Then he thought about the chair, which was so comfortable sometimes he thought of sleeping in it rather than going home. When was the last time he'd been home? Newt wondered. Not to his apartment in D.C., but his *home* in Pennsylvania? It seemed like ages. So long he could barely remember what his parents' faces looked like. Then Newt felt hands on his shoulders and someone calling his name. He realized it was Maggie.

"Newt. Newt. Wake up!" Maggie said.

Newt opened his eyes to find Maggie standing in front of his chair, shaking his shoulders. "What's wrong?" Newt asked.

"What's wrong? You *froze*, that's what's wrong," Maggie said.

"No, I didn't," Newt said. "You asked me about interns, and I was thinking about whether it was a good idea or not."

"That was ten minutes ago, dude," Chad said. "We've been trying to shake you out of it. You were stiff as a mannequin. I was about to splash some ice water on you."

Newt's condition, SPMD—Selective Paralytic Mutism Disorder—was rearing its ugly head. As he feared it would. Drifting into periodic states of suspended animation, where he could neither speak nor move, was very disconcerting for those who witnessed it. Newt decided it was better to simply come clean and tell them the truth.

"I stopped taking my meds," Newt said.

"What?" Maggie said. "Why on earth would you—"

"You know how the meds cloud my thinking. I need to be able to think clearly right now."

"Well, you can't think if you're catatonic," Maggie snapped. "Jesus. Does Pipi know?"

Newt shook his head. "No, and don't you dare tell her."

Maggie lowered herself back in her chair. "Damn it, Newt," she said, but Newt ignored her.

"Excuse me, but I thought you called us here to talk about a case," Chad said.

"Yes," Newt said. "Have either of you heard of the *Catch Me If You Can* killer?"

Chad shook his head. Maggie said, "I don't think so."

"The guy's name was Doyle Slade. He was the son of an Irish diplomat, born in New York in 1948, one year after the opening of the United Nations building. His parents divorced a couple of years later, and he moved with his mother to Kansas City. The mother worked as a nurse at St. Luke's Hospital, while Doyle got into trouble with drugs and petty theft. After his fifth arrest, he was given a choice: enlist in the military or go to jail. He enlisted in the Navy in 1968, traveled the world on various ships, and was honorably discharged in 1971. He rented an apartment in Oceanside, California, and for all intents and purposes, it appeared he'd turned his life around. Then the killings started."

Newt explained the details of the report he'd received about the dead teenagers at the Eureka drive-in and the calling card. When he was done, he dropped the bomb. "I want the two of you to go to Eureka and check things out. The police are clueless, which is good, so we need to be on top of this."

"And you want us to go there? Like, together? Me and Chad?" Maggie asked.

"Why not?" Newt asked. "Is there some reason I should be concerned?"

"Not on my end," Chad said eagerly.

"Why do you want Chad and I involved with this Slade guy if it's a serial killer case?" Maggie asked. "You're supposed to be on serial killers, and we're supposed to be on ghosts."

"Sorry, I failed to mention Slade died of liver cancer in 1997."

Maggie and Chad exchanged looks and Maggie said, "Okay, got it."

"What about the interns?" Chad asked.

"The interns? Uh, that's a hard no," Newt said.

"Why?"

"Think about it, Chad. The idea ghosts exist and are murdering people is so classified we don't want anyone else in the building to know," Newt said. "We can't input the files using interns—if we did and something leaked, we'd have a hundred million views on TikTok by Thursday."

Chapter Twenty-One

Noah Ashley lay in bed in the caretaker's house, staring at the ceiling, and realizing what a total shit he'd been. Jumping on Onyx for threatening Abigale Dietz was—after a bit of reflection—exactly what she should have done. Abigale was not easily deterred. She needed to be put on her heels. There was no other way she'd back off her plan of turning Crimson Cove into just another tourist trap with stores selling three t-shirts for $20. Noah needed a way to make it up to Onyx. But how?

Noah climbed out of bed, walked to the garage, pulled the canvas tarp off his motorcycle, and thought about the last time he'd taken her out—not just to town, but really let it out on Route 1. But first, he had an important situation to take care of.

* * *

Noah had invested his heart and soul in getting Noah's Grille up and running, and an ungodly number of hours to make it a success. So, the idea that Carlos had abandoned it so easily ticked him off. He'd be damned if the place was going to be taken back by the bank and turned into a 7-11.

"Have you ever met Mickey Spilatro?" Ellen asked once Noah had arrived at the restaurant.

"No, first time," Noah said. "Anything I need to know, other than the fact he's a gangster?"

"He's short. He gets pissed off when people say anything about it."

"How short are we talking?" Noah asked as he counted the money in the cash drawer. "Are we talking Joe Pesci short, or Peter Dinklage short?"

"I don't know who Peter Dinklage is, but Joe Pesci sounds right, though you never know how tall people are in the movies. Tom Cruise doesn't look short, but people say he is."

"And he's got a temper?"

"Tom Cruise has a temper?" Ellen said.

"No, I'm asking about Spilatro—does Mickey Spilatro have a temper?"

"See the wall?" Ellen said, pointing.

Noah glanced behind him and saw a gaping hole in the wall behind the bar about three feet off the ground. "Are you saying Mickey Spilatro did that?"

"Yes."

"Because of the money Carlos owes him?"

"Yes."

"Does Mickey carry a gun?" Noah asked, going back to counting the cash.

"I don't know, probably," Ellen said. "Speak of the devil..."

Noah looked through the window and saw a black Cadillac Esplanade pull into a parking spot. "Big vehicle for a little man," Noah said. "If he's as short as you say he is, I wonder how he can see over the steering wheel."

Ellen giggled, then said, "I think he uses a seat cushion, or maybe a child booster."

Noah and Ellen watched as Spilatro jumped down from the car and push through the front doors of the restaurant. He was dressed in a black sharkskin suit, with a silver necktie and an unlit cigar clenched between his teeth. To complete the look, he was wearing a dark gray fedora. The man looked like something out of central casting for a Scorsese movie. But Ellen had his height wrong—Spilatro was nowhere near as tall as Joe Pesci. More like Danny DeVito.

"Where's Carlos?" Spiltro snapped, not bothering to say hello.

"Carlos is gone," Ellen said.

"Gone? Gone as in he ran out for some cannoli? Or are you saying he's *gone* gone, as in, he flew the coop?"

"He left two days ago, and no one has seen him since," Noah said.

"And who are you?" Spilatro said, turning in Noah's direction.

"I'm the new Carlos."

"This is Noah Ashley," Ellen interjected. "He's—"

"Noah, huh? Noah as in *Noah's Grille*? That's your name on the front of the building?"

"That's me," Noah said. "You want something to drink?"

"No, I don't want something to drink," Spilatro said in a harsh tone. "What I want is my frickin' money, that's what I want. You got my money, you're my new best friend. If not, what are you doing here?"

"Like I said, I'm the new Carlos. If you want your money, you deal with me now."

Spilatro looked over at Ellen and said, "The balls on this guy. Did you explain the situation to this goombah?"

"He knows Carlos borrowed $200,000 from you," Ellen said. "And I told him what you threatened to do to Carlos and me if we didn't pay."

"Good, but it's $218,000 now," Spilatro. "You forgot about the vig."

"What?!" Ellen said, shocked. "What's the vig?"

"It's the interest on the loan," Noah said.

"That's correct," Spilatro said turning back in Noah's direction. "I'm an entrepreneur, and entrepreneurs are entitled to a profit. Isn't that right, Mr. restaurant owner?"

"Come on, let's sit," Noah said, taking a seat at a table.

Spilatro shrugged and said, "Why not?" and climbed into the seat opposite Noah. "You got somewhere I can hang my hat?"

Noah didn't answer.

Spilatro removed his hat and placed it on the chair next to his. "We used to own this place. My family, back in the day."

"The Owl," Noah said.

"That's right, Faustino Spilatro was my great grandfather," Spilatro said. "Hell of man, tough as nails—Vegas tough. They don't make 'em like that anymore, do they?"

"Let's talk about the money," Noah said, changing the direction of the conversation. The last thing he wanted to do was get into a pissing match about what an evil person The Owl had been, and the pain the Spilatro crime family had brought down on the residents of Crimson Cove in the past. It was better to drop it.

"Okay, talk."

"I don't have the money," Noah said. "Not even close."

"Then that's a problem."

"But there's something I *do* have," Noah continued.

"Being?"

"Skills," Noah said. "I can cook, and I know how to run a restaurant—a *profitable* restaurant."

"Keep talking," Spilatro said.

"I propose you give me a few days to get the restaurant back open, and then you can come by every Monday, and I'll make a payment."

"How much?"

"I figure $2,000 a week is possible."

Spilatro snorted, then said, "At two thousand a week, plus the interest at ten percent per week, you could never get there."

"Yeah, about the vig," Noah said. "There isn't going to be any vig."

"You want me to waive the vig?" Spilatro scoffed. "Why would I do that? I ain't runnin' some kind of goody-two-shoes non-profit."

"You want your $200,000 back?" Noah said. "Then that's the deal, take it or leave it. $2,000 a week for the next two years, then we're done."

Spilatro remained silent for the next minute, then said: "I want it every week, no exceptions. You're one dollar short and we're gonna have a problem."

"Short? Don't worry about us being short. We won't be short," Noah said, glancing at Ellen who was doing her best to keep a straight face.

"You're a smart ass, huh, Ashley?" Spilatro said. "What makes you think I won't take the money for the next two years, then kill the two of you to send a message to the rest of the schmucks around here?"

"I don't know," Noah said. "Probably for the same reason I'm not going to have you killed in your sleep."

"The fuck? Who the fuck do you think you're talking to?" Spilatro said, rising to his feet, his face flushing with anger. "One more crack like that and you've signed your death warrant."

Noah stood and glared down at Spiltro. "And if you don't take the deal, you just signed *yours*, Mickey," Noah said. "You don't know who *I* am, do you? You *do* realize who my wife is, right?"

It took several seconds, then Spilatro's face went slack.

"That's right," Noah said. "Onyx Webb is my wife. And I promise you, take the deal or you'll never have a good night's sleep for the rest of your life."

* * *

The first time Noah had ventured down Route 1 on his bike, he was taken by the rugged beauty of the Oregon Coast—the ocean on one side, and a sea of Douglas firs and spruce trees on the other. And the smell. It smelled... *green*.

It was in a place called Otter Rock that Noah finally saw it: a quaint hotel nestled among the trees, feet from the ocean. It was perfect.

Noah turned in, parked the bike, and entered the office.

"Welcome to the Otter Rock Lodge," a young girl said from behind the counter. "Checking in?"

"No, I need to make a reservation."

"How many in your party, and what dates are you looking for?"

"Just me, and just one night," Noah said. "Tonight."

"Hang on and let me see if we have anything, it's a really busy time." The girl typed on the keyboard and then sighed. "Oh, darn, we only have one room."

"Well, I'm only looking for one room."

"I know, but it's more than you probably want to spend since it's just you, I mean."

Noah said the room was only for himself because he had no plans for anyone to know Onyx was there. "How much?"

"Like I said, it's expensive because it has an ocean view, a very large bed, and mirrors on the ceiling."

Noah pulled out his wallet. "How much?"

"$325," the girl said sheepishly.

"I'll take it," Noah said. Compared to the $2,000 per week he'd agreed to pay Mickey Spilatro for the next two years, $325 seemed like a rounding error.

*   *   *

When Noah got back to the lighthouse, he put the bike in the shed and then found Onyx in the foyer playing the piano.

"You want to hear about my day?" Noah said. Onyx looked over but continued playing. "I got Carlos and Ellen off the hook for the money they owe Mickey Spilatro, without interest, I might add."

"How did you manage that?"

"I told him if he didn't take the deal, I was going to send you over to kill him."

Onyx stopped playing. "You threatened Mickey Spilatro?"

"Yep."

"After you gave me hell for threatening Abigale, *you* threatened someone? Using *me* as the threat?"

"Well, it worked," Noah said. "Oh, and I rented us a room for the night. Tonight."

"You rented us a room?" Onyx said. "What in God's name for?"

"I wanted to say I was sorry, and I thought..."

Onyx released a long breath and tried to calm herself. After 70 years of being a ghost, she'd learned few things burned more energy than anger.

"It's a beautiful place, Onyx, down at Otter Rock, very romantic, nestled in the trees," Noah said, "with an amazing ocean view."

"A beautiful place? Nestled in the trees? Look around, Noah—we live in a lighthouse with a view of the ocean that's so beautiful they named the place Crimson Cove. How much better could the ocean view possibly be?"

Chapter Twenty-Two

Doyle Slade could not remember being so tired in his entire life (or death, for that matter.)

He'd spent the last twelve hours hauling crates, feeding animals, and building bleachers. The worst part was raising the canvas roof of the big top tent. Being one of ten people pulling on a rope with all your might was exhausting for any man, but for a ghost? It sucked your energy. Like steam escaping a tea kettle, the water eventually evaporates if left on the stove too long. So, everyone cheated. They pretended to be pulling the rope, but they held back. Which made the job take three times as long to complete.

Slade knew this to be a fact because he, too, had held back. His survival depended on it.

Even with holding back, the amount of energy he'd expended was significant. He felt like an empty vessel, light, virtually floating in the air. This is what the living saw sometimes, hence the vision of a ghost floating at the bottom of a bed or in a graveyard. It was days like this that made him wonder what he was even doing, trying to stay.

Early on, the circus made sense. Being surrounded by fellow ghosts, who understood what it was like to be dead hiding in plain sight, provided a feeling of comfort. Of belonging. Maybe it was time to go it alone?

And then there was Dolly and her damn schedule. Each ghost had a day when they were allowed to go to town. His day was still a week away, and he knew he'd never make it. Screw Dolly. He refused to be treated like a child any longer. He'd go when he damn well felt like it. Like he'd done the previous week in Eureka. Taking the two teenagers at the drive-in wasn't only necessary, it was fun. The look on those kids' faces when he opened the door and climbed in the back seat of the car. The terror in their eyes.

Just like the old days, back when he was alive.

*   *   *

Slade waited in his trailer until it was late enough to not be seen by too many people. But he couldn't wait too late, however—if he did, there might not be anyone out at all. On the weekends, he could go as late as 2 a.m. This was a weekday, so he needed to leave earlier. He glanced at his watch. It was 11 p.m. Almost time to go. And he still needed to put on his clown makeup.

As per his routine, Slade started by laying out all his materials: thick white cream, powder, blue, red, and black face paint, and his brushes and face sponges. He hated the process when he'd first started, now he looked forward to it. He found it calming somehow. In truth, he didn't *need* to put on the makeup. It had become part of his ritual.

Serial killers loved their rituals.

The time required to properly apply his makeup was usually half an hour, but only if he was making himself performance-ready. Applying clown makeup for going to town late at night, he'd only need fifteen minutes.

Slade put a headband on to hold his hair back, then started by painting his entire face white. Face paint was an art, and like any artist, he needed a blank canvas on which to work. He liked using a sponge rather than a brush. The sponge was faster.

Next, he painted on what he considered the most important part of his clown face: the eyebrows. Most clowns focused on the mouth. This was a mistake. Eyebrows were the key, the more dramatic the better. His were high, arching, and jet black. He finished by using a smaller brush to apply matching black eyeliner for definition.

Slade grabbed another brush and painted his lips a bright ruby red, which he outlined in blue. He painted large blue circles on his cheeks, with a smattering of black freckles. Finally, he drew large trademark blue tears at the corner of each eye to complete the look.

When he'd decided to go the clown route, Slade had no idea how scared people were of clowns. He'd taken in a matinee when the circus was passing through Tucson a few years earlier. The title of the movie was *It*. Stupid title, but a great movie. Scary AF.

He missed popcorn, though. Eating for ghosts was strictly a non-starter. He'd made the mistake of having a hot dog once and found out the hard way. It wasn't pretty. To make up for the popcorn, he'd taken the theater cashier in the washroom right before closing.

Hopefully, Crimson Cove had a theater. Most small towns did. He made a mental note to check it out.

*　*　*

Ulrich stood in the darkness, watching the clown's trailer, waiting to see if Dolly was right.

Dolly had summoned Ulrich earlier in the day and asked him to do her a favor. "I want you to keep your eye on the clown," Dolly said.

"Okay. May I ask why?"

"He's the one not following the schedule," Dolly said. "I want you to follow him."

"And if you're right?"

"If he so much as sneezes without my permission, I want you to end him."

Twenty minutes later, Slade emerged from his trailer, in full clown makeup. He glanced around to make sure no one was watching. Satisfied he was alone, Slade headed off into the darkness.

* * *

Ulrich stayed as close to the clown as he could, but knowing the man was a ghost and could hear even the slightest snap of a twig, he had to maintain some distance, or he'd be discovered. He wasn't afraid of the clown, but he had no desire for a confrontation—not if he could avoid one. Even with his superior size, Ulrich knew that the best fight was always the one that could be avoided.

The clown wove his way through the trees, heading due east, at a pace Ulrich determined to be around three to four miles per hour. Where he was going was anyone's guess, but it seemed like it was more than a casual stroll in the woods—the man had a destination in mind.

Ulrich had no idea how far they'd walked but, based on where the moon was in the sky when they'd started until now, it was two hours, so they'd probably gone six to eight miles.

Ulrich's greatest challenge came when the clown exited the woods and entered a large clearing. If Ulrich followed him through the clearing, he would be spotted for sure. He had to hold back and wait, hoping he could pick up the trail later.

And then Ulrich saw it.

The lighthouse.

Ninety-two feet from the foyer floor to the top, the cast-iron structure stood at the edge of the cliffs, watching over the cove like a sentry on guard duty—the flame dancing at the top of the tower, just as he remembered.

He also remembered how much he hated the nightly task of hauling kerosene up the 103 steps to the tower. The state of Oregon had considered upgrading to electric but other priorities always ate up the State's funds. Besides, it wasn't the responsibility of the state legislators to climb up and down the damn thing—as the owner, it was his.

Off to the left, Ulrich noticed two graves. He walked over so he could read the names on the gravestones. One of the stones was etched with the name of Onyx's father, André Webb, who went by the name of Catfish—a man who didn't care for Ulrich and did everything within his power to keep her from marrying him.

The second gravestone bore the name Katherine Keane, someone Ulrich had met years earlier but didn't know very well. All Ulrich knew about Keane was that she and Onyx had both been kidnapped by someone the papers called the Child Snatcher of St. Louis. What was the kidnapper's name? Ulrich tried to remember, but like so many other things, he couldn't recall it. In any case, Onyx and the Keane woman must have been close. Why else would she be buried here?

Then there was a third grave, this one was unmarked. Could it belong to Onyx? Or perhaps it was *his* grave. Yes, it probably was, Ulrich decided. Buried in an unmarked grave seemed like something Onyx would have done, and something he probably deserved.

Then Ulrich shifted his gaze to the caretaker's cottage, and to the right side of the building where the bedroom was located—the bedroom in which his loving wife set him on fire seventy-five years earlier.

A moment later, a light came on in the room.

Someone was there.

Chapter Twenty-Three

Serial killer Stan Lee Mungehr was lying on the concrete slab in the ten-by-twelve-foot room that had served as his home for over a month. He was on his back, looking up and daydreaming about the various ways he intended to torture Newt Drystad if the opportunity ever presented itself, even though he knew it was unlikely.

When you're locked in a room in the basement of a building in God knows where—fantasies of taking a pair of pliers to the man who put you there were all you had.

Stan Lee heard footsteps echoing off the concrete walls in the distance and sat up. He felt naked without his prosthetics, and his stumps ached worse than he could ever remember. They were dry and cracked to the point of bleeding. He learned early on that asking for lotion was pointless.

Making sure he didn't get what he asked for was part of the game that was being played.

The footsteps grew louder. How many people? It was more than one person. That he could tell for sure.

When the door opened Stan Lee saw Special Agent Newt Drystad standing there. In shorts. Legs in full view for Stan Lee to see. The legs shined and shimmered in the florescent lighting as if the man had just rubbed lotion on them.

Once, several weeks earlier, they sent in a female agent in a short skirt. For whatever reason, that didn't get to him as much as this. Well played, Stan Lee thought.

"Well, if it isn't Spider-Boy," Stan Lee drawled, using his well-practiced Southern Gentleman accent.

Newt turned and headed for the door.

"Wait!" Stan Lee said. "I apologize for my rude behavior."

Newt stopped and turned around. "Let's get something straight. I'm in charge here."

"And *here* is, where exactly?"

"Here is *here*," Newt said, waving his hand, "and you're in no position to demand anything."

After a moment Stan Lee said, "Is there any chance of getting my prosthetics back, Agent Drystad?"

"It's *Special* Agent Drystad, and we'll see," Newt said.

"Some people would consider this cruel and unusual punishment," Stan Lee said.

"That's humorous, coming from someone who murdered fifty women, sawed their legs off, and kept the legs in glass containers filled with formaldehyde. You do see the irony, don't you, Stan Lee?"

Stan Lee remained silent.

"But I might be willing to make a trade."

"A trade?"

"Yes," Newt said.

"What kind of trade did you have in mind?"

"Your prosthetics in exchange for information."

"What kind of information?" Stan Lee asked.

"Your story," Newt said. "I want your story. All of it, with nothing held back. And all of it, the truth."

"What makes you think I'll tell you the truth?"

"Because I think you *want* to tell me the truth," Newt said. "I think you're hungry to explain why you've done the horrible things you've done. I think you want to someone understand you."

"And that someone is *you*, Special Agent?"

"Yes."

"And if I do as you ask, if I share my deepest, darkest secrets with you, then I get my legs back?"

"No," Newt said. "You're never going to get your legs back—but I will return your prosthetics."

A full minute of silence passed, then Stan Lee said: "Very well. Where do you want to start?"

*   *   *

Newt leaned forward and pressed the red record button on the video camera perched on the tripod next to his chair. "Why don't we start with the first person you killed. When was it and why did you do it?"

"You know this already, Special Agent Drystad, don't you?"

"I know who you killed, and how you killed her," Newt said. "What I'm interested in is, why?"

Stan Lee took a deep breath and exhaled loudly as if he was already exhausted by the session. "Very well. Her name was Juniper."

"Juniper Cole?" Newt said. Stan Lee nodded in the affirmative, but Newt knew Stan Lee was lying. And he wasn't surprised. Asking for honesty and getting honesty were two very different things. All that mattered was he'd gotten Stan Lee to engage with him. "Go on," Newt said.

"What do you want to know?"

"Why Juniper? Of all the kids at the prom that night, why her?"

"Pure chance," Stan Lee said. "I was looking for someone to kill, and she was in the wrong place at the wrong time."

"You said you were looking for someone to kill, but that isn't true, is it? You were looking for a girl to kill."

"Yes."

"Why a girl?"

"They're easier to take," Stan Lee said.

"That's not the reason, is it, Stan Lee?" Newt said. "What's the real reason?"

Stan Lee remained silent.

"Tell me about the prom," Newt prompted. "Not the prom you took Juniper from, I'm talking about *your* high school prom."

Stan Lee shifted uncomfortably on the concrete slab and glanced toward the corner of the room. "Don't look to her for answers," Newt said. "I want to hear from *you,* not her."

Stan Lee began to shake, then steadied himself and said, "I don't know what you're talking about."

"Sure, you do, Stan Lee. I'm talking about your imaginary friend," Newt said. "What's her name?"

"I said, I don't know what—"

"It's okay, Stan Lee," Newt interrupted what he knew was about to be another denial. "It's just the three of us here, right? You, me, and your friend—the friend you created to help you cope with the world. Say her name."

A minute went by in total silence.

"There's nothing to be ashamed of," Newt said. "Most kids have imaginary friends. But as normal children assimilate into the world, they grow out of it. You didn't. Your assimilation never took place. It got interrupted—first by seeing your mother murdered, and then the trauma you experienced at the Dunning asylum. My best guess is that's the moment she appeared. Am I correct?"

Once again, Stan Lee's eyes shifted to the corner of the room. Newt jumped from his chair and in Stan Lee's face. "What's her name?" Newt screamed as loud as he could.

"Kara," Stan Lee said finally. "It's Kara."

Newt took a step back and lowered himself back in his chair. "Good. Now I want you to tell her you're fine, and that you can trust me. That I have your best interests at heart, and you don't need her help, okay?"

Stan Lee nodded.

"Say it, Stan Lee," Newt said sternly. "Tell her—"

"I don't need her help," Stan Lee said.

"Don't tell me," Newt said. "Tell *her,* say it to *her.*"

Stan Lee looked to the empty corner of the room. "It's okay, Kara. You can go," Stan Lee said, wiping away a tear from the corner of his eye. "We can trust Special Agent Drystad. He's a friend."

Newt reached over, hit the stop button on the camera, and stood up. "I'm going to grab lunch. You want me to bring anything back? I love a good BLT sandwich, you want one?"

Stan Lee wiped his face with his shirt and nodded.

"Good, BLTs it is," Newt said. "Then we'll get back to Juniper Cole."

Chapter Twenty-Four

O nyx stood at the top of the lighthouse, gazing at the gray of the ocean as she did every day at sunset. The only color Onyx could see was a thin line of crimson as the sun went down over the ocean. Other than those few seconds of color, Onyx lived in a gray lighthouse surrounded by gray trees beneath a gray sky.

The lighthouse was purchased in 1937, a gift from her first husband, Ulrich, for $5,800, which was a royal sum at the time. Only later did Onyx discover Ulrich had murdered the previous owner so the lighthouse would come up for sale.

Ulrich had walked Onyx blindfolded through the woods and finally, they reached a clearing and said, "Okay you can look now." Admittedly, it was a magical moment.

For the next two years, Onyx was the happiest she'd ever been, spending her days painting and her nights standing at the top of the lighthouse with the sound of the ocean waves crashing on the rocks below. For the first time since leaving the Louisiana bayou, Onyx felt like she was home.

For Ulrich, however, owning the lighthouse was pure hell. He'd failed to read the list of responsibilities required of him in Clause 26 of the purchase agreement, which read:

"Purchaser agrees to provide ongoing maintenance and upkeep of physical structure, land, and foliage, in addition to all daily tasks associated with the operation of the structure for its intended purpose."

By buying the lighthouse, Ulrich had unknowingly trapped himself in a grueling, thankless job that provided a laughably meager eighty-dollar monthly stipend to cover his time and effort maintaining the place. His days were spent painting, caulking, patching, spackling, sanding, mopping, waxing, mowing, cutting, planting, trimming, and filling in potholes in the 156-foot dirt road that led from the main highway.

And as if that wasn't enough, the owner was responsible for ensuring the lighthouse remained lit from dusk to dawn, which required carrying twenty-eight gallons of lamp oil up the 103 steps of the spiral staircase to the top of the lighthouse. He would have enjoyed more freedom had he been convicted for killing the previous owner and put in prison.

To make his existence tolerable, Ulrich began spending money he'd stolen from the Vegas mob, even though he knew doing so might attract unwanted attention. These purchases included a guitar, radio, shotgun, phonograph, his and hers bicycles, and one of every tool offered in the Sears catalog. "And a dinner jacket?" Onyx asked. "Who are we going to see, Ulrich? This is not New York or San Francisco. We live in a lighthouse in the middle of nowhere!"

And that was the problem. Ulrich was trapped in a lighthouse in the middle of nowhere. And it drove him mad.

As Onyx's anger grew, Ulrich changed direction and began spending money on her instead. A Singer sewing machine was the first thing to arrive, followed by art books, paints, fifty-foot rolls of canvas, dozens of pairs of women's shoes—in random styles and colors—and when she casually mentioned how nice it would be to have a typewriter, Onyx found herself standing on the front steps of the lighthouse signing for a Remington Rand Model-5 and three cases of red and black typewriter ribbons.

But then Ulrich did the unthinkable when he purchased a Mercedes Benz sports car. "What I wouldn't give for my old friends in Berlin to see me cruising down the autobahn in this!"

"What then, Ulrich? If they could see you in this car, what then?" Onyx asked.

"Then they would see what a success I have made of myself."

"No, Ulrich," Onyx said, shaking her head. "What they would see is what a fool you have become. Tell me, how much did this car of yours cost us?"

Ulrich said nothing.

"Tell me, Ulrich!" Onyx yelled. "I am your wife, and I have a right to know."

"Ten thousand," Ulrich said finally.

"Dear God, Ulrich," Onyx said. "You've gone mad. What's next? What craziness should I expect next?"

Onyx had no idea that Ulrich had reconnected with his mistress, Claudia, and that she would convince Ulrich to poison her to death. In the end, Onyx got the last laugh, dousing him in kerosene and setting him on fire. In the process, Onyx was seriously burned and three days later she would die in the woods, attacked by a pack of wolves. The whole thing was like an insane soap opera.

Unlike Ulrich, Onyx did not remain dead. She found herself as a ghost, straddling the line between the world of the living and the world of the dead. Seventy years later she fell in love with Noah.

If ever there were opposites, it was Ulrich and Noah.

Ulrich was lazy. Noah was hard working.

Ulrich did nothing but complain. Noah rarely said a word about the things that bothered him.

Ulrich was rough. Noah was tender.

Ulrich was selfish. Everything Noah did was with her in mind.

Because of Ulrich, Onyx was a ghost. Noah married her knowing she was a ghost.

On top of everything else, Ulrich had an unsatiable need for sex, and she'd always accommodated him. Yes, it was in a time when women were subjugated to the home and submitted to their husband's every sexual desire. But still.

The more she thought about Ulrich, the worse Onyx felt about the way she'd treated Noah. He'd try to do something nice by renting the room down at Otter Rock, and what did she do? How did she repay him? She knew she had to fix what she'd done.

One way would be to pack a bag and tell him she wanted to go after all. But she didn't. She wanted to stay in the comfort and safety of the lighthouse.

The love between her and Noah wasn't gone, but Onyx knew it wasn't as strong as it once had been. And sex? When was the last time they'd made love? The mere fact that she could not remember was an indication of a problem.

Onyx checked her reflection in the mirror and was pleased with the image looking back at her. No scars. No crow's feet at the corner of her eyes. The small lines that could once be found at the corners of her mouth were gone as if rubbed away with a pencil eraser. She was thirty-nine forever.

So why check her appearance? The only reason was to see if she needed makeup to mask any grayness.

Satisfied, Onyx descended the spiral staircase and headed over to the caretaker's house. She entered the bedroom and opened the bottom dresser drawer. It was where she kept her most intimate apparel. A drawer she had not opened for way too long.

Shame on her.

Onyx found Noah asleep in the bedroom down the hall and quietly pulled back the covers. Noah opened his eyes and looked up at her in surprise. "What is this?"

Onyx climbed on top of Noah, leaned down, and pressed her lips against his, then softly replied: *"This is us being us."*

* * *

After they'd made love, Onyx stayed in bed with Noah until he drifted off, then quietly climbed out of bed. Then, out of nowhere, she felt a chill run down her spine as if someone was watching. She spun around and saw the silhouette of a man looking through the window. She took a step forward, and as she did, the form disappeared.

Onyx threw on her nightgown and rushed outside just in time to see a man running away. She hurried after him but the man managed to reach the far edge of the clearing and disappear into the woods, not far from where the wolves had ended her life so many years earlier.

Though she could not see the man's face, there was something familiar about him. His height, the brutish way in which he carried himself. Another chill went down her spine.

Even from behind, she knew who it was.

It was the man she'd murdered seventy years ago.

It was her ex-husband.

It was Ulrich.

Chapter Twenty-Five

A very tall, very thin blonde flight attendant approached holding a tray with two tall, thin glasses of champagne. She set the glasses on the table between Maggie and Chad, then sauntered off.

"This wasn't necessary," Maggie said.

"I like champagne," Chad said, lifting his glass and taking a gulp of the bubbly liquid.

"No, I meant there was no reason to book a private jet. The FBI was paying for the trip."

"I didn't book the jet, it's mine," Chad said. "And if it got around that I'd flown Delta, people might think the family has money problems. Flying commercial was out of the question."

"When did you buy a jet?"

"Right after you dumped me," Chad said, picking up Maggie's glass and holding it out toward her. "Here, drink your champagne."

"We're on official business. It's against regulations."

"No one's here to find out, Maggie. I won't tell if you don't."

Maggie released a long breath, took the glass, and drained it in three big gulps.

"That's my girl," Chad said.

"I'm not your girl, Chad."

"I know. But I still don't understand why," Chad said.

"You want to know why? You *really* want to know why? It's because of *this*," Maggie said, waving her hand. "This isn't real. None of this is real."

Chad took a sip of his champagne. "Tastes like $200 of *real* to me."

"See. There's never a minute when everything isn't about money," Maggie said.

"Okay, so what if I got rid of all my money?"

"*What?*"

"You heard me," Chad said, leaning forward and taking Maggie's hand. "What if I gave away my money—donated it all to the ASPCA or cancer research—would you be willing to get back together?"

Maggie pulled her hand away. "You're nuts. You know that, right?" Maggie waved her hand to get the flight attendant's attention. "Can I have another glass of champagne, please?"

"Answer me," Chad said. "If I was poor, do you think you could love me again?"

The flight attendant arrived with another glass of champagne, and Maggie drank it down as quickly as the first. "I'm going to sleep. Wake me up when we get there."

* * *

Maggie was still trying to shake off the aftereffects of the champagne when Chad's plane set down at the private airstrip in Eureka, California. There was a limo waiting for them on the tarmac. Maggie insisted they rent a car.

Once at the Eureka Police station, she and Chad were left sitting in the waiting area for twenty minutes. It was a case of the local police trying to flex their muscle and show them who was in charge. This was one thing Hollywood got right. It was the same everywhere.

Eventually, a man approached them. "Mind if I see some ID?" Maggie and Chad opened their FBI identification wallets and allowed the man to inspect them. "I'm detective Walsh. What seems to be the problem?" Walsh did not offer to shake their hands, nor did he offer them anything to drink.

Again, more games.

"There's no problem," Maggie said.

"Except no one here called the FBI," Walsh said.

"Just standard follow-up on a recent murder case."

Walsh screwed up his face. "Murder case? We aren't working any murders right now."

"Sure, you are," Maggie said. "The dead kids at the drive-in?"

"Oh, that. The coroner already determined the cause of death to be natural causes. Open and shut. Anything else?"

"Nope, that's it," Maggie said and looked over at Chad. "Let's go."

"Mind if we take a look at the file?" Chad said.

"Well, that could take some time," Walsh said. "Everything on the case has already been sent to the archives. I can put in a requisition if you want, but it could take some time."

"Not necessary," Maggie said. "Come on, Chad."

"How long are we talking? To get the file?" Chad prodded.

Maggie grabbed Chad by the elbow and led him out of the station.

Once they were outside, Maggie said: "What in the hell was that?"

"What do you mean? We're here to see the file, aren't we?"

"No, Chad, we're here to see if there has been any kind of real investigation, which obviously there hasn't. Like he said, it was open and shut. This is good for us. Besides, Newt's already seen the file. If there was anything we needed to know, he would have told us."

Chad threw up his hands. "Then why are we here?"

"We're here to investigate."

"That's what I was trying to do," Chad said.

"No, you were trying to look like a big-shot FBI agent."

*   *   *

"I told everything I know to the police already," the drive-in manager said.

"Humor us," Maggie said. "So, you woke up about six in the morning, and then what?"

"I went outside to leave and that's when I saw the red Camaro," the manager said.

"What kind of red?" Maggie pressed. "Bright red? Maroon? Candy apple red?"

"Candy apple," the manager replied. "Custom paint job, probably. Shiny."

Maggie glanced at Clay, but the importance was lost on him. "And you say their skin was gray?"

The manager nodded. "And wrinkly, like old people. Real old, like they were in their sixties."

"Anything else?" Chad asked.

"Well, there was one other thing," the manager said. "It might be nothing, but…"

"What?" Maggie prompted.

"Earlier that night, around dusk, I thought I saw someone standing at the far end of the parking lot. He caught my eye because of the way he was dressed."

"How was he dressed?" Chad asked.

"Like a clown."

Chapter Twenty-Six

When the phone had rung 30 minutes earlier, Abigale almost didn't answer it. Thank God she did.

It was from a customer at the Dietz Theater, informing her that one of her employees had cut his hand opening a metal can of nacho cheese sauce. The cut was bad enough that they drove him to the emergency room.

"Okay, thanks," Abigale said. "I'll check on him in the morning."

"No, you don't understand," the man said. "The person who drove him was the other employee. There's no one running the place, there are only customers." Abigale grabbed her cell phone and dialed Aaron, telling him to meet her at the theater as fast as he could. By the time she got there, the movie had ended, everyone was gone, and the lobby was in a clouded haze of burned popcorn smoke. Then she thought about the money.

Abigale opened the register drawer and was happy to see it still had cash in it. If someone had taken money, they would probably have stolen it all. People in small towns like Crimson Cove tended to be fairly honest, for the most part.

That's when Abigale heard footsteps approaching from behind. "It took you long enough," Abigale said, turning around and expecting to see Aaron walking up. It wasn't Aaron. It was a clown.

"I'm sorry, but the theater is closed," Abigale said. The clown stood there, smiling at her. Or maybe he wasn't smiling, she thought—maybe it was his makeup. The clown raised his arm and held out his hand in Abigale's direction. She looked and saw he was holding a card. "What? What is that?"

The clown reached his hand out a bit further, close enough that Abigale could read the five letters that were printed on it.

CMIYC? The letters meant nothing to her. "I think you'd better leave," Abigale said.

A moment later, the clown was on her, shoving her backward into the popcorn machine, the glass door coming off its hinges and shattering on the cement floor. Abigale tried to run, but the clown reached out and grabbed her scarf, pulling her backward. The clown tightened his grip on the scarf, pulling it harder and harder. Abigale clawed desperately at the scarf, but it was futile.

Eventually, the room went black.

* * *

Slade walked to the front door of the theater, turned the bolt to the locked position, flipped the open sign to closed, and returned to the concession stand. Hopefully, she was still alive. There was no way to suck the life out of a dead person.

He knelt over the woman and placed his fingers on her neck.

Good, a pulse.

When Slade was alive, he choked his victims to death. Always from the front, never from behind. Nothing made a killer feel more powerful than watching the life drain from someone's eyes. He did not understand shooting people, like that guy David Berkowitz. What was that about? Pull the trigger and run?

No, choking was the way to do it. Up close. Personal. Intimate.

In this case, the woman had been wearing a scarf, which was helpful. His energy was so low that he could feel his hands shaking. Now, he was seconds from feeling alive—well, as alive as a dead person could feel.

Slade placed his left hand behind the woman's head and raised it toward him. He leaned down and was about to put his mouth over hers when he heard footsteps. Somewhere outside. He wasn't worried. He'd locked the door. He paused. Then he heard the jingle of keys as they turned in the lock. A moment later:

"Abby? You here?" a man called out. "Abigale?"

Damn it.

Slade considered taking the man too but thought better of it. Taking a woman in his weakened state was one thing. Taking a man was another.

But this was why he'd come, wasn't it? To get energy. Here was his chance.

"Abigale! Where are you?" the man called out again.

Closer.

In the end, Slade did something he'd never done before. He decided to run.

Chapter Twenty-Seven

N ewt Drystad leaned back in his Herman Miller Aeron chair reading a file with his feet on his new Herman Miller foam foot pillow. The pillow, which was basically a block of foam inside a leather case, was designed for people who sat for long periods working at a computer. It elevated the feet, as well as supported them. More importantly, it placed your lower spine in a neutral position, helping relax your muscles and distributing torso weight more effectively.

The pillow set Newt back $275—more accurately, it set the bureau back $275 since he'd expensed it, even though he knew he probably shouldn't have. Per the manual, only necessary items could be expensed, and the pillow was far from necessary. But Newt had leverage to do things like this, knowing Pipi would never kick it back. Yes, she could hang him out to dry on the policy violation, but *he* could hang *her* out by exposing the fact she was a ghost—in particular, a ghost who needed to go out and kill someone every few weeks. As expected, Pipi signed off on it, and no one said a word.

Newt tossed the file he was reading on the desk and retrieved the file labeled Stanton Lee Mungehr. He was pleased with the progress he'd made with the serial killer, but there was still so much more to learn.

Newt had established that Stan Lee was an organized serial killer, as opposed to the disorganized variety, but knowing it didn't tell the whole story. At best it described a killer's pattern, but it didn't identify their motives.

Newt wanted to understand motives.

Motives were crucial to understanding what drove a person to do what they did; in other words, what made them want to kill—what made them *tick*.

Newt believed all serial killers fell into one of four "types" or categories: Hedonistic, Visionary, Mission, and Power/Control.

Hedonistic killers often killed for sexual gratification, usually involving rape and/or torture. They were driven by lust or were seeking a thrill.

Visionary killers usually murdered because they believed God, or some other power, was commanding them to kill. They were usually suffering from some form of psychosis, like the Son of Sam had been.

Mission-oriented serial killers felt it was their responsibility to rid society of certain groups of people, like prostitutes or to clean the streets of the homeless.

Finally, there were killers whose primary motivation was power and control. To this group, it was about dominating their victims.

Motivations rarely fit into one category and often overlapped. But in Mungehr's case, he fit into only one category. He never raped a single girl he took. No one told him to do it. And he wasn't on a mission.

In Stan Lee's case, it was about achieving power and control over his victims. To Newt's studied mind, the serial killer's primary motivation was the result of deep-seated feelings of inadequacy, powerlessness, and the fear of rejection. Dominating others gave him a feeling of empowerment. This was the reason he cut off his victim's legs and kept them as souvenirs.

Did Stan Lee believe that collecting enough legs would somehow replace the legs he had lost? It was an interesting question. The answer would help him understand his motivations.

Newt kicked away his foot pillow and left the comfort of his Herman Miller chair for the first time in two hours and stood up. He grabbed his gun and FBI ID and pulled a bottle of meds from his desk drawer. He didn't want to take them because they clouded his thinking. But Maggie was right—he was freezing more often, sometimes drifting in a catatonic state for minutes at a time.

Newt opened the bottle, removed one of the yellow and black pills, and popped it in his mouth.

* * *

Rather than sitting in his regular position on the concrete slab on the far side of the cell, Stan Lee was sitting in the wheelchair Newt had arranged.

"You look happy," Newt said as he set up the video camera and took his seat.

"I had a dream last night," Stan Lee said. "Want to hear it?"

"Sure," Newt said. "I've got time for anything you want to discuss."

"I was back on the farm. My Oma was pinning a carnation on my lapel, a light blue carnation. She said the color went nicely with my eyes, then she got a camera and took my picture. Then, suddenly I was sitting in the passenger seat of a pickup truck driving down a dirt road."

"Whose truck, do you know?" Newt asked,

"Jimmy Teagarden," Stan Lee said.

"This Jimmy Teagarden, he was a friend?"

"No, he was a dick," Stan Lee said, annoyed. "Do you want to hear the rest of the dream?"

"Go on."

"Well, the next thing I remember Jimmy's girlfriend started teasing me about the carnation, telling me light blue was popular with legless faggots. Then she reached down and started rubbing me."

"Masturbating you?"

"No, she was rubbing one of my stumps," Stan Lee said. "She was saying they felt weird, rough, like the outside of a cantaloupe. No, not a cantaloupe, like the outside of a coconut."

Newt remained silent. He couldn't wait to see where this was going.

"I started apologizing, telling her I usually put lotion on them, but I forgot," Stan Lee continued. "That's when she pulled a plastic bottle of Jurgens from her purse and squirted a large dollop of white lotion into her hand and started massaging my stump, asking me how it felt."

Again, Newt said nothing, giving Stan Lee time to search his memory.

"Then, like dreams tend to do, there was a time jump," Stan Lee said. "I found myself surrounded by a group of kids, all wearing masks and robes, like from one of those devil worship movies. Then one of the kids walked up and asked me if I'd ever been in a parade. I started begging them not to do it, but they ignored me. They took off my clothes and duct-taped me to a metal pole."

"It wasn't a dream, was it, Stan Lee? It's a memory," Newt said. "You're talking about the night of the homecoming dance, your freshman year in high school."

Stan Lee nodded. "Very good. You've done your homework."

"They dressed you up like a scarecrow and paraded you out in front of everyone."

"Yep. Five hundred people in the bleachers, all laughing and pointing and chanting their stupid song:

Scarecrow, scarecrow, raggedy and worn,
Your hat is old, and your clothes are torn.
Your arms and legs are made of hay,
Out in the field, keep the crows away.

Stan Lee, Stan Lee, strapped to your pole,
With legs of hay and a heart made of coal.
Out in the field, pecked by the crows,
Eating your eyes and pecking your nose."

"Is this why you took Juniper Cole and cut her legs off?" Newt asked.

"I don't know, you tell me," Stan Lee said.

"The night you took Juniper, what was she wearing?" Newt asked.

"A dress."

"What color was the dress?" Newt pressed, already knowing the answer.

"I don't remember," Stan Lee said.

"Sure, you do, Stan. It was blue—light blue, the same as the carnation your grandmother pinned on you the night of the homecoming dance. It wasn't chance that you picked Juniper, it was the dress. That's what attracted you to her, wasn't it? It was the dress."

"When do I get my prosthetics back?" Stan Lee asked.

"Soon," Newt said. "Now tell me about the night you killed Juniper and took her legs."

"There's nothing to tell," Stan Lee said.

"Did she ask you what you planned to do?"

"Juniper was a smart girl, maybe the smartest of all," Stan Lee said. "She already knew."

"What did you do with Juniper's legs?" Newt asked. "They were the only set of legs we didn't find."

"I took them with me just before the FBI raided my house," Stan Lee said.

"Why? Why hers?"

"Because she was special."

"Special how?"

"She was innocent and pure," Stan Lee said. "And she didn't beg."

"Is that why you did what you did, to hear them beg?" Newt asked.

Stan Lee remained silent for several long seconds, as if thinking, then said, "No, I just wanted them to understand."

"To understand what...?"

"What it was like to lose my legs, the way I did."

"Again, what did you do with Juniper's legs?"

"I don't remember."

"I am going to ask you one last time, and if you don't answer me, the wheelchair is leaving with me," Newt said. "What... did you do... with Juniper... Cole's... legs?"

"Honestly, I don't remember," Stan Lee said. "I swear."

*   *   *

Once Newt Drystad was gone, Stan Lee grabbed the rails of the wheelchair and used his arms to raise himself as far as he could, then back into the seat. Then he did it again, and again, counting the reps as he went... *three, four, five...* until he reached fifty, and paused.

Stan Lee rested for a minute, then began again. He was determined to be in the best physical condition possible should the opportunity to strangle Newt Drystad ever present itself.

"Why'd you lie?" Kara asked from her position seated on the concrete slab to Stan Lee's left.

"About what?"

"About Juniper Cole's legs. You *do* remember what you did with them, right?"

Of course, he did.

Once he'd realized the FBI was closing in on him, he'd placed the glass container with Juniper Cole's legs in the back of the van with a few belongings and took off. He wanted to keep the legs, but Kara felt having a pair of severed legs in the back of his vehicle was a bad idea, should he get pulled over.

Giving in to Kara's incessant pressure, he'd rented a five-by-five temperature-controlled storage unit at a *Store-It-Cheap* facility in Ogallala, Nebraska. He'd paid $249.82 in cash for a six-month rental. Six months should have been plenty, and it would have been.

Had he not been caught.

Now, three months later, the three-foot-tall glass container with Juniper Cole's legs inside was sitting on a concrete floor in storage locker B122, covered by a brown and green blanket.

He wanted them back.

And the clock was ticking.

Chapter Twenty-Eight

Ulrich sat on the ratty little sofa in Mohawk Joe's trailer, deep in thought while carefully wrapping his hands in white Mueller's athletic tape. Growing up in Germany, as part of the Soaring Schröders high wire and trapeze act, he'd learned to take care of his hands. As a ghost, it wasn't necessary. Ripped skin was not painful like it had been when he was alive, but old habits were hard to break. It also looked more professional. The audience expected it.

"I never bothered to tape my hands," Mohawk Joe said from a chair on the other side of the trailer.

"Maybe that is why Antoinette was unhappy with you," Ulrich said without looking up. "You have a bad attitude."

Mohawk Joe snorted and said, "I'm dead. I think I'm entitled to have a bad attitude."

"Perhaps."

"By the way, where were you last night?" Mohawk Joe asked.

Ulrich didn't answer.

"Did you hear me, Ulrich? I asked where—"

"I went by the lighthouse."

"What lighthouse?"

"Where I used to live. With Onyx."

"Holy shit," Mohawk Joe said. "What made you decide to do that?"

Ulrich didn't want to talk about following the clown and chose to simply say, "Curiosity."

"So, it's still there? The lighthouse?"

Ulrich nodded. "Yes, it was still there. And something else..."

"What?" Mohawk Joe said.

"Not what, who," Ulrich said.

"No! Are you saying you saw—?"

"Yes, I saw Onyx."

Mohawk Joe jumped up out of his seat like someone had set fire to it. "Holy shit!"

Ulrich nodded. "You can say that again."

"Did she look the same?"

"Just as I remember her," Ulrich said. "Just as beautiful, maybe even more so."

"Did you talk to her?"

"No," Ulrich said.

"Did she see *you*?"

"I'm not sure, she might have," Ulrich said. "She chased me into the woods, but I lost her."

"Then she saw you."

"She saw someone looking through the window," Ulrich said. "She may not know it was me, it could have been anyone."

"So, what are you going to do?"

Ulrich tossed the empty tape roll on the trailer floor. "I'm not sure there is anything *to* do." The two men sat in silence, then Ulrich added: "It seems she has a new man."

"Oh?"

Ulrich nodded.

"Well, you can always go back and take him," Mojo quipped. "Right?"

Ulrich knew that, under normal circumstances, this is exactly what he would have done—he'd have killed the man with his bare hands. And he'd have enjoyed it. Yet he hadn't. He'd seen another man making love to his wife in their bedroom, but rather than kill him, Ulrich had turned tail and run away.

Why?

Then it hit him. The realization of the obvious: It was no longer *his* lighthouse. And they weren't making love in *his* bedroom. And Onyx was no longer *his* woman.

Those things were a lifetime ago.

Ulrich was dead. A dead man who had no desire to spend time hurting people, bringing them pain and heartache. He'd done enough of that to others to last a lifetime. And an *afterlife* time, too. In any case, it was time to report the status of his actions to Dolly.

*   *   *

Ulrich stood at the edge of Dolly's desk, towering over her as she leaned back in her chair smoking her stupid cigarettes. If there was one thing he hated, it was feeling like a child being chastised by a parent.

"I followed him, as you asked, but he lost me," Ulrich said.

"How hard can following someone be?" Dolly asked. "You should have been able to hear his footsteps from a mile away."

"And he could hear mine," Ulrich said, "so I had to stay back"

"I'm disappointed in you," Dolly said, stubbing out her cigarette. "Maybe I need to get a better man for the job?"

"Yes, maybe you do," Ulrich said.

When Ulrich exited Dolly's trailer, he was surprised to find Mohawk Joe waiting at the bottom of the steps. "What are you doing here?" Ulrich asked.

"I don't know," Mohawk Joe said. "Willy told me Dolly wanted to see me, that's all I know."

"Be careful," Ulrich snorted. "Dolly is a conniver. Whatever she asks, it's best to say no."

Mohawk Joe watched as Ulrich walked off and then climbed the steps to Dolly's trailer feeling like a condemned man heading to the gallows. A minute later, he understood Ulrich's warning.

"Wait. Are you asking me to kill the clown?" Mohawk Joe said.

"He's not following the schedule," Dolly snapped. "He's become a liability to the circus. If he keeps it up, we'll have to move again. Is that what you want to happen?"

"Well, no, of course not."

"Good, then it's settled," Dolly said lighting up another Sorbaines.

"I don't know," Mohawk Joe stammered. "I'm not sure if I can, there's something evil about him."

"There's something evil about all of us," Dolly said blowing a stream of smoke in Mohawk Joe's direction.

"How would I do it?"

"The same way you take anyone else," Dolly said.

Mohawk Joe thought for a moment, then nodded. "When does it need to be done?"

"Five minutes ago, but I'll give you until tomorrow morning. If the clown is not gone by then, pack your bags and go, you're of no use to me. You do realize I don't need you, right? Ulrich has replaced you as Antoinette's partner, so you serve no useful purpose unless you do what I tell you to do."

Chapter Twenty-Nine

It was a few minutes after 5 a.m. when Sheriff Clay Daniels arrived at the hospital and took the elevator to the fourth floor where Abigale Dietz had been rushed to hours earlier. He found Abigale's brother, Aaron, nervously pacing in the hallway.

"Took you long enough," Aaron said.

"How is she doing?" Clay asked.

"Someone almost strangled her to death, Clay, but other than that she's doing peachy," Aaron snapped.

"Is she conscious?"

"No, they've got her on a respirator."

"Did you see the person who attacked her?"

Aaron shook his head. "No, whoever it was, they ran off. What are you going to do about this?"

"What do you think?" Clay said. "I'm going to find out who did this and arrest them."

"Come on, Clay. We both know who did this. It was Onyx Webb."

"You don't know that."

"Really? Onyx threatened to kill Abigale two days ago, and now this happens? Who do you think did it? There was no money missing, Clay. It wasn't a robbery."

"Come on, Aaron. We both know—"

"Here we go, let's blame the victim."

"I'm not blaming Abigale, but we both know she tends to exaggerate things."

"What is it with you?" Aaron demanded. "Why are you always defending Onyx? I don't suppose it has anything to do with you and Noah being best buddies. Maybe you're not the right person to investigate this."

"Call me the minute she's awake, okay," Clay said, then walked away. There was no reasoning with Aaron when he was upset.

"You arrest Onyx today!" Aaron called out. "If you don't, I'm calling the FBI."

"Don't bother," Clay said over his shoulder. "I called them an hour ago."

* * *

Calling the FBI was the last thing Clay wanted to do. Abigale had survived the attack and no murder had been committed. Since there was no proof that any state lines had been crossed, which would have given them jurisdiction, calling the FBI made him look incompetent. After all, movies always showed the local police getting bent when the FBI showed up—now here he was calling them in.

But there were a few reasons to do it:

First, Clay had a connection to Special Agent Newt Drystad. They weren't friends, exactly, but they'd been involved in a case together months earlier.

Second, Clay had no reason to believe Onyx had attacked Abigale. Doing so would be stupid, which meant someone else had done it. Clay took pride in his work in law enforcement, but he knew his limitations. He was a small-town sheriff. With just himself and a couple of deputies, he was ill-equipped to handle the situation.

Finally, Newt Drystad had been to the cove before, and he knew Onyx Webb was a ghost.

Chapter Thirty

With the exception of a few late-night diners, the streets of Washington D.C. were empty, and Newt Drystad was still at his desk. This was not because he enjoyed working late. It was because he'd just awoke from yet another episode.

The last Newt remembered he was getting ready to leave for the night. He'd turned off his computer, and...

It had been 6:13 p.m.

Now was almost midnight.

Newt opened his desk drawer and grabbed a bottle of pills. He didn't want to take them—he hated what they did to him, how they dulled his thinking—but he had no choice. If someone discovered him in the middle of an episode, the consequences were far worse. He'd most certainly be suspended and placed on medical supervision.

He shook a yellow and black pill from the bottle and swallowed it.

Newt turned the computer back on and grabbed his cell phone to see if he had any messages. There was only one. It was Maggie. It read: *Got something. Call me.* Newt hit the call symbol and waited. He knew she would still be up since it was only nine in California.

Maggie answered on the first ring. "Why did it take so long for you to call?"

Newt ignored the question. "What's up? What have you got?"

"You were right. The detectives at the Eureka P.D. did a half-assed job. They've pegged the night manager as their prime suspect."

"The *night* manager?" Newt said. "It's a drive-in, Mags. *Night* manager is redundant."

"Okay, fine, they think the *manager* is good for the murders."

"Based on what?" Newt asked.

"Based on the fact the kid had gone out with the dead girl a couple of times."

"That's it?"

"And he lied about it."

"Did they establish a motive?"

"Nope."

"Do they have a theory as to how this kid sucked the life out of two healthy teenagers?" Newt asked.

"Negative," Maggie said.

"So, they're focused on a suspect with no motive or ability to commit the crime."

"Good summary."

"So, what's your take? It's not the manager, then—?"

"Definitely a ghost," Maggie said. "But there's a twist."

"Okay."

"The killer might have been dressed as a clown."

"A clown?"

"Yeah. The *manager* remembers seeing someone dressed like a clown hanging around earlier. Said he seemed out of place."

"I'd imagine," Newt said. "Unless it was someone's birthday party." Or a circus, Newt thought.

"Another thing," Maggie continued. "Might be nothing, but, the car the kids were in was candy-apple red. To quote the manager, *'It was really shiny,'* unquote. Might have been what drew the killer's attention to them."

Newt knew the only color a ghost could see was red. "Okay, go on."

"We stopped at four places in the vicinity of the drive-in; the grocery store, dry cleaner, bank, 7-11, and guess what we found."

"Advertisements for a circus."

"Bingo."

"This circus, is it still going on?"

"No, it left on Thursday," Maggie said.

"Headed where?"

"No idea."

Newt didn't know, either, but he had a hunch. "I need the two of you to go to Crimson Cove, Oregon."

"Okay, why Crimson Cove?"

"Two other kids were found up there, both dead, in a car crash."

"Probably coincidence," Maggie said.

"Yeah, probably, but I think you should go," Newt said. "Do you remember Clay Daniels?"

"The sheriff? Of course."

"Daniels called me this morning and told me the owner of the local theater, Abigale Dietz, had been attacked."

"Is she alive?"

"Yes, she is, but barely."

"Okay, we're on it."

"Where's Chad?"

"He's here in the car, with me," Maggie said.

"He hit on you yet?" Newt asked.

"Jesus, Newt. Besides, if he did, I'd have brushed him off."

"Okay. Tell him I said, good job."

"For not hitting on me?" Maggie asked.

"No, for doing a good job."

Chapter Thirty-One

Onyx was playing the piano in the downstairs foyer of the lighthouse when Noah's cell phone rang. He answered it, listened for a minute, then said, "I'll call you back." By the look on Noah's face, Onyx could tell something was wrong.

"That was Clay," Noah said, his face turning red with anger.

Onyx turned the page on her sheet music. "So, what's his problem this time?"

"Someone attacked Abigale Dietz," Noah said.

Onyx stopped playing. "Attacked her? Is she okay?"

"No, she's not. She's in the ICU, on a respirator."

"Do they know who did it?"

"I was hoping you could tell me," Noah said.

"How would I know—"

"Where were you last night?" Noah asked, cutting her off.

"You know where I was, Noah," Onyx said. "I was here—in bed—with you."

"And afterward?"

Onyx remained silent.

"Onyx, I'm going to ask you only once and I expect you to be honest with me. Did you attack Abigale Dietz?"

Onyx paused, then said, "No. And I have no idea who did."

"I woke up around midnight, and your side of the bed was empty," Noah said.

Onyx said nothing.

"That's it? That's all you have to say, nothing?"

Onyx remained silent, then said, "You know I don't sleep."

"Do you realize the shitstorm that's coming down on us?" Noah asked.

"For the last time, I had nothing to do with it," Onyx said. Onyx stood up, crossed the foyer, and started up the spiral staircase that led to the top of the lighthouse.

"You know," Noah said, "you're so worried about Abigale trying to turn Crimson Cove into the ghost capital of the Pacific Northwest. You did more to make that happen than Abigale ever could."

Chapter Thirty-Two

D oyle Slade was one royally pissed-off clown.

The evening before he'd ignored Dolly's ridiculous schedule and made his way into the city to find energy, which was a nice way of saying to kill someone and suck the lifeforce from their body. Unfortunately, he hadn't realized how far Crimson Cove was from where the circus had set up.

The trek into town took almost two hours by foot, which by his calculations was a good six miles. By the time he'd gotten there, he was dragging.

After failing to find easy prey on the street or in the back alleys, Slade entered a movie theater and finally found what he was looking for; a woman behind the candy counter, busy counting money in the cash register, facing away from him.

Alone.

The prudent thing to do would have been to rush the woman from behind and take her quickly before she even knew what was happening. But that was not his style. Yes, he needed her energy, but he also wanted to see the fear in her eyes when she realized she was about to die.

Instead, he'd screwed up.

Now, here he was, ten hours later, more exhausted than ever. He'd walked twelve miles in all, and for what? Nothing. Add to that, Dolly decided she wanted to do a complete show rehearsal, with every member of the troop required to perform their routines from start to finish. In front of no one.

Jesus.

Slade opened his makeup kit and began laying the materials on the table in the order of their use: the thick white cream on the far left, followed by the powder, then his face paint—blue, red, and black, left to right—and finally his brushes and face sponges. He was a man with enormous flaws, the least of which was his insatiable desire to kill, but no one could ever accuse him of a lack of organization and discipline.

Slade looked in the mirror and was terrified at what he saw. His skin was the lightest shade of gray he had ever seen, transparent to the point of being able to see completely through himself as if he were nothing more than mist. Where was he going to muster the energy to do Dolly's rehearsal? If he went much longer, he'd disappear altogether. A ghost's worse fear.

And then he thought of something.

The mirror.

When Slade was a teenager, his parents—who were devout Catholics—had covered the mirrors in the house with black cloth to keep dark forces from coming into the house. His mother even claimed she would catch a glimpse of her dead father looking in on her through the glass. He thought his mother was full of shit. Now he knew better. The dead could transport themselves from one place to another through mirrors.

Slade had only traveled by mirror one time, and it hadn't gone well. After that, he vowed never again. It was time to reconsider, he had no choice.

The mistake he'd made on his previous attempt was entering the mirror without having a clear destination in mind. Without having a destination, a ghost could end up anywhere. Which is what happened. Slade found himself walking aimlessly in a dark gray void as if under a sky blanketed with clouds during the intense thunderstorms he remembered as a child growing up in Oklahoma. The experience frightened him to his core. Fortunately, he had not ventured far from the mirror and was able to find his way back.

So, what destination could he use? It had to be somewhere that would have a mirror, somewhere people lived, with someone he could take. Otherwise, what was the point? And it could not be a crowded place—it had to be out of the way.

And then he thought of a place.

The night before, on his way into Crimson Cove, he had passed a lighthouse, perched on the cliffs high above the ocean. How much more out of the way could one get than that? And someone did live there. He knew because he saw a light on in one of the rooms in the house next door.

It was a good plan, Slade thought. Besides, what other choice did he have? Staying here and doing nothing was a death sentence. He would simply fade away.

Slade walked to the full-length mirror in the corner of the trailer, closed his eyes, and formed a picture of the lighthouse in his mind. Then he stepped forward toward the mirror and disappeared into the glass.

Chapter Thirty-Three

Newt prided himself on having few addictions, but he was unquestionably addicted to caffeine, ingested in the form of espresso.

When he and Maggie first became a thing, they invested in a La Marzocco GB/5 espresso maker, which sounded more like a sports car than a coffee maker. A professional-grade machine, the GB/5 was a double boiler that extracted espresso and steamed milk at the same time with minimal temperature variance. It also featured an articulating steam wand that could be easily moved into multiple directions on its pivot base, which allowed the barista to steam and froth milk to perfection and personal preference.

The only con to the GB/5 was it wasn't something you pulled out of the box and was good to go. Getting the unit up and running involved getting the correct plumbing, adjusting settings, and more, all before you could even consider pulling your first shot.

Newt waited for the machine to finish foaming, then lifted the tiny ceramic espresso cup to his lips and took the first sip of the morning. As expected, it was glorious. Of course, with a price tag of $15,500, it should be.

While Newt wanted to believe espresso was his only addiction, the truth was far different. He was also addicted to Maggie and the pursuit of serial killers. Without Maggie, serial killers, and his morning espresso, he didn't know how he'd survive.

Newt had a decision to make. Should he give Stanton Lee Mungehr back his prosthetics? He knew he should. What he was doing, keeping Mungehr in the secret underground facility at St. Elizabeth's was not only illegal—it was also immoral.

On the other hand, hadn't Mungehr abandoned his right to be treated fairly through his heinous, murderous, sadistic acts? Once upon a time, Newt would have been the one making the case for the distinction between right and wrong, or good and bad, behavior. Morality said innocent prisoners ought to be freed. If that was true, then the inverse was also true. The guilty should not be freed.

But that wasn't the question at hand. Stan Lee Mungehr was never going to go free. Ever. The question was, should he be given his legs back?

Newt looked at his watch. It was 7:30. The morning rush hour traffic in D.C would still be outrageous. There was no reason to hurry.

*   *   *

Stanton Lee Mungehr was lying on his back on the slab of concrete that served as a bed when the guard let Newt into the cell. "Good morning, Stan Lee," Newt said.

Stan Lee did not look over, his eyes focused on the ceiling overhead. "Aren't the clouds beautiful, Special Agent?"

Newt glanced up at the gray pock-marked cement. "The clouds?"

"Yes, the clouds," Stan Lee said. "You do see them, don't you?"

Newt remained silent.

"Besides their beauty, the best thing about clouds is that they let you predict incoming weather. Like, when clouds are high in the sky, over 20,000 feet up. Like cirrus clouds, the feather-like, wispy ones. And cirrocumulus, the ones that look like cotton patches. Sailors used to take down their sails when they saw them, fearing there might be a hurricane over the horizon."

"Where'd you learn so much about clouds?" Newt asked.

"My favorites are cumulonimbus," Stan Lee continued, ignoring the question. "Do you know why I like cumulonimbus clouds best?"

"No, but I'm guessing you're going to tell me."

"It's because they're large and dark—big billowing motherfuckers that don't give a shit about anything—their big bulging tops towering in the sky on hot, humid days, clouds that bring showers, then thunder and lightning," Stan Lee said. "That's what I remember most growing up on the farm."

"Are you saying you had a stormy upbringing?" Newt asked.

"No, I'm saying I like pretending I'm anywhere but here," Stan Lee said. "What about my prosthetics?"

"They're in the hallway," Newt said.

Stan Lee sat up and looked at Newt for the first time since he entered the cell. "And I get them today?"

"If you're good," Newt said.

Stan Lee clenched his fists and screamed, "I want my God damn legs!"

"Tell me about your mother first," Newt said.

"No, you give me my legs first."

Newt remained silent, then he turned and exited the cell. A minute later he returned, a pair of prosthetic legs under his arm. "Tell me about your mother," Newt said.

Stan Lee took a deep breath, and said, "What exactly do you want to know? She was a stripper raising two boys, and she died too young."

"She didn't die, she was murdered."

"Died, murdered, whatever."

"No, not whatever," Newt pressed. "Tell me about the guy who murdered her."

"His name was Rocky Dredge. My mother worked in his bowling alley."

"A bowling alley that was also a strip club, right?"

"Yes."

"So, your mother was a stripper."

"You know all this."

"Humor me, and I'll give you your legs," Newt said. "You're ten minutes from getting them back, so tell me the story."

"Dredge thought my mother had stolen money from him, which she hadn't. They fought. I tried to get him off her, but he was too strong. He punched her, and she fell and hit her head. That's it."

"But that's not it, is it Stan Lee? You're leaving out the part where Rocky Dredge kicked you in the head and left you for dead."

Stan Lee said nothing.

"And then they took you to Dunning?" Newt asked.

Stan Lee nodded. "Yes. The same night. Can you imagine that? I watched my mother get murdered and three hours later they put me in an asylum."

"Yes, about the asylum," Newt said, "there aren't any records about your time there. Tell me about that."

"Be careful," Kara said appearing from thin air in the corner of the room. "Don't tell him about the experiments, Stan, that could ruin everything."

"I don't remember much about the asylum," Stan Lee said. "Those years are a blur."

"You remember nothing?" Newt pressed.

"Not a thing," Stan Lee said. "I know they did some experiments they weren't supposed to do, but I don't remember anything else. Memories are like clouds sometimes, they're there, but when you reach out to grab them, they disappear, like mist."

Stan Lee glanced over to the corner of the room at Kara. "Jesus. Memories are like clouds? This guy is super smart, so don't be an idiot and try to outwit him. Just say you don't remember. And quit talking about experiments!"

"I want to be helpful, Special Agent, but I just don't remember. My time there is like a big black void. Now, can I have my legs back?"

*   *   *

Stan Lee waited for Special Agent Drystad to leave before continuing his conversation with Kara, who leaned casually against the door jam. "Good job," Kara said. "We're one step closer to executing the plan."

Yes, the plan.

The plan was the only thing that kept Stan Lee sane and functional during his incarceration, and included three steps:

Step one was to get his prosthetics returned to him. Escaping without his prosthetics would be impossible.

Step two was to get the guard to let him out of his cell so he could see an area of the building that was outside his cell.

Step three was the hardest part, which was to use his ability to astral project himself out of his cell. This is what Newt Drystad was poking around about.

Stan Lee had learned how to astral project himself while part of sensory deprivation experiments conducted during his incarceration at the Dunning Asylum. When asked about his time there, he lied.

Of course, he could remember. The pain inflicted upon him by Dr. Lilith Pandor wasn't simply unimaginable, it was unforgivable.

Lilith Pandor made her bones as a researcher on Project MK Ultra, the CIA's top-secret mind-control program involving research into the area of astral projection utilizing the most advanced sensory deprivation chambers in the world.

Unfortunately—even with state-of-the-art facilities—Lilith's research showed no progress, and she was terminated from the project. Refusing to abandon her work, she set up a secret lab in an abandoned basement laboratory at the Dunning Asylum on the outskirts of Chicago.

Pandor believed the missing ingredient was to experiment on subjects who had experienced head trauma. That's where Stan Lee came in.

During his mother's attack, Stan Lee had been kicked in the head by his mother's murderer, resulting in severe and ongoing epileptic seizures. Lilith believed the vibrational brain wave frequency created by the seizures would allow subjects to have out-of-body experiences.

For almost three years Stan Lee was taken to a hidden room in the basement of the asylum, stripped of his clothes, forced to wear a leather hood with electronic sensors, and placed in an oblong, plastic coffin filled with water and Epsom salt that caused him to float on the water's surface.

Once in the box, time and space ceased to exist. Nothing did. And though he'd been told the water *was* there to make him dream, the dreams were never good. Even the best dreams—the ones where Stan Lee went places and saw amazing things he'd never seen before—made him feel sick.

Disoriented.

Lost.

It was like dreaming while wide awake, floating in a sea of silent black clouds as if he were in outer space.

Unfortunately, the progress was slow, and Lilith was desperate to prove her theory, that soldiers could be trained to astral project anywhere in the world and become virtual killing machines. After 234 attempts, it finally happened.

Stan Lee found himself standing outside a house peering through a window decorated with spider webs and paper skeletons. Halloween night. He pressed his face against the glass to get a better look and saw three young girls drinking steaming cups of cider or hot chocolate from large ceramic mugs that seemed too big for their small little hands.

At first, he assumed it was just another dream. Then he felt the weight of something in his hand. A knife. It felt real. It *was* real. And he knew what he was there to do.

When he emerged from the tank covered in blood, Lilith Pandor believed she'd proved her theory, and that Stan Lee was her golden ticket back to the CIA.

In the end, Pandor was half-right. She'd proved her theory that astral projection was possible, but she would never make it back to the CIA. Stan Lee saw to that.

"Can you still do it?" Kara asked. "Can you use your mind to astral project your ass out of here?"

"I don't know," Stan Lee said.

"Well, you better figure it out."

Chapter Thirty-Four

Maggie was behind the steering wheel of the Avis rental car, doing her best to navigate the twists and turns of Route 1 along the Pacific Ocean in the pitch blackness of a moonless night. And she was pissed.

For perhaps the first time ever, Chad had done what Maggie had asked, sending his private jet back to New York. It was his way of proving he could slum it. The problem was when Newt asked them to head up to Crimson Cove, there were no flights available the next day. The only option was to drive.

Maggie glanced over at Chad who was sound asleep in the passenger seat. They'd agreed to switch places driving every hour for the 350-mile trip—which was three hours ago now. Maggie studied Chad's face as he slept, remembering how she'd felt about him once upon a time. She had truly loved him. And Chad truly loved impressing her—and everyone else—with his family's money. He'd asked her if she could love him again if he changed. The answer didn't matter. She'd fallen in love with Newt. And that was that.

Chad stirred in his seat, then yawned. "What time is it?"

"Two hours past your turn to take the wheel," Maggie said. It was another fifteen miles before Maggie found a place to pull over on the narrow two-lane highway without falling off the side of a cliff.

"What was the big deal with the color of the car at the drive-in?" Chad asked once he began driving.

"Ghosts see the world in black and white. The only color they do see is a specific shade of red."

Chad nodded. "He was drawn to the color."

"Probably," Maggie said. "A bright red car in a sea of gray would stand out like a beacon."

"Tell me more."

"About ghosts?"

"Yes."

"What do you want to know?"

"Abilities and vulnerabilities, for starters," Chad said. "I mean, I know they need energy, and they'll kill people to get it. Beyond that, I don't know anything."

"Okay, let's start with energy," Maggie said. "To remain in the living plane, ghosts must take energy from humans. The more energy they take, the more alive they appear."

"Like Pipi Esperanza."

"Yes, like Pipi."

"Just so we're clear, you're telling me the head of the FBI is killing people?" Chad said.

Maggie released a long breath as she contemplated how to answer. "The simple answer is, yes. But it's complicated. There are good ghosts and there are bad ghosts, just like there are good people and bad people. Good ghosts follow a code. They only take people who are very sick or evil; people who are *in* pain or *causing* pain. They see taking someone who is terminally ill—"

"...as helping?" Chad said.

"Yes, to them they are helping."

"Oh, so Oregon would have more ghosts than other states because euthanasia is legal," Chad said.

Maggie decided to let the sarcastic comment slide.

"The ghost we're looking for—the one who killed the teenagers at the drive-in—is one of the bad ones," Chad said.

"Exactly," Maggie said.

"Okay, so Pipi Esperanza must be killing a lot of people to look so alive," Chad said. "She had me fooled."

"How about we stay clear of Pipi and talk about ghosts in general, okay?"

"Fine."

"When ghosts lose energy, they lose their color. Lose enough energy and they eventually become transparent."

"Is there any slime, like in Ghostbusters?"

"If you want me to continue, you need to take this seriously," Maggie said.

"No, I am interested. Really."

"One crazy thing is that ghosts appear as perfect versions of themselves when they return," Maggie said. "Scars, age lines, crows-feet, skin blemishes, are gone—even tattoos and piercings."

"What about severed limbs?"

"They come back."

"That's pretty freaky."

"Listen, I need to get some sleep or I'm going to be useless," Maggie said. "Can we pick this up later?"

"Yeah, get some rest."

Chapter Thirty-Five

S lade created a vision of the lighthouse he'd seen on his failed mission the night before and stepped into—and through—the mirror. Instantly and miraculously, he found himself gazing through the mirror from the other side into a room he'd never seen. The room had curved walls and besides a piano and some paintings on the walls, it appeared to be empty.

Slade reached out his hand and watched it slide through the glass as if he were reaching into water, then stepped forward and directly into the room. He was indeed alone.

The room was circular, about thirty feet across, with a spiral metal staircase that ascended upward, confirming what he assumed to be true—yes, he was in the lighthouse.

The question now was, should he go up the staircase to see if anyone was there? He turned and gazed at his reflection in the mirror and saw that he was on the verge of being invisible—the stereotypical ghost the movies got right.

Slade figured the most logical step was to try the house where he'd seen the light in the window the night before. He walked to the door and reached for the knob, but when he did, he made an amazing discovery: his hand went straight past the knob and through the door as if the wood were not even there. He could walk through solid wood.

Walking through walls was not something ghosts could do. Or at least, that's what he believed. Then he knew the awful state he was in—so transparent he was like vapor. Mist. If he didn't take someone soon, he would dissipate completely and cease to be.

Just as he'd done with the mirror, Slade stepped forward and passed through the door and found himself outside—only now he was face-to-face with a woman.

The woman had long jet-black hair and striking features. To describe her as beautiful was an understatement.

What surprised Slade most was what happened next. The woman did not shriek or recoil, as one would assume someone would when seeing a ghost. She asked, "What are you doing in my lighthouse?"

Slade remained silent. What should he say? Finally, he said, "I was looking for energy."

"You will not find it here," the woman said. "I suggest the beach, at the base of the cliffs. It is a place the homeless tend to gather."

Slade held out his hand and said, "I am almost gone. I won't make it."

The woman paused, as if thinking, then said: "Several seconds, that's all, understood?"

It took Slade a moment to get what she was suggesting, and then understood: she was offering him some of her energy. "Understood," Slade said.

The woman stepped forward and placed her lips against his and instantly Slade felt the flow of energy enter him as if it were an electric current. Seconds later, the woman pushed him back, away from her.

The woman was still as beautiful as before, but her skin lacked the luster it had moments earlier, and her hair was no longer shiny as silk, but dull and lifeless. Then he looked down at his hands and saw that they had some color and were no longer transparent.

"You are also a ghost?" Slade asked.

The woman ignored the question and said: "This is my home, my lighthouse. You are not welcome here again."

Slade nodded and began walking across the clearing toward the tree line, then turned back. "Thank you," he said.

The woman nodded, then pointed toward the trees.

"Will you please tell me your name?" Slade asked.

"It's Onyx," the woman said. "Now, go quickly before I change my mind and put an end to you, as I probably should have."

Chapter Thirty-Six

Noah stood in the shadows at the rear of the theater, knowing it was probably a bad idea for him to be there. But he needed to know what was going on.

Under normal circumstances, the event would have been limited to the twenty-two official members of the Crimson Cove Merchant's Association, but Aaron Dietz decided to open the meeting up to the entire town. As a result, the place was packed. Channel 9 even sent a TV crew.

Aaron Dietz went to the podium on the stage and banged the gavel. "This emergency meeting of the Crimson Cove Merchant's Association is now in order. As you know, my sister, Abigale, is in the hospital in critical condition after being attacked two nights ago in this very theater. Now, I asked Sheriff Daniels to come here today to address the situation, but he declined. But he assures me, he's investigating and—"

"Investigating my ass!" someone shouted. "Clay Daniels is as worthless as his old man was."

Aaron banged the gavel and the room calmed down.

"Excuse me, Mr. Dietz," a woman called out. "Sherice Brown, with Channel 9, Portland. It is our understanding that the FBI is getting involved. Can you verify this?"

"Thank you for the question," Aaron said. "And, yes, I can confirm the FBI will be lending their assistance in this matter. Agents from D.C. are on the way, as we speak, and they will be assuming control of the investigation. As such, I have complete confidence the perpetrator will be caught and prosecuted to the full extent of the law."

"Maybe it was someone from this damn circus setting up outside of town," someone yelled. "Circus people are always bad news."

"Circus-schmurcus," someone yelled back. "We all know it was Onyx Webb."

Well, that was fast, Noah thought.

"That's right," another person yelled. "We've turned a blind eye to this for far too long. I've got no problem with her killing transients and drug dealers, but this is unacceptable."

As if on cue, the rear doors of the theater swung open, and a man and woman strode in. It was obvious from how they were dressed, and the way they carried themselves, that they were from the FBI.

Maggie and Chad proceeded down the center aisle and climbed the steps to the stage. "I'm Special Agent Margaret McCord," Maggie announced. "The man to my left is Special Agent Chadwick Chatterton. And as of right now, this meeting is over."

*   *   *

When Noah returned to the lighthouse, he could hear music playing and headed straight up the spiral staircase to let Onyx know about the mess she'd caused.

"Who cares what a handful of shop owners think," Onyx said, trying to minimize the situation.

"It wasn't a few shop owners, Onyx. Aaron opened the meeting to the public, everyone in Crimson Cove was there. And they want blood."

"Well, they'll be disappointed seeing that ghosts don't have blood and do not bleed."

"Clay called in the FBI."

"No, he didn't. He wouldn't," Onyx said, her voice tinged with concern. "We have an understanding, an agreement."

"Maybe it's not what we thought."

"When do they arrive?"

"They're already here. Oh, and Channel 9 sent Sherice Brown to cover the meeting," Noah said. "You're going to get questioned, there's no way to avoid it, so you're going to need a better alibi than you were out in the woods by yourself, taking a stroll under the moonlight."

Onyx stepped to the window and looked out at the ocean, thinking. Noah was probably right. This wasn't going to go away by itself. In the past, she'd always been able to count on Clay Daniels to protect her. Things had changed. But the bigger issue was that Noah believed she was guilty, like everyone else. That couldn't stand.

"I wasn't, as you put it, simply taking a stroll in the moonlight," Onyx said.

"Go on."

"After we'd finished making love, once you'd drifted off to sleep, I had the feeling someone was outside. I could feel eyes on me. I went to the window, and I was right. There was someone outside. A man."

"There was a man outside, watching us?"

Onyx nodded.

"What did you do?"

"I followed him into the woods."

Of course, you did, Noah thought, but said: "Did you get a good look at him? Is it someone you recognized?"

"Yes."

"Well, who was it?" Noah said angrily.

"This is why I didn't tell you the truth," Onyx said. "I knew this was how you'd react. I was afraid you'd go and do something stupid."

Noah took a deep breath to calm himself, then said: "Okay, I promise not to do anything stupid. Just tell me who it was."

"It was my late husband," Onyx said, then went silent allowing what she'd said to sink in.

Finally, Noah's eyes went wide. "Are you saying—are you saying that...?"

"Yes. It was Ulrich."

Chapter Thirty-Seven

Aaron Dietz led Maggie and Chad down the hospital hallway to the ICU. "She's been in and out of consciousness," Aaron said. "She's off the ventilator, but she still can't speak."

"I'll take it from here," Maggie said when they got to the door. "Chad will escort you back to the lobby and I'll rejoin you when I'm finished."

"Hold it, wait one minute," Aaron snapped. "There's no way you're going in there without me."

"Do you want our help?" Maggie asked.

"Yes, but—"

"Then I'll meet you in the lobby."

* * *

Maggie showed her ID to the nurse outside and entered the room and was pleased to see Abigale was awake and sitting up. She flashed her ID once again, and said, "Hello, Abigale? I'm Special Agent Margaret McCord with the FBI. I have a few questions regarding the attack on you the other night. Is that okay?"

Abigale pointed at her throat.

"Yes, I realize you can't speak. If I ask you yes and no questions, can you nod or shake your head?"

Abigale shook her head ever so slightly. It was obvious she was still experiencing considerable discomfort.

The signs of the attack were visibly noticeable; areas of redness and swelling from the ligature, scratch marks on both the right and left sides of her neck from clawing at the scarf, and it was clear she was having trouble swallowing. Also, her entire right eye was red, the result of blood leaking from ruptured capillaries.

"How about holding up one finger for yes, two fingers for no, and nothing if you don't know. Would that work?" Abigale held up a single finger on her right hand, indicating yes. "Good," Maggie said.

"Let's start with the obvious. Did you see who attacked you?"

Abigale held up one finger and Maggie made a note in her notepad.

"Was the attacker someone you knew?"

Abigale held up two fingers.

"Was the attacker male?" Maggie continued.

Abigale raised a single finger.

"Did he say anything before he attacked you?"

Abigale held up two fingers.

"Do you think he intended to kill you?"

Abigale held up one finger.

"Do you think he targeted you, specifically?"

Abigale did not respond.

"Okay, we're almost done," Maggie said. "Last question: Was there anything about him that stood out? Anything that seemed odd or unusual?"

Abigale held up one finger.

Maggie handed her notepad and pen to Abigale and said, "Write down what it was, and be as specific as you can."

Abigale took the pen from Maggie's hand and scribbled in the notepad, then handed the pad back to Maggie.

Maggie looked down to find a single word on the page. It said:

CLOWN.

Chapter Thirty-Eight

Security guard Winston Young—the man assigned to watch serial killer Stanton Lee Mungehr in the secret prison cell in the basement of a shuttered church owned by the government—found himself in a crisis of conscience. His job, for which he was being paid handsomely, required that he follow the orders given to him by the FBI. On the other hand, as a human being, he felt he had a responsibility to do what was right.

The orders being given to him by FBI agent Newt Drystad were wrong. Very wrong. Winston felt it could be classified as cruel and unusual punishment. And unlawful.

Winston had served his country as a soldier for eight years, enlisting in 1998, three years before the attack on the World Trade Center, and left the service after four tours of duty in 2006—just after the civil rights atrocities at Abu Ghraib.

Winston had learned a few things since then. For one thing, while Article 92 of the Uniform Code of Military Justice makes it a crime to disobey a lawful military order, it was illegal to give an order to torture a prisoner. What were the defensible arguments that interrogation techniques are legal? There were none. Any soldier who was given an illegal order is not only *allowed* to disobey it—they're *required* to disobey it.

This is what happened when the illegal actions taken at the Abu Ghraib prison were made public in 2004. Eleven soldiers were found guilty of prisoner abuse, even though they had been given orders to do so by their commanders. Several of the soldiers involved tried to assert that they were following orders as a defense. None were successful.

Admittedly, this wasn't the army. The rules were a bit gray. In any case, Winston had a decision to make: Follow the orders given to him by Special agent Drystad of the FBI—or disobey them because to his mind they were illegal.

Stanton Lee Mungehr had been locked in his ten-by-twelve-foot windowless concrete cell for thirty-nine days. Sleeping on a concrete bed. No blankets. No pillows. The lights in the cell were on 24 hours a day. Urinating and defecating in a metal pail. All of it on the stumps of his amputated legs.

The legs.

That was another thing. The man had begged for his prosthetic legs to be given back to him, only to be denied. It was only yesterday that the prosthetics had been returned. That was cruel and unusual punishment for sure. And probably illegal.

Winston had the sense that Mungehr was being held without due process—they'd locked him up and thrown away the key. But that wasn't entirely true. The FBI hadn't thrown away the key.

They'd given it to him.

Winston looked down at the key in hand and asked himself the question Christians often asked themselves when they encountered a difficult situation: WWJD?

What would Jesus do?

Winston had no idea. He wasn't a Christian. But that wasn't an excuse for not doing the right thing. The only question Winston needed to answer was: What should *he* do? He knew where to start.

Mungehr had asked him if he could be allowed to leave his cell, even if only a minute. *'Handcuff me to a wheelchair, roll me around in the hallway, carry me in your arms, I don't care—just let me out for a few minutes. Leave my prosthetics in the cell, I'm not going to run away! Please,"* Mungehr said.

Winston decided that granting this request was the least he could do for the man. Yes, he had killed people. Women. In the most horrendous and heinous ways. But what he'd asked for seemed reasonable, especially since he'd suffered so much at the hands of the government.

He decided that when he reported for his shift, he would let Stanton Lee Mungehr out of his cell, even if just for ten minutes.

*   *   *

Stan Lee heard a key turning in the lock of his cell door and immediately began rubbing his stumps for the visual effect it would have on the guard who he knew was probably bringing lunch. He had no clock or watch with which to tell time but based on his growling stomach it was probably a safe bet.

"What's this?" Stan Lee asked though he thought he knew.

"It's me doing the right thing," Winston said. "Come on."

"Dear God, thank you, thank you," Stan Lee said with great emotion in his voice, half of which was a true sign of gratitude, and the rest for effect. "You can handcuff me if you want, I'd understand."

"There's no need for that," Winston said. "I don't think there's anything to fear from you. You're not big enough to take me, and I don't think you can outrun me on those things. You're not going to run, right?"

"No, sir," Stan Lee said, putting his prosthetics on and pulling himself to his feet.

"Good," Winston said, pointing down the hallway and having Stan Lee walk in front of him. Smart.

One door, Stan Lee said to himself as he walked. "Where are we going?"

"Lunch," Winston said.

Two doors, Stan Lee said to himself.

They kept walking, passing the third door.

"Here," Winston said when they reached the fourth door. "You've got twenty minutes, not a second longer." Winston swung the door open, and Stan Lee was directed into a small open-air courtyard bathed in sunlight. There was a table against the wall. On the table was a bag from Subway and a drink.

Stan Lee felt his cheeks become wet with tears and wiped his eyes with his sleeve. The tears were not for effect. They were real. "Thank you," Stan Lee said. "I will not forget this."

*   *   *

"Where did you go?" Kara asked once Stan Lee had been returned to his cell and the door locked behind him.

"To a courtyard, down the hall to the right."

"Did you count the number of doors?" Kara asked.

"Of course," Stan Lee said. "Four."

"Good. So, if you project yourself there, you can find your way back to the cell?"

"Four doors down, four doors back. Easy peasy."

"Did you see anyone else, were there any other guards?" Kara asked.

"No," Stan Lee said. "I think I may be the only person being held here."

"Good. So, let's review the plan."

"I know the plan, Kara," Stan Lee snapped. "Astral project to the courtyard. Kill the guard. Get his keys, then let myself out of the cell. Escape."

"When are you going to do it?" Kara asked.

"Does it matter?" Stan Lee asked.

"Think, Stan Lee!" Kara shouted. "It matters for lots of reasons. For one thing, you have to do it when the guard is here. How else are you going to get the keys to the cell if he isn't here with the keys?"

She had a point.

Stan Lee had determined the guard worked in shifts, twelve hours on and twelve hours off, from 8:00 a.m. to 8:00 p.m., seven days a week. The balance of the time—the from 8:00 p.m. to 8:00 a.m.—he was pretty sure he was the only person in the building.

"I'm thinking you should do it after dinner," Kara said, "when you know he'll still be here."

"Or I could do it in the middle of the night when he's *not* here," Stan Lee said.

"Jesus, Stan, think! How are you going to kill him if he's not here?"

"But why kill him at all?" Stan Lee asked.

"Because he's got the keys, you idiot! For the plan to work you've got to get back in your cell."

Damn it, she was right again. "Okay, I'll do it after dinner. Any thoughts as to how I should kill him?"

"Does he have a gun?"

"Yes."

"Then shoot him with it," Kara said.

"You make it sound simple," Stan Lee said. "It's not. He's a big guy, I'd have to take it from him, overpower him somehow."

"Then walk up from behind and hit him over the head with something, I don't know, figure it out."

It was a shame, Stan Lee thought, that he had to kill someone who had been so kind and thoughtful as Winston Young had been. But what else could he do?

He wanted out.

He *had* to get out.

Chapter Thirty-Nine

Clay Daniels pulled his police cruiser over to stop at the curb opposite the Ocean View motel, turned off the engine, and closed his eyes. His sleep had been restless at best for the last two nights, and a wave of exhaustion was hitting him hard. The nap was short-lived, however, when the passenger side door swung open, and Chad slid into the seat.

"Special Agent Chad Chatterton," Chad said, holding his hand out. "You always keep your cruiser doors unlocked when you sleep?"

Clay ignored the comment and shook Chad's hand with a firm grip. "Where's Agent McCord?"

"On a status call with D.C. She said we should go on ahead and she'll catch up asap."

Clay started the engine, did a U-turn, and hit the gas.

* * *

The circus was larger than Clay expected. Carnivals try to pass themselves off as being a bigger deal by calling themselves circuses. Circuses had tents, performance acts, lions, elephants, clowns, jugglers, and cotton candy. Carnivals were mostly comprised of rides, photo booths, rigged games, and cotton candy. Selling cotton candy was one of the few things they did have in common.

The difference between circuses and carnivals wasn't only their size, it was also their business structure. A circus was usually operated by an owner, with employees. Carnivals, on the other hand, tended to be a collection of concessionaires and ride owners, each running their businesses independently. As such, circuses tended to be close-knit families; carnivals were dysfunctional collections of the dregs of society.

What Clay found himself looking at was a combination of both circus and carnival, owned and run by a woman named Walbruga Oesterreich, which he assumed was German.

When he was young, Clay dreamed of running off and joining the circus. But over the years he'd seen many a circus come to Crimson Cove and learned the truth about circus life: long days, heavy lifting, lots of moving around, and more animal shit than you can shovel. The fantasy of being part of a close-knit romantic culture was just that, a fantasy.

"Impressive," Chad said as they walked the exterior of the large tent, watching the workers buzz around them like bees. "How many people do you think are part of an operation like this?"

"At least thirty, maybe forty?" Clay said. "Come on, let's buy tickets and get inside."

Once they were seated, Chad got out his cell phone and started taking pictures. Especially of the clown, since Abigale Dietz claimed her attacker was dressed as one.

"Why we don't bring the clown in and sweat him," Clay said.

Chad turned and shot Clay a look. "Sweat him?"

"Well, that's what you guys do, right?"

"You watch too many old movies," Chad said. "No one sweats anyone at the FBI. We interrogate."

Clay shrugged his shoulders. "You say tomato..."

Ten minutes later, Maggie arrived. "Well, I learned something interesting."

"Something good?" Chad asked.

"Not good or bad, just interesting," Maggie said. "The name you gave me, Walbruga Oesterreich? Interesting background. Went on trial for the murder of her husband."

"Huh. Convicted?" Clay asked.

"No, she got off, hung jury," Maggie said. "The interesting part, though, is when the trial took place."

"I give," Chad said.

"The trial was in 1922."

Maggie took a seat next to Chad and motioned toward the clown. "Did you take pictures?"

"Yep," Chad said.

"Did you say the lady that runs this thing was alive in 1922?" Clay asked.

"Seems so," Maggie answered.

"Huh. So, the circus is owned by a ghost," Chad said.

"That's my assumption," Maggie said.

Great, Clay thought to himself. More ghosts.

Chapter Forty

Dolly had no desire to fill the role of the circus ringmaster, but she had no choice. What started as a temporary gig until a replacement could be found had lasted for over a decade. With no end in sight, she'd had a candy-apple red ringmaster suit custom made, along with a matching red top hat and cane.

She checked her watch to see it was 15 minutes past 7 p.m.

Dolly walked from her trailer, positioned herself near the rear of the tent, and peeked through the slip in the canvas. The clown was doing his job, which was making the audience laugh and getting them engaged. As much as she loathed the man, he was extraordinarily creative with impeccable comic timing and improvisational ability. It was a shame she needed to terminate him. Assuming the Indian would do the damn job.

When she heard the musical cue, Dolly pulled on the flap in the canvas. She stepped through the opening, bathed in the spotlight, the crowd going wild with excitement. She took her position in the center of the ring, then struck a dramatic pose, and waited for the crowd to quiet in anticipation.

Finally, it was the moment Dolly had come to live for if there was such a thing as living when you're dead: getting to deliver the greatest seven words that could be spoken to an audience under the big top:

Ladies and gentlemen, children of all ages...

It was showtime.

* * *

Maggie, Chad, and Clay sat in the bleachers, blending in with the rest of the crowd, when the clown reappeared to the delight of the audience, this time wearing an outlandishly large pink wig, oversized pink shoes, and an enormous hot-pink bra. As everyone was busy laughing at the man's antics, a large wheel was rolled into the center of the big top, and the next act was ready to go.

Chad pointed his cell phone at the clown and took several more pictures, as Clay pulled out a pocketknife and started cutting an apple. He popped a chunk of apple in his mouth, chewed it, then noticed Noah working his way down the aisle in their direction.

"How'd you find me?" Clay asked as Noah squeezed in next to him.

"I know where Onyx was when Abigale was attacked," Noah said. "She didn't do it."

"We know," Clay said.

"You know? Does that mean you know who did it then?"

"Later," Clay said, cutting another chunk of apple and holding it out to Noah.

Noah ignored the apple slice on the tip of the knife. "No, tell me now."

Clay pointed at the clown and Noah said, "What? The clown?"

"Yep, we're pretty sure it's him."

"Seriously?"

Clay nodded. "Abigale says it was a clown who attacked her, and this circus appears to have just one clown."

"So, go arrest him!" Noah shouted over a roar of laughter and audience applause.

"We will," Clay said calmly, taking a final bite of the apple and dropping the remainder through his feet beneath the bleachers. "Be patient, okay, Noah? Give us some time."

"Fine," Noah said and stood up. "I'll let Onyx know she's no longer a target."

"Man, you just got here," Clay asked. "Come on, sit for a bit. We never get a chance to hang out anymore. We'll order a couple of Rogue Ales and enjoy the show."

"Nah. I can't think of anything worse than wasting a night at the circus."

Chapter Forty-One

Serial killer Stanton Lee Mungehr put on his prosthetics and then laid on his back, doing his best to relax his mind and body as he was taught to do while part of Dr. Lilith Pandor's program at the Dunning Asylum. Which was hard to do on a bed made of concrete. So, he started by pretending he was lying on a bed of feathers.

"How do you get off an elephant?" Kara said from the corner of the room.

"Leave me alone, I'm trying to relax."

"No, you're not, you're talking to me."

"Shut up," Stan Lee said.

"Make me," Kara challenged.

"I said, shut up."

"Okay, answer my question and I'll go away. How do you get down off an elephant?"

"I don't know," Stan Lee said. "How?"

"You don't get down off an elephant, you get down off a goose."

Stan Lee snorted at the cleverness of the joke. He prided himself on his intelligence and making up jokes was one way to prove his superior mental abilities.

"Want to hear another?" Kara said.

Stan Lee did not respond. He was trying to ignore her. It was easier to perform astral projection alone, in a state of total and utter relaxation, than it was with someone else in the room. Now he had to deal with Kara's incessant chattering.

"No, go away," Stan Lee said, closing his eyes.

"A photon is going through airport security and the TSA agent asks, *'Don't you have any luggage?'*" The photon replies, *'No, I'm traveling light.'* Traveling *light*, get it?"

Jesus.

Stan Lee closed his eyes and tried to clear his mind. *Concentrate on your body,* he thought to himself. He started by relaxing his shoulders, then the muscles in his hands, curling and uncurling his fingers. Then he moved on and did the same thing with his imaginary toes.

He'd learned it was impossible to force yourself into a hypnagogic state; he had to *sink into it*—to allow his mind and body to approach sleep, but without losing consciousness.

Eventually, his thoughts began to fall away.

The key to astral projection was achieving the right vibrational frequency that made it possible to separate his mental self from his physical body. Traveling light, he thought.

Light.

Become the light, he thought to himself.

Be the light.

Stan Lee shifted his focus to the courtyard where he'd been taken for lunch, and on the details of the place. *Hold the picture in your mind's eye,* he thought.

Once he had the picture firmly in his mind, he thought about the bricks on the walls in his cell. Then the cracks between the bricks. Then he imagined himself walking toward the bricks and gliding through the wall as if it were nothing but smoke.

Then it happened.

Stan Lee found himself standing in the courtyard. *Is this real?* he thought. There was only one way to find out. He walked to the door and took the knob in his hand. It felt real.

He turned the knob, then pushed the door open several inches and looked through the crack into the hallway. Stan Lee could barely believe it. He *was* out of his cell.

Now he had to find something heavy.

* * *

Winston Young reached into his glove box and rummaged around for the extra pack of cigarettes he buried beneath the vehicle's owner's manual. He'd told his wife he'd quit, and for the most part, it was true. The only time he smoked was when he was bored, which on this assignment was every minute of every day.

After he located them, Winston shook a Marlboro from the pack and lit it. The fact that his name was Winston and he smoked Marlboros was not lost on him.

After he smoked the last of the cigarette, he put the Marlboros back in their hiding place and returned to the building. Once inside, he locked the door behind him and headed down the hallway toward the courtyard where he'd left his cell phone on the table.

And found the door open.

Not much, just a few inches. But open.

He never left a door open.

Ever.

Winston took the knob in his hand, and cautiously pulled the door toward him. Then looked around.

The courtyard was empty, but the table was lying on its side.

And one of the legs was missing.

"Hey," a voice said from behind him, and he turned to find Stan Lee standing there holding the table leg. A half-second later Winston found himself on the floor looking up. There had been no time to shield himself from the blow. There would be no time to shield himself from the second blow, either, nor the third or fourth, or fifth.

No good deed went unpunished.

* * *

Stan Lee tossed the blood-covered table leg to the floor and knelt next to the security guard's motionless body. "Sorry, old chap," he said. "I had no choice."

In truth, he *did* have a choice. There were *always* choices.

He'd considered only knocking the man out, tying him up, and leaving him alive. But what if he got away and called for help? Or, what if someone called the police when he failed to return home after his shift? That could not be allowed to happen. Stan Lee needed to put as much time and distance behind himself and Newt Drystad as possible.

Stan Lee rummaged through the guard's pockets, found the key chain, and headed up the hallway counting the doors as he went.

First door.

Second door.

Third door.

Stop.

The third key he tried worked. Stan Lee opened the door and gazed at himself, sound asleep on the concrete slab. A moment later, a sensation swept over him, like the feeling one had just before one passed out.

Then he sat bolt upright on the concrete bed, awake.

The cell door was open.

A set of keys lay on the floor.

He'd done it.

"You're the man, Stan," Kara said from the doorway. "So, what's next?"

"I want to get a burger, or some pizza," Stan Lee said, "maybe both."

"Then?"

Stan Lee didn't know. He hadn't thought that far ahead. All that mattered was that he was free.

"Get the keys," Kara said.

Stan Lee grabbed the keys off the floor and headed down the hallway to where the security guard lay in a pool of blood. What a shame. Stan Lee rummaged through the guard's pockets until he found his wallet, which contained fifty-three dollars in cash, a Visa credit card, a Blue Cross health insurance card, and pictures of his wife and kids. He took the money and the cards, then he took the man's watch and placed it on his wrist.

"Take his gun," Kara said. "And his badge."

Stan Lee hated guns. Guns were tools of unskilled killers. But he grabbed it anyway.

"Good, now get a move on," Kara said from behind him.

"Yeah, I will," Stan Lee said. "But I have one more thing to do."

Chapter Forty-Two

Maggie, Chad, and Clay watched as the spotlight swung to a man dressed in all black, with a black hood covering his face. The man in black pointed at the clown, then curled his finger, summoning him over. The clown ran over. Then the man pointed at the clown's bra. The clown reached inside the bra and produced two oranges, to the crowd's laughter.

Chad took more pictures of the clown to get his face from every possible angle.

The man pointed at the wheel and the clown ran over, holding the oranges at arm's length, shaking wildly. Seconds later, two knives were hurled through the air, each one striking an orange, pinning them to the wooden wheel behind the clown.

The clown wiped his forehead in relief.

Next, a beautiful young woman appeared. The clown strapped the woman to the wooden wheel and spun it. The man in black produced six large knives. The audience held its collective breath as the first knife was hurled through the air, nearly missing the woman. It was the same for the next four knives. The final knife, however, missed its mark and went directly into the woman's shoulder. The audience gasped in horror, and for a moment everyone sat in a frozen state of shock.

Without hesitation, the clown reached up and pulled the knife from the woman's shoulder. Then he shocked everyone by plunging the knife into his chest to more gasps, then he quickly pulled it back out, declaring, "It's a fake knife!" The audience erupted in applause.

Maggie leaned toward Chad and said, "That look like a fake knife to you?"

Chad shook his head. "It looked more like a nice save of a trick gone wrong."

"Better take pictures of everyone, just in case."

*   *   *

The next amazing act you are going to witness is called Escape or Die," Dolly exclaimed with exuberance from the center of the ring. "This death-defying stunt was originally performed by the great Harry Houdini! But here, today, to recreate it, I give you escapologist extraordinaire, our own Daring Darlene!"

The audience cheered as Antoinette entered the ring, a long blonde wig covering her short brunette hair. The truth was most everyone in the circus played multiple roles to help keep costs down. The fewer ghosts to feed, the better.

Antoinette waited in the spotlight as a large wooden chest was set beside her in the center of the ring. She dramatically extended her arms as Mohawk Joe placed handcuffs around her wrists. Antoinette tugged on the cuffs to show she was indeed restrained, then climbed into the chest. Mohawk Joe slammed the lid of the chest closed and produced a handful of nails from his pocket. He used a hammer to pound the nails into the lid. To finish the effect, Mohawk Joe hid the chest behind a cloth partition, so it could no longer be seen by the audience.

"Ladies and gentlemen, look at your watches," Mohawk Joe shouted. "There is only a small amount of air in the chest. If three minutes pass and the lid doesn't open, the lovely Darlene will have met her fate and shall be delivered to the heavens."

The tent went eerily silent as everyone nervously looked at their watches. Seconds later, Antoinette pushed her way through an opening in the partition to the cheers of the audience. What they didn't know was a skeleton key to the handcuffs had been secreted in a compartment inside the chest. Antoinette was out of the handcuffs before Mohawk Joe had finished nailing the lid shut. Each nail had been driven through a previously drilled hole that was slightly larger than the nails themselves—all Antoinette had to do was push on the lid and it would easily pop open.

That was one of the great things about circus tricks. Everyone knew they were tricks, but no one cared. The truth didn't matter. They were there to be entertained.

As the audience cheered Daring Darlene's great escape, Mohawk Joe left the center ring and exited the tent where he found Ulrich waiting for him. "What did Dolly want earlier?" Ulrich asked.

"Nothing much," Mohawk Joe said.

"Nothing much, my ass," Ulrich said. "She wanted you to kill the clown."

Mohawk Joe said nothing.

"Are you going to do it?"

"She told me she'd toss me out of the circus if I don't," Mohawk Joe said.

"She won't," Ulrich said. "She knows you might rat her out to the authorities. Dolly is all about self-preservation."

"Truth is, I'm not sure I can," Mohawk Joe said. "When I was in the Army, they'd send me behind enemy lines at night with nothing more than a knife. I caught six Krauts once, all by myself, and scalped every man, one at a time. But the clown? He scares me."

"Then don't," Ulrich said. "Let me handle it."

"No, you already saved my life once," Mohawk Joe said. "I can't let you—"

"I said, I'll handle it."

Chapter Forty-Three

For as long as Mable Stark could remember, she'd wanted to work with lions.

Mable joined her first circus in 1911, the year of Haley's Comet, and married famous lion trainer, Louis Roth. In February 1916, she was severely mauled by a lion trained by her husband. The lion bit Mabel's arm and rolled her over several times, but Louie came to her rescue by firing six shots at the cat with his revolver. He had no intention of killing one of his prized cats—the gun was loaded with blanks. Fortunately for Mable, the tactic worked, and the lion released her.

Dolly walked to the center ring. "From the earliest times in recorded history, man has wanted to prove he is stronger than the wild beasts that roam the jungle." Dolly turned and pointed dramatically as a canvas tarp was pulled back, revealing a large cage containing three lions. "Many a man has tried, but most have failed. And I wish to apologize to those of you who paid good money to be here because we have been unable to find even a single man willing to try."

The audience released a collective groan of disappointment.

"But, while no *man* is willing to risk death by taking on the challenge of taming such savage beasts, we have found a woman! Ladies and gentlemen, the one and only Mable Stark, queen of the lion tamers!"

Mable Stark entered the tent to the cheers of the audience and declared: "Bring me my whip!"

The clown ran out, handed a whip to Mable, then quickly fled the ring to immense laughter.

"See the claws on these beautiful but deadly beasts? They are sharp, over three inches in length, and can slice through human flesh like a hot knife through butter. And then there are the teeth, able to rip a gazelle into pieces, housed in jaws that can open wide enough to fit a human head."

Mable walked to the cage, swung the metal door open, and entered.

*　*　*

Up in the bleachers, Maggie, Chad, and Clay looked on as Mable Stark controlled the lions with her whip, making them leap.

"You think the lions are ghosts, too?" Chad asked.

"I don't know," Clay said. "Is that possible?"

"I'll be back in a bit," Maggie said getting to her feet. "I'm going to take a look around."

"Do you want me to come along?" Chad asked.

"No, I'll be fine."

*　*　*

Maggie had spent the last hour observing everything going on inside the circus tent. Now she wanted to venture into the areas behind it. To do that, she needed props. She stopped and bought some cotton candy from a vendor's cart, then three helium balloons from another. Nothing said *clueless spectator* more than cotton candy and balloons.

It took only a few minutes for Maggie to realize how big the operation was. There were two 18-wheel semi-trailers, one of which held cages for the large animals, a gasoline tanker truck, a collection of smaller cargo trucks and vans, and at least twenty individual trailers like what one would see on location at a film shoot. It was nowhere the size of Cirque du Soleil, or the circuses of old with hundreds of employees and train cars filled with exotic animals, but it was impressive, nonetheless.

Maggie had no idea of what she was looking for, exactly. But, like shopping for a gift in a store, she'd know it when she saw it.

Maggie made her way out from the visitor's area to what looked like the operations and employee section. On one hand, the employee area had the look and feel of what one would expect. There was nothing that jumped out at her, but still, something seemed off. Then Maggie realized what it was: it was the absence of food. Out front, where the public was allowed, there were carts selling hotdogs, popcorn, and hot pretzels, plus food trucks selling chicken wings and pizza by the slice, and soft drinks.

All these employees, but no catering trucks? Maggie wondered. There was no smell of food wafting through the air. No mess tent or picnic tables where employees would gather while they ate. Was it possible that—?

"Excuse me, young lady," a male voice said from behind. "Can I help you with something?"

Maggie turned around and found herself face to face with the clown.

"Uh, no, I—I was looking for the, uh, bathroom," Maggie stammered.

The clown looked her up and down, then said: "There's a ladies' restroom right back this way. I'll show you." The clown turned and took several steps, but Maggie was frozen. "Are you coming?" the clown asked, smiling.

"I better be heading back," Maggie said. "My husband is probably wondering where I am."

Maggie turned and started in the direction of the main entrance. *Don't look back,* she thought. *Don't let him see any fear.* Maggie walked straight ahead, then when she got to the edge of the main tent, she finally glanced behind her.

The clown was gone.

*   *   *

Maggie was still a bit shaken when she got to her seat. It wasn't only because she knew the clown had attacked Abigale and was probably responsible for the two teenagers at the drive-in. There was something else that spooked her, perhaps more than anyone she'd ever encountered. Either dead or alive. It was like coming face to face with pure evil.

"Where in the hell have you been?" Chad said. "I was about to come looking for you."

"Have you been taking pictures of everyone?"

"Yeah, you asked me to, so—"

"That program you wrote two years ago, the facial recognition one, is that on your laptop?"

"Yeah, why?"

"Tell me your laptop is in the office."

"It's locked in the drawer of my desk," Chad said.

"Good," Maggie said. "We need to send pictures of every performer to Newt right now."

*   *   *

Newt got off the phone with Maggie and checked his email. The file with the photos had arrived.

Though Maggie told him not to bother with the FBI's facial recognition program, Newt felt it was still worth a try. She was right. There were no matches. Instead, she'd instructed Newt to use the WFRS program on Chad's laptop. WFRS stood for Web Facial Recognition Search. Chad wrote the code back when he was part of the FBI's Information and Technology Branch—or ITB, for short—whose mission was to modernize the agency's aging information technology infrastructure.

The FBI had recognized the need to modernize its computer systems going back to the late 1990s, but as it was with all large bureaucracy-driven governmental agencies, the work had been postponed multiple times, primarily due to budget constraints. It wasn't that they didn't have the money. They did. It was that they kept redirecting the funds to other "priorities." By the time Chad joined the ITB in 2010, the FBI was reliant on computer systems running on 1980s technology. Eventually, Chad had enough of the constant project postponements, and he started writing software programs on his own. This was strictly forbidden, of course. Were someone to find out, he could go to prison for the rest of his life. Out of an abundance of caution, Chad quit working on them. They never saw the light of day.

WFRS was one of these secret programs, designed to search through trillions of digital photos stored on the World Wide Web, not only those in the FBI's files. It was stuff like this that made Newt believe Chad was the best computer guy the FBI ever had, and why he wanted him back.

Newt retrieved the key to the Ghost Division offices from his desk drawer. Now all he had to do was break into Chad's desk.

* * *

Maggie, Chad, and Clay looked on as a woman in a skimpy purple outfit rode a white horse bareback doing acrobatic tricks. "She should be an Olympic gymnast," Clay said, "not trotting around in some rinky-dink circus."

Maggie was about to respond when her phone rang. "It's Newt," she said as she answered the phone. "What did you find out?"

"You were right. None of them were in the FBI system, so I ran them through Chad's WFRS program," Newt said. "You got a pen?"

Maggie pulled her notepad and a pen from her purse. "I'm ready, go."

"The lion tamer's real name is Mary Hanie—stage name, Mable Stark. Born in Kentucky, December 10, 1889."

"She's dead, I assume," Maggie said.

"Yes, date of death April 20, 1968. Next, the weightlifter, the woman of steel, Katie Sanswina. No date of birth available, but I know when she died."

"When?"

"January 12, 1952."

Okay, got it."

"Next, the high wire guy is Charles Blondin, aka Jean-François Gravelet, born in Saint-Omer, France, February 28, 1824. Deceased, February 22, 1897."

"That name rings a bell," Maggie said.

"It did with me, too," Newt said. "He was rather famous. The first person to walk over Niagara Falls on a tightrope. He was Karl Wallenda before Wallenda was even born."

"What about the rest?" Maggie asked.

"I'll email you what I got, but it's pretty much the same."

"Meaning?"

"Your hunch was right," Newt said. "They're all dead. It's a ghost circus."

Chapter Forty-Four

Antoinette stood at the entrance to the tent, waiting to be introduced as the circus' grand finale—the trapeze act. A few feet away, Slade was looking into the audience, studying the girl he'd run into minutes earlier. There was something about her that intrigued him. He wasn't sure what it was, but he felt something flutter inside him when he'd talked to her. Maybe it was her clothes, he thought. The sharp navy blazer over the starched white cotton blouse. And holding the cotton candy and balloons? She looked like a schoolgirl, coming into the age where she'd be interested in boys, and they'd be even more interested in her.

And then it hit him.

She reminded him of his first kill. It had been so long ago, that he'd almost forgotten the girl's face. How she looked when he'd strangled her.

Slade made up his mind, then and there.

He wanted to take her.

He needed to take her.

Whoever this girl was, she wasn't leaving the circus alive.

"You're a freak, you know that?" Antoinette said in Slade's direction.

"Takes one to know one," Slade responded, his eyes still trained on where Maggie was seated. "Let's say we meet up at my trailer later, you and me."

Antoinette turned toward Slade, but before she could speak, Willy walked up and stood between them. "Antoinette, we need to talk," Willy said.

"Not now, I'm about to be introduced."

"It's important," Willy said.

"Well, whatever it is—"

"I slept with Dolly," Willy blurted.

"What?"

Slade snickered and shook his head. "I think I'll take my leave and let the two of you rip each other's heads off." Then he walked away.

"You slept with Dolly?" Antoinette hissed.

"Yes, but it's not my fault," Willy whined. "She seduced me. It happened so fast."

"It always happens fast with you, Willy."

Willy let the insult regarding his sexual stamina slide and said, "Dolly, she always gets her way. You know that. It's not my fault—"

"Get out of my sight," Antoinette growled. "I never want to see your face again for as long as I live, Willy. You may be handsome on the outside, but you'll always be ugly on the inside."

Willy's shoulders slumped and he looked like he was going to cry. "Please, Antoinette, I'm sorry."

"You're a sorry excuse for a man!" Antoinette screamed. "Now go!"

As she watched Willy walk away, Antoinette had two competing thoughts. The first was: How dare Dolly do this to her? She'd had enough of the woman. Dolly had driven her to the breaking point. And the second thought was:

Relief.

That Willy had admitted to sleeping with Dolly honestly didn't bother Antoinette. Yes, Willy was gorgeous, and she looked good on his arm. But that was all. She never really loved Willy. Besides, what was love to a ghost?

In any case, Willy's admission meant that Antoinette was free—free to *do* whatever she wanted and *be* with whomever she wanted.

Antoinette shifted her gaze to the opposite side of the tent where Ulrich was waiting. She had spent so much time with Ulrich she'd begun to feel comfortable with him. More than comfortable, perhaps. Were her feelings more than professional? Dear God, was it love? She had no idea.

The things that made love special to the living— daydreaming about another person, the euphoria of that person's touch, the passion of sharing their bed—ghosts felt none of that. Those things were gone. All that was left for a ghost was the *memory* of what love used to feel like.

But ghosts *did* feel anger. And jealousy. And humiliation. And betrayal. *Especially betrayal.* Plus, if Willy had slept with that old hag, what did it say about her? The situation was unacceptable. Something needed to be done to restore order to the universe.

In a moment of pure inspiration, Antoinette decided to use her newfound freedom to teach Dolly a long-overdue lesson. *You like to set fires and watch them burn, don't you, Dolly?* Antoinette thought. *Well, two can play that game.*

Screw the show, Antoinette thought. She turned and stormed from the tent, making a beeline for the supply trailer where she found a 15-gallon Roughneck gas canister and checked the fuel gauge. It read nine gallons—more than enough for what she had in mind.

The Roughneck had a handle and wheels on the bottom, which made it easy to maneuver, even for someone as slight as she was. It also had a nozzle with two settings: pour and spray. Antoinette turned the knob to spray and rolled the cart to the back corner of the tent and started spraying gasoline on the canvas.

For years Antoinette had told Dolly she was an idiot for not coating the canvas tent with a fire retardant. Every circus she'd ever performed with did so. Dolly refused. The chances of fire were low, and the need to save money was high, Dolly said. "Well, the odds of a fire just went up, bitch," Antoinette said aloud.

It took Antoinette just a couple of minutes to cover the entire backside of the tent, then she stopped. This way the backside of the tent would go up in flames, giving people plenty of time to escape through the main entrance. She had no desire to kill anyone.

Then Antoinette realized she'd forgotten one important thing:

Matches.

The most logical place to find matches was from someone who smoked. She looked around and spied the supply trailer. The supply manager was a smoker. She raced to the trailer, climbed the stairs, and tugged on the handle. It was locked. She pounded on the door and waited. Several seconds later the door flew open.

"What do you want?" the supply manager barked, a cigarette dangling from his gray lips.

"This," Antoinette said, then she reached up and snatched the cigarette.

Chapter Forty-Five

N
ewt was in his car, headed for St. Elizabeth's, and he was worried. As was his custom, he called Winston Young—the agent he'd assigned to guard Stanton Lee Mungehr—to let him know he was coming. Young didn't answer. The calls went straight to voicemail.

Young always answered on the first ring. Always.

This wasn't good.

Newt had taken a calculated risk by assigning a single agent to guard duty because the fewer the number of people who knew they had Mungehr in custody, the better. Which was why he'd chosen St. Elizabeth's.

Located in the southeast corner of the District of Columbia, St. Elizabeth's was a hospital built in 1855 by the federal government to house a growing population of indigent, mentally ill residents. At its peak, the facility housed eight thousand patients and had a fully functioning medical-surgical unit. Now it was little more than an empty shell, owned by the U.S. Department of Homeland Security, but under the jurisdiction of the FBI.

One could say it was a black site. Of sorts. It certainly wasn't a place where prisoners were subjected to any kind of torture, aka, "enhanced interrogation" techniques.

Newt knew he was walking a line with the interrogation techniques he was using with the serial killer. Or maybe *straddling* the line was more accurate. Keeping his prosthetics from him *could* be considered torture. As was making the man urinate and defecate in a metal pail, which remained in his cell for days on end before being dumped. As was making him sleep on a concrete slab with no mattress or sheets or pillow.

But Newt had his reasons.

And his justifications.

Stanton Lee Mungehr was among the most prolific serial killers in history, having taken the lives of at least thirty women the FBI knew about, and perhaps many more.

In Newt's mind, the man had forfeited his right to humane treatment. The man was subhuman. He deserved nothing.

Yet, deep down, he knew he was wrong.

But he wanted results. There were things he wanted to know. Needed to know. And Mungehr was his once-in-a-career ticket to the answers.

Newt believed there was some sort of moral equilibrium holding the universe of humans together, something that created balance, in the same way, the spinning of the earth on its axis kept it in balance. This balance, he believed, consisted of two parts: good and evil.

Stanton Lee Mungehr was evil, doing the wrong thing at every turn. Pure and simple. This could not be refuted. There was no world in which Newt wanted to live in which the man's actions could be considered good.

Newt believed he—or at least, people *like* him—were the counterbalance. But what if he was wrong? What if his actions, no matter how right he felt they were, no matter how he justified them, were unacceptable to the universe? What if, in his zeal to do *good*, he'd crossed the line to the side of evil?

The questions he was grappling with were simple: *Had he tortured Stanton Lee Mungehr by denying him the basics of life?* And, if so: *Did what he was learning from the man justify the means?*

The answer to the first question was: *Probably.*

The answer to the second question was: *He hoped so.*

Newt pulled out his cell phone and dialed Winston Young again. Again, the call went straight to voicemail. Had something bad happened? Had his plan gone wrong? He would know in ten minutes.

*   *   *

Newt steered his car into the parking lot off of Sycamore and pulled around the building and held his breath. Would Winston's car be there?

It wasn't.

Newt unlocked the glove box and grabbed his FBI-issued Glock 5. He exited the vehicle and rushed to the door, expecting it to be locked. Winston always kept the door locked and Newt had to get him on the phone to open it when he visited. He reached for the knob and turned it.

The door was unlocked.

Newt cautiously opened the door and saw the body lying on the floor twenty feet away, near the entrance to the courtyard.

It was Winston Young, lying in a pool of drying brown blood.

Newt holstered his gun and approached the body, instantly concluding the cause of death was likely a blow to the head. Multiple blows.

Winston's holster was empty. The metal chain that held the keys to the building and Mungehr's cell was gone, as were the keys themselves. The man's wallet was lying on the floor next to him.

There was only one last thing to check.

Newt made his way down the hall to Mungehr's cell.

The door was open.

The cell was empty.

The worst-case scenario had come true.

Then Newt saw the note lying on the concrete slab. It was a hand-drawn picture of a spider with a short poem:

A hungry Spider made a web
Of thread so very fine,
Your tiny fingers scarce could feel
The little slender line.
I am hungry, very hungry,
Said the spider to a fly.
If you are caught within my web,
You very soon should die.

*   *   *

Newt sat at his desk and rubbed his eyes. He'd spent the previous six hours scouring through thousands of documents gathered over the years on serial killer Stanton Lee Mungehr, known to the public as The Leg Collector. While one of the bureau's strengths was its thoroughness, it was also a weakness. *'Leaving no stone unturned'* created a lot of unnecessary documents, many quite unnecessary, making it all the harder to find what one was looking for. It was like an Easter egg hunt at a chicken farm.

It also didn't help that Newt had no idea what he was looking for. How would he know if he'd found *it* when he found it if he didn't know what *it* was?

There were three questions he needed to consider:

1. *How did Stanton Lee Mungehr escape?*

2. *Where was Mungehr likely to go?*

3. *Should he tell Director Pipi Esperanza or leave her out of it?*

The only good news was the fact that Mungehr didn't have a passport. Due to post-9/11 security measures, it was unlikely he could make it out of the country. Even so, it was a big country, and he had at least a two-day head start.

Newt finished reviewing the files in the fourth storage box and set it aside. Which to review next? Then he saw the box labeled: *Dunning Asylum.*

Information on Mungehr's time at the Dunning Asylum was scarce, and what was available was general in nature—things about the *asylum*, not on his experiences while there.

Newt sorted through the box and spied a file labeled: *Experiments/Dr. Lilith Pandor.*

According to the file, during the Cold War, the Central Intelligence Agency became convinced the communists had discovered a drug or method that allowed them to control the human mind. So, the CIA began its secret program. The program was called MK-ULTRA.

Created by a chemist named Sidney Gottlieb, MK-UTRA was the most sustained research of its kind ever conducted. One of the researchers was a woman, Dr. Lilith Pandor.

Many of the program's participants suffered greatly from the intensity of the experiments. Still more committed suicide once the program was terminated.

Ultimately, Gottlieb concluded the level of mind control desired was not possible. Lilith Pandor disagreed, and Gottlieb fired her.

At the end of Gottlieb's time with the CIA, he destroyed what were assumed to be all the records about MK-ULTRA. Years later, duplicate records were discovered in the basement of the secret laboratory at Dunning run by Lilith Pandor.

Newt flipped past more documents and stopped on what was a letter written by Lilith Pandor to her ex-boss, Sidney Gottlieb, at the CIA. A portion of the letter read:

"You continue to barrel your way down the wrong path, believing the secret to mind control will be found in drugs. It's not. My research suggests sensory deprivation techniques imposed on subjects who have suffered serious head trauma will successfully be able to astral project themselves from one location to another. How can I be so sure? Because I have found such a person. His name is Stanton Lee Mungehr. Allow me to prove it to you, Sidney. I am not lying!

"Jesus," Newt whispered aloud. As unbelievable as it seemed, this had to be how Stan Lee did it—by astral projecting himself out of his cell, killing Winston Young, and then releasing his physical body from his cell.

Newt shook his head in disbelief. Two hours ago, he would have told anyone who asked that astral projection was a fairy tale. But why? Why hadn't he considered it? Because it seemed impossible? Once upon a time ghosts seemed impossible, too, but now he knew better on both counts.

Newt also realized this was why Stan Lee wanted his prosthetics returned to him so badly. Astral projecting to another part of the building and killing Winston Young was a plan he could not complete without them. It was also why he'd refused to discuss his time at Dunning; he'd been planning his escape all along.

The big question Newt faced now was: *Should he tell Pipi?*

The director had placed her faith in Newt, which allowed him to sequester Stanton Lee Mungehr outside the normal channels. Now, because of his actions, one of the most prolific serial killers in history was loose and on the run.

An even bigger problem was lying in a pool of blood on the floor in the basement of St. Elizabeth's hospital. A missing serial killer was one thing—a dead FBI agent was another.

Newt tossed the file on the desk and stood up, released a deep breath, then grabbed his gun and his badge from the desk drawer. There was a good chance Pipi Esperanza would be asking for them once he told her what had just gone down.

Chapter Forty-Six

Maggie and Chad sat on the bleachers in the circus tent, watching the circus and waiting for Clay to call. He'd gone into town to show Abigale Dietz the picture they'd taken of the clown.

"Did Newt say anything about the clown?" Chad asked. "Anything definitive on him yet?"

Maggie shook her head. "No. Newt says there were no matches, probably because of his makeup. But he's sure it's Doyle Slade."

"So, let's go arrest him," Chad said.

"When Clay calls with a positive ID, *then* we'll go after him."

They didn't have long to wait.

"What have you got?" Maggie asked when her cellphone buzzed seconds later.

"It's him," Clay said.

"For sure?"

"One-hundred percent," Clay said. "Abigale started shaking like a leaf the moment she saw the picture."

"Good work," Maggie said. "What's your E.T.A?"

"I'm two minutes out, max."

Maggie looked to the rear of the tent where the clown waited. It seemed like he was staring in their direction. No, not in their direction, but directly at *her*. "Okay," Maggie said. "As soon as you get here, we'll take this asshole down."

* * *

Dolly waited for the applause to die down, then strode confidently to the center of the ring. "And, now our grand finale, we bring you the death-defying aerial artistry of the Amazing Antoinette and the Unbelievable Ulrich!"

Dolly waited for Antoinette and Ulrich to walk in from opposite sides of the tent into the center ring, but Ulrich was alone. Antoinette was nowhere to be seen. "Where is Antoinette?" Dolly hissed.

Ulrich shrugged. "I have no idea, I'm not her babysitter. Maybe she—"

Without warning, the band launched into playing *The Stars and Stripes Forever*, a tune used by circuses as a distress signal.

Someone in the bleachers stood and screamed, "Fire! Fire!"

Dolly spun around and watched in horror as the entire back wall of the circus tent was suddenly engulfed in flames. "Be calm, and everything will be fine!" Dolly shouted. But her words were ignored as 300 people simultaneously jumped from their seats and began running for the exits.

The long metal chute used to lead the lions into the big top was blocking one of the side entrances, making it impossible to pass, and the fire had already spread past the emergency exit on the opposite side of the tent. The only way out of the tent was through the main entrance, which quickly became a crushing mass of people pushing and screaming.

* * *

Maggie and Chad were halfway down the main aisle of the bleachers getting in position to arrest Doyle Slade the minute Clay got there—then someone yelled *'Fire!'* and all hell broke loose.

"Holy shit," Chad said, pointing at the back wall of the tent.

Maggie scanned the scene unfolding around her and saw the rapidly spreading flames, and the mass of humanity racing toward the single exit. "We've got to get control of this or—"

Suddenly two gunshots rang out and everyone instinctively stopped and looked, including Maggie who saw Clay standing inside a makeshift exit he'd cut into the tent wall from the outside.

"This way!" Maggie screamed, waving people at the back of the charging herd to go to the other exit. Within seconds the bottleneck at the main entrance began to lessen, and moments later they'd gotten everyone out of the tent, which was now filling with black smoke.

Maggie and Chad made their way to the hole Clay had cut in the tent wall and stepped out into the fresh air. "Is everyone out?" Clay asked.

Maggie shook her head, coughing. "I don't know… I think so."

"Where's Chad?" Clay asked.

It was only then that Maggie realized Chad was not behind her. Without hesitation, Clay dashed through the hole into the tent and disappeared into the smoke.

A minute later, Maggie felt someone tap on her shoulder. When she turned, it was Chad. "Oh, my God, what happened to you?"

"I got lost in the smoke, but somehow I managed to find the main entrance," Chad said coughing. Then he glanced around and said, "Where's Clay?"

* * *

Willy was standing about a hundred yards away when the tent went up in flames, and his first thought was Antoinette. He glanced at his watch. By his calculations, she should have been in the middle of her act at that moment. Wasting no time, he took off running in the direction of the tent. Moments later, to his great relief, he found Antoinette standing outside the inferno, gazing up at the flames.

"Oh, my God, you're okay!" Willy shouted. "You got out!"

"I never went in," Antoinette said still gazing at the fire, the corners of her mouth curling up in what looked to Willy like a smile. "Do you like it?"

"What? What are you talking about?"

"The fire," Antoinette said. "I set it because of you. This is your fault."

"Because I said I cheated on you?"

Antoinette nodded.

"Jesus, Antoinette," Willy said. "I didn't sleep with Dolly!"

"You didn't sleep with Dolly?" Antoinette said, confused.

"No, I only said that to make you jealous," Willy said. "You'd been spending so much time with Ulrich, and I—oh, my God, this *is* my fault."

"Oh, whatever," Antoinette said. "Dolly had it coming anyway."

Suddenly the sound of wood creaking and groaning could be heard, followed by a loud snap. Antoinette and Willy looked up to see the large center tent pole falling toward them from above. Willy grabbed Antoinette's arm and tried to pull her back, but he was a second too late. The pole crashed down directly on top of Antoinette, pinning her to the ground.

Antoinette tried to wiggle her way out from under the pole, but it was impossible. She was trapped. Willy ran to the end of the pole and grabbed it, doing his best to lift it off her. It was so heavy, that it barely budged. He tried again, feeling the energy draining from his body as he did.

"Willy, don't," Antoinette pleaded when she saw the color draining from him. Willy ignored her. He squatted down as low as he could, bending at his hips and knees and grabbing the flaming pole with both hands. "I've always loved you, Antoinette," Willy said.

Willy strained to lift the tentpole, but it was so heavy and required so much energy to lift that Willy turned transparent right before Antoinette's eyes.

"No! Willy, don't!" Antoinette screamed.

Willy ignored her and pulled his shoulders back, grunting like an Olympic weightlifter, and used his legs to raise the pole off the ground as much as he could, just enough for Antoinette to roll out from beneath the log.

Antoinette looked up to see the little that remained of Willy and an overwhelming feeling of guilt washed over her.

"Willy, I never—"

"It's okay," Willy said as the final bit of energy drained from him. "Even before we ever met, you were the woman I dreamed of."

And then he was gone.

Chapter Forty-Seven

Stan Lee Mungehr was behind the wheel of a styleless, navy-blue Chevrolet Impala sedan, something he would never, under normal circumstances, be caught dead in.

This was not a normal circumstance.

He'd just killed a man—an FBI agent, no less—and was on the run. No doubt the FBI was losing their shit by now, having put a BOLO on the car he was driving. He needed to secure new wheels as soon as practical. Ideally, something stylish.

The easiest way to get a different car would be to rent something from Hertz or Avis. Unfortunately, that was not an option. He didn't have a driver's license, credit card, or car insurance. And he couldn't take the chance his photo had been sent to every car rental company already.

Same with train stations.

And bus lines.

And airports.

"Just keep driving," Kara said from the passenger seat. "The important thing right now is to put as much distance between you and D.C. Besides, there's a good chance they're not looking for you at all."

"How do you figure?" Stan Lee asked.

"Think about it, Stan. The FBI hates bad publicity."

She was right. And an escaped serial killer was about the worst publicity possible. They may be looking for him, but they sure as hell weren't informing the public. They were looking as quietly and as discretely as possible.

"This is good," Stan Lee said under his breath. "This is very good."

But he still needed to change cars. Logic required it.

The freeway sign overhead read: Memphis, 56 miles. Time to get something to eat, a few hours of sleep, and then a different car.

*   *   *

Stan Lee sat in the parking lot at a small BBQ joint called Corky's on the outskirts of Memphis with a large brown bag of food in his lap. It had been ages since he'd had good bar-b-que, and the restaurant had just the right look to it: an older place, with lots of character, not one of those crappy-ass chains.

Twenty minutes later, he'd polished off a whole slap of pork ribs, a side of baked beans, a quart of potato salad, and two pieces of cornbread slathered in butter.

Stan Lee wiped his chin, started the car, and worked his way back to the freeway. An hour later he pulled into a rest area off the interstate, parked the car, and removed his prosthetics.

"Take a nap, Stan," Kara said from the back seat. She was right. Better to wait until dark. He set the alarm on the watch he'd taken off Winston Young for midnight, then leaned back and closed his eyes, his stomach still full of bar-b-que. Minutes later he was fast asleep.

*   *   *

In the dream, Stan Lee was sitting in class in high school, listening to the teacher drone on about how the Statue of Liberty was a gift from the people of France when the bell rang, and everyone stood to leave. Except him. He looked down and saw he had no legs, just a pair of bloody stumps. "Get up, Stan, it's time," he heard a girl say from behind him. He looked over his shoulder to see Kara standing there.

"What?"

"I said, get up, it's time."

Stan Lee opened his eyes to see he was sitting in the front seat of the car he's stolen from Winston Young, on the far edge of the rest area.

"Kill the alarm," Kara said. "We've got work to do."

Stan Lee scanned the parking lot to see there were only three cars other than his.

The first was a silver Mercedes. Too flashy.

The second was a red jeep. Not his style.

The third car was a gray Toyota Camry, parked on the opposite side of the lot, with a woman asleep behind the wheel.

Perfect.

He looked around the car to see what he might be able to use to kill the woman. There was nothing.

"There's probably a jack in the trunk," Kara said. "You can use it to smash the window."

"I don't want to break the window," Stan Lee said. "I've got to drive the car."

"Okay, then tap on the glass, and when she opens the door, hit her in the head. Easy peasy."

Stan Lee nodded. It was as good a plan as any, so he strapped his prosthetics back in place, then got out of the car. When he opened the trunk, he was pleased to see there was indeed a spare tire, jack, and tire iron. He grabbed the tire iron and slinked through the darkness toward the Camry. But just as he got to the rear bumper, the car door suddenly opened, and the dome light came on. Stan Lee crouched down behind the car and could hear the woman talking on her cell phone.

"There, is that better?" the woman said loudly. "Uh, huh, okay good. No, I was exhausted, so I pulled off at a rest stop. Yes, I'm going to run to the rest room then I'm leaving. I'll be there in about three hours. Yes, I love you, too. Bye."

The woman exited the vehicle and closed the door, then walked in the direction of the restrooms.

"Look in the car," Kara said from behind him. "Maybe she left her keys."

Stan Lee crept along the side of the car and looked through the driver's side window. Son of a bitch, Kara was right. The woman had left her keys in the ignition!

With no time to waste, Stan Lee dropped the tire iron to the ground and hurried back to the Impala. He grabbed his things from the car, then headed back to the Camry and slid down behind the steering wheel.

"What are you waiting for?" Kara asked. "Go!"

Stan Lee started the car, backed up, then drove away.

*   *   *

Stan Lee had driven less than a mile before he realized his mistake. "Fuck!" he yelled, pounding his fists on the steering wheel. How could he be so stupid?

The entire reason for switching cars was to get something no one would be looking for. For that to be the case, he needed to kill the woman, not leave her alive. With her phone, no less. She'd be calling her husband or the police in less than ten minutes.

"You've got to go back," Kara said.

"I know."

"Well, turn around."

"I can't turn around!" Stan Lee screamed. "I'm on the goddamn freeway."

Two miles later Stan Lee got off the freeway and got back on, heading in the direction he'd just come from.

When he pulled into the rest area, he was relieved to see the only car left in the lot was Winston Young's Impala. A second later, his headlights flashed on the woman, standing in the spot where her car had been, looking around in bewilderment.

"Hit the gas," Kara said.

Stan Lee nodded and pressed the accelerator down, aiming the car directly at the woman. The woman's bewilderment turned to shock when she realized the car was barreling in her direction and picking up speed.

The Camry was going forty miles per hour when it struck her, sending her flying backward like a rag doll to the pavement. She didn't stand a chance.

Stan Lee parked, got out, then dragged the woman's body to Winston Young's Impala and lifted it into the trunk. Fortunately, the woman was petite, around a hundred pounds, and the arm workouts he'd done in his cell came in very handy. But it was still exhausting.

"Okay, are we good to go?" Kara asked from the passenger seat of the Camry.

"I think so," Stan Lee said, his breath labored.

"Then let's get out of here."

"Wait, there's something we missed."

It was the woman's cell phone.

Stan Lee turned on the headlights and searched the pavement with his eyes. There it is.

"Well, get it!" Kara snapped.

Stan Lee hopped out of the car, retrieved the cell phone from the ground, and a few seconds later he peeled out of the lot, surprised at how hard his heart was beating.

"That was intense," Kara said from the back seat. "You know, a small bump would be so nice right now."

No, Stan Lee thought. He needed to stay alert and level-headed. Drugs were out of the question.

Stan Lee's drug of choice was Ketamine. It was something he used to drug the girls he was abducting. Now and then, he'd use a bit himself, just to calm his nerves. It leveled him out.

"Come on, Stan," Kara prompted. "Memphis is the perfect place to score some K."

She was right.

Memphis was a big city. All big cities had neighborhoods where drugs could be found.

Assuming one knew where to look.

"Why don't you just get it over with," Kara said.

"I'm going to," Stan Lee said.

"I'm not talking about the drugs," Kara said. "I'm talking about killing Newt Drystad. You know you want to. You know it's inevitable. Besides, aren't you tired of running?"

She was right. That was the only solution. After three days of zig-zagging around the country, looking over his shoulder, he wanted it over with. He needed to kill Newt Drystad.

He'd go to Memphis.

Buy drugs.

Then head back to Washington D.C.

Juniper Cole's legs would have to wait.

Chapter Forty-Eight

Mohawk Joe was livid with himself. He'd become such a coward, having grown comfortable being part of the circus. He knew that if he didn't do as Dolly had asked, he'd be cast out. Ostracized. Alone. Screw that. Even though Ulrich had offered to kill the clown, Mohawk Joe knew it was his fight. Now, all he had to do was find the face-painted freak.

Where would he be amid all this chaos? Mohawk Joe wondered. Maybe he'd want to get away. Okay, so how would he do it? He'd steal a vehicle.

Mohawk Joe worked his way around the outside of the still-burning tent and went to the parking area. And that's where he found him. The clown was kneeling over a man he'd just taken, rifling through his pockets, in search of car keys no doubt.

The clown found the keys, stood up, and said, "I was wondering when you'd show up. I know Dolly asked you to take me out."

"I have an idea," Mohawk Joe said. "How about you shut up and we just get on with it."

The clown smiled and took a step toward Mohawk Joe, then stopped and looked to his left to see Ulrich standing there. "Oh, look, it's the Giant German. Come to party, too?"

"What are you doing here?" Mohawk Joe asked.

"We agreed I'd handle this, Joe," Ulrich said.

"And I changed my mind."

"How adorable, a lover's spat," the clown giggled.

"Trust me, I've got this," Mohawk Joe said ignoring the clown.

Several seconds passed. Ulrich nodded and started to walk away, then Slade said: "Hey, Ulrich, did you know I kissed Onyx?"

Ulrich stopped, then spun around. "What did you say?"

"I said, I kissed your wife."

"Shut up," Ulrich spat. "You know nothing about Onyx."

"Oh? I know she lives in a lighthouse out on the cliffs. I know she's a ghost, like the rest of us. And I know she's a great kisser."

Ulrich clenched his fists and felt the energy drain from his face as he and the clown stared each other down, waiting to see who was going to make the first move. As it turned out, neither man did.

They were interrupted.

"Ulrich, over here," he heard a woman's voice say from behind him. He turned and looked to see Antoinette standing there, her clothes burned away, leaving her virtually naked.

"Oh, looks like Ulrich has a new girlfriend," Slade said. "Wait till Onyx finds out you've been cheating on her."

"What's he talking about?" Antoinette asked as Mohawk Joe ran over to where she was standing, took off his shirt, and wrapped it around her.

"Joe, are you still willing to take care of this asshole for me?"

"It would be my pleasure," Mohawk Joe said matter-of-factly, taking a step forward toward the clown.

"You're giving your friend a death sentence," Slade said. "You do realize that, right?"

"We've *all* been given death sentences," Ulrich said.

* * *

Antoinette led Ulrich through the smoldering debris of the circus and stopped him behind Dolly's trailer, one of the few structures that survived the inferno.

"So, what happened to you?" Ulrich asked.

"I had a run-in with a burning tent pole," Antoinette said.

"Where's Willy?"

Antoinette didn't answer. Instead, she said: "I need your help, doing something dangerous."

"Dangerous? What?"

"It's time to give Dolly what she deserves," Antoinette said.

"If you want to take Dolly, take her," Ulrich said. "No one is stopping you."

"I don't want to simply *kill* her," Antoinette hissed. "I want to teach her a lesson she'll never forget. I want her final miserable moments on this earth to be spent thinking about one thing. Me."

* * *

Dolly knew the jig was up. The circus she'd spent her life building was over, destroyed beyond repair. The only option left to her now was to run. And to run, she needed money—money she kept in a safe hidden under the floor of her trailer.

Dolly kept her head down, trying not to be recognized as she wove her way through groups of spectators watching the Crimson Cove Fire Department fight the final burning remnants of the big top tent. She had no idea how the fire started, but if she ever found out, there would be hell to pay.

When she arrived at her trailer Dolly noticed a large trunk sitting at the bottom of the steps, with the lid propped open. What was *that* doing there? she thought as she climbed the steps and opened the door.

"Hello, Dolly," Antoinette said.

"What—?"

Antoinette lunged forward and shoved Dolly, sending her hurtling backward through the air—directly into the open trunk. It took Dolly a moment to get her wits about her. By the time she did, Ulrich stepped forward and slammed the lid closed.

Antoinette climbed down the steps and secured the chest from the outside with an iron padlock she'd found in the supply trailer, all the while singing, *"Hello, Dolly—well, hello, Dolly—it's so nice to have you right where you belong."*

* * *

It was a full mile from where the circus had been staged to the edge of the cliffs. The path was not an easy one to navigate, weaving through the pine trees on bumpy ground. Fortunately, ghosts were able to see in the dark, and Ulrich knew the most direct route, having once lived nearby.

"Are you sure this is what you want to do?" Ulrich asked. "It's rather cruel."

"Cruel? The only thing that's cruel around here is locked back there in that chest," Antoinette said.

Ulrich shrugged, glancing at the magician's chest being pulled by May Wirth's white show horse behind them. If he'd learned one thing in his life, hell hath no fury like a woman scorned. Onyx had taught him that lesson the hard way.

The trip took over an hour, but eventually, they exited the woods and arrived at a clearing overlooking the Pacific Ocean. In the distance, Ulrich could see Onyx's lighthouse—the lighthouse they'd once shared as husband and wife, off in the distance, the flame at the top glowing in the dark.

"Let's do this," Antoinette said.

Ulrich detached the chest from the horse and slid it over until it was balanced on the very edge of the cliff. "I suppose you want to do the honors?" Ulrich said.

Antoinette nodded.

Then she stepped forward and kicked the chest as hard as she could, sending it toward the crashing ocean waves below.

"Feel better?" Ulrich asked.

"Better than she does," Antoinette said. "How long do you think she's got before the last of her energy is gone?"

"I don't know," Ulrich said as the pair watched the chest bobbing in the ocean as it drifted out to sea.

"I've been thinking," Antoinette said. "You're the best partner I've ever had, Ulrich, and I've been doing this for a long, long time. What if we worked out an act, something wonderful, something better than anyone has ever seen before?"

"Join another circus?" Ulrich asked.

Antoinette reached out and took Ulrich's hand. "Do you believe in fate?"

"Fate? Yes, probably."

"I think we'd be great together—come with me."

Ulrich turned and looked over the cliffs in the direction of the lighthouse. "I wish I could, but I've got some unfinished business to deal with."

Antoinette leaned in and kissed Ulrich full on the lips. "We'll find each other somehow. Fate has a way of doing that."

Chapter Forty-Nine

Ulrich worked his way through the tall pines to the edge of the clearing and gazed at the flame burning atop the lighthouse. He remembered what a horrendous job it had been, hauling a full canister of lamp oil up the 103 stairs, and wondered if Onyx was doing the exhausting task herself, or was it her new man?

He shifted his gaze toward the caretaker's house and noticed a sliver of light escaping through the door of the shed and headed in that direction. He peaked through the opening and saw it wasn't Onyx. Instead, it was the man tending to a motorcycle—the same man Ulrich had seen in bed with her a few nights earlier when he watched them through the window. What a strange feeling. Once upon a time *he* had shared Onyx's bed and stood in that same shed working on the Mercedes Benz he'd imported from Germany. *Men and their women,* Ulrich thought. *And boys and their toys.*

Suddenly, a hand grabbed the collar of his shirt and pulled him backward, away from the door. He spun around and found himself face to face with Onyx.

"My God, Onyx, you scared the hell—"

Onyx held her index finger to her lips and signaled for Ulrich to follow her toward the lighthouse.

Once they were far enough away to not be heard, Onyx said, "I've accepted that you are a deeply-flawed man, Ulrich, but you've reached a new low—you're also a peeping Tom now?"

"You knew it was me the other evening?"

"Why have you come here, Ulrich? What do you want?"

"I came to say I'm sorry."

"Sorry? Sorry for what, Ulrich—for what, losing our money? Being a lying, cheating, murdering thief? For trying to poison me to death?"

"All of it, Onyx, I'm sorry for all of it," Ulrich said. "You are right. I am a deeply flawed man, or at least I *was*. I'm not the same now, I've changed."

"*You've changed?*" Onyx snorted. "Because you died, you think you've changed? People never change, Ulrich. Even in death, we remain who we were."

Ulrich shook his head. "No, you're wrong."

"Really? Tell me, Ulrich, kill anyone lately?"

Ulrich thought about having just helped Antoinette send Dolly to a watery grave. "Okay, and you, Onyx? How long has it been since *you've* taken a life?"

"You are right, I am in no position to pass judgment on you. In the end, we both turned out to be murderers."

"Is that your way of saying you forgive me?"

"Is that what you came here for? Forgiveness?" Onyx asked.

"Yes, I am asking for that which I do not deserve. I am asking to be forgiven," Ulrich said.

"With what we have done, I'm not sure any of us will ever be forgiven," Onyx said. "But I do offer understanding."

Understanding was the best Ulrich was going to get.

Or deserved.

"How did you come back? Do you know?" Onyx asked.

Ulrich shook his head. "I have no idea. It felt like I was sleepwalking in some kind of unconscious state, then suddenly I was looking through a mirror at Mohawk Joe."

"The Indian?" Onyx spat.

Ulrich knew there was no love lost between Onyx and Mohawk Joe, and he'd wished he'd not mentioned him. But it was too late. "He summoned me, somehow, by thinking about me. He just drew me to the circus."

"Mohawk Joe is part of a circus?" Onyx asked, surprised.

"We both are," Ulrich said. "I'm doing a high wire trapeze act. At least I was, before the fire."

Ulrich turned and pointed in the direction he'd come from, through the woods. Onyx closed her eyes and concentrated her attention, hearing the faint sound of sirens wailing in the distance. "Were people hurt?"

"I don't think so," Ulrich said. "But the police are rounding up people from the circus for questioning. They'll be holding people in jail cells. If they hold them long enough, they're bound to discover some of them are ghosts. I had no choice but to run."

"I understand," Onyx said. "Come with me."

*　　*　　*

Noah was in the shed, on his hands and knees, cleaning the buildup of brake dust and grime from the aluminum alloy wheels. He retrieved a bottle of Boden's cleaner from the cabinet, shook it well, and sprayed a generous amount on a cotton cloth. He rubbed the cloth on both sides of the wheels, careful not to get any of the spray on the discs or the calipers. The cleaner smelled like formaldehyde but worked like a charm.

"Noah," Onyx's voice came from behind him. Noah turned around and was shocked to see Onyx standing there, but not alone. A man was standing there with her—a man

Noah recognized from old photos. It was her ex-husband, Ulrich.

"What is this? Why is *he* here?" Noah managed.

"There is no time for squabbles," Onyx said. "The police are rounding up the ghosts from the circus. He needs to get away. Give him the keys to your motorcycle."

"What? I'm not—why are you helping him?" Noah asked. "After all he did?"

"Please, Noah," Onyx said. "I'm asking you to do this. For me."

Every fiber of Noah's being wanted to lash out, to tell them both to go to hell. But he didn't. "Here," Noah said, tossing the keys through the air to Ulrich. "She's got a tall first gear. If you start from second gear, you'll slip the clutch."

Chapter Fifty

Maggie locked her car and headed toward the elevators in the basement garage in the building next to the FBI offices and pushed the up-arrow button. As usual, Pipi Esperanza's car was already there.

Maggie didn't bother looking for Newt's car, since she knew Newt was still in bed, right where she'd left him a half-hour earlier. Newt didn't have 9 to 5 hours. He'd be in when he felt like it, and his mind was fully rested.

Newt.

Maggie was still amazed at Newt's genius. His ability to do computer-like calculations in his head. His photographic memory. His ability to make connections between things that looked unconnected to everyone else. It was what had attracted her to him in the first place.

The next two hours were spent reviewing her notes and using them to write a detailed summary of the events in Crimson Cove. Reports were part of the job. But this report mattered more than most since a local police officer had died while assisting their investigation. Clay Daniels deserved her best effort. If ever there was an example of going above and beyond the call of duty, running back into the burning circus tent to save someone's life clearly qualified.

Maggie made a mental note to send flowers to Clay's funeral, on behalf of the bureau.

Now, she needed to decide what she was going to do regarding the situation with Chad. Should she tell Newt that Chad hadn't exactly moved on from their relationship?

Maggie knew she probably should.

She also knew she probably wouldn't.

Not because she worried Newt would think she cheated on him. She knew he wouldn't. What worried her was losing Chad from the team. Chad was the second smartest person she knew—and he was rich.

But Chad's money didn't matter. The money was a turn-off, for two reasons. First, it was all he ever talked about—his entire identity was wrapped up in what he owned. Second, his wealth made Chad lazy. He didn't have to work. He wasn't driven.

To Maggie, the most important thing to her was catching bad guys. And no one did it better than Newt.

*   *   *

"Tell me about Crimson Cove," Newt said when he got into the office.

"It's all in there," Maggie said, pointing at the report she'd dropped on Newt's desk an hour earlier.

"I'm sure it is," Newt said. "I want to know what *isn't* in the report."

What wasn't in the report was any mention of ghosts. Such information couldn't go in the official report. Ghosts didn't exist. Especially killer ghosts who sucked the life out of people so they could stay in the living plane.

Only crazy people believed in ghosts.

And crazy didn't sell well at the bureau.

"The whole thing was a cluster," Maggie said. "At least no civilians died."

"Awful about Clay Daniels," Newt said.

"Yes, Chad feels horrible by the way. He blames himself."

"That's reasonable," Newt said. "Did you see Onyx?"

Maggie shook her head. "Onyx has been keeping a low profile—well, she *did* apparently threaten Abigale Dietz, but other than that."

"Why did she threaten her?"

"Abigale wants to use Onyx to turn Crimson Cove into the Ghost Capitol of the Pacific Northwest," Maggie said.

"Terrific," Newt said. "So much for keeping ghosts a secret. Anyway, there's something I have to tell you, and it's confidential."

"Okay."

"Mungehr's gone," Newt said.

"You transferred him? Where?"

Newt shook his head. "No, I mean he's *gone*."

"Oh, no, no, no," Maggie said, shaking her head violently from side to side. "Please don't tell me—"

"He escaped," Newt said.

"Escaped! How in the fuck could he escape?"

"You ever hear of MK Ultra?"

"Of course—the secret CIA program from the 1950s."

Newt nodded. "Part of that program included astral projection. Stan Lee was one of their subjects."

"And we're just finding this out?"

"I missed it," Newt said. "It was buried in thousands of pages of reports from 20 years ago."

Maggie shook her head and let out a long breath. "We've got to get him back. He's not going to stop killing, you know that, right?"

"Yes, Maggie, I am *very* aware of that. I am also aware that if he does, the murders are on me."

"That's not what I'm saying."

"I know."

"Did you tell Pipi?" Maggie asked.

Newt nodded.

"How did she take it?"

"Not well," Newt said.

"She's letting you deal with it?" Maggie asked.

Newt nodded but said no more. While he hated keeping things from Maggie, in this case, it was best to leave her out of the loop.

Newt couldn't tell Maggie that an FBI agent had been murdered during Mungehr's escape because Pipi hadn't decided how to handle it yet. He knew was the FBI was good at two things. The first was catching bad guys. The other thing was covering their tracks when they screwed up.

"Stan Lee is going to come after you, you know that, right?" Maggie said. "He's going to want revenge."

Newt shook his head. "He's long gone. We're not going to see Stanton Lee Mungehr for a long, long time."

Chapter Fifty-One

Doyle Slade slid into the corner booth opposite the bar in an Irish pub in the not-very-safe part of downtown Lincoln, Nebraska, and waited for the waitress to come. When she did, he ordered a Bud Light and sat there pretending to sip from it to avoid looking out of place.

The waitress came by a half-hour later, eyed the still-full beer mug, then left. Slade realized that ordering a beer and not drinking it was not the norm, so he poured half of it on the floor under the table.

Behind the bar, a game played on the television. Slade hated sports and paid no attention. When the game ended, Katie Couric appeared on the screen. Slade hated Katie Couric, too, but her guest caught his attention.

It was someone he recognized. The woman from the theater in Crimson Cove, the one he let get away.

"So, Abigale, please tell our viewers about the frightening attack on your life."

"Turn that up, will you?" Slade said loudly. The bartender grabbed the remote control and increased the volume.

"Yes, Katie, it was extremely frightening," Abigale continued, her voice hoarse. *"I was closing the theater when a man came in dressed like a circus clown."*

"Dressed like a clown?"

"Yes, it was like something out of a Stephen King movie," Abigale said.

"Go on," Katie nudged.

"Well, when I told him to leave, he shoved me into the popcorn machine. The Dietz Theater is known for our popcorn," Abigale said. *"I tried to run, but the man grabbed my*

Hermes silk scarf, something I'd picked up on a recent trip to Nordstrom's in Seattle."

Katie pointed to the red and black scarf tied in a stylish French knot around Abigale's neck. *"Is that the scarf?"*

"Yes," Abigale said. *"The only reason I'm wearing it today is to hide the garish welts on my neck."*

"What happened next?"

"He began choking me. I must have passed out, because the next thing I knew I was on a respirator in the intensive care unit."

"And this man, the one who strangled you, he's still at large?" Katie asked.

Abigale nodded and said, *"Yes, the FBI believes he escaped during the fire. But there's something else, something really disturbing."*

"Tell us," Katie said breathlessly.

"I'm convinced the person who tried to kill me was..."

"Was, what?"

"I believe he was dead."

"Wait a second," Katie said. *"Are you saying the man who attacked you was actually a—"*

"Yes, I'm saying he was a ghost," Abigale said. *"I was in the wrong place at the wrong time. Had my brother not come along when he did, I wouldn't be here to do this interview."*

"So, you believe ghosts are real?"

"Real? Yes, of course, they're real," Abigale said. *"We've got one right here, in Crimson Cove, whose been here for seventy-five years. Her name is Onyx Webb, and she lives in the lighthouse. I'd go so far as to say Crimson Cove, Oregon, is the ghost capital of the Pacific Northwest."*

Slade sat in the corner booth of the bar and pushed his beer mug around the table, thinking. Not about the woman on the television, he couldn't have cared less about her. He was thinking about the female FBI agent he'd run into. The one who reminded him of his first kill sixty years ago. God, how he wished he could have taken her. He would have if it weren't for the fire.

Slade pulled out the cell phone he'd taken off a truck driver at a Pilot Flying J truck stop in Casper, Wyoming, two nights earlier, only to find it was dead again. Of course, it was.

Ghosts not only sucked the life from the living, they also drew energy from surrounding power sources. Like cell phones. Flickering lights, television static, and cold spots in the middle of an otherwise warm room were often the result of ghost activity.

Slade tossed a five-dollar bill on the table and exited the bar, stepping out into the darkened street. He needed to find somewhere he could get online. Six blocks from the bar he found a 24-hour FedEx office and went inside. Two minutes later he was navigating the FBI's official website.

It was ridiculous how much information the government made available online. He clicked on the Field Offices tab and scrolled through the list, which appeared in alphabetical order: Albany, Boston, Cleveland, Detroit, El Paso, Honolulu...

Slade smiled when he came to Indianapolis because it made him think about the stupid Indian who thought he could take him. When the moment came, the Mohawk chickened out, of course, and ran away like a little bitch. He knew he should have gone after him, but the circus grounds were swarming with police by then, and it was more important to get away. So, when no one was looking, Slade grabbed a cop car and simply drove away.

Slade scrolled down the list until he found the FBI location he was looking for: Washington D.C. A minute later, he was staring at a photo of Special Agent Margaret McCord.

Dark brown hair. Light green eyes. A serious look on her face. Yep, it was her.

The website did not list employees' home addresses, of course, just their names and titles. Having her home address would have made it easier, but that was okay with Slade; he didn't want it to be easy. Half the fun was in the hunt. An hour later, he boarded a Greyhound bus headed for Washington D.C.

Chapter Fifty-Two

Stan Lee Mungehr wasn't exactly sure what was happening. One second, he was heading on the I-80 West on his way to Ogallala, Nebraska, with the intent of retrieving the container holding Juniper Cole's legs, and the next moment he was on the I-80 East, heading in the exact opposite direction. He didn't even remember turning around.

Maybe it was anger.

Maybe he wanted revenge.

Maybe he was sick and tired of looking over his shoulder.

"Maybe it's the Ketamine?" Kara asked.

"Don't start," Stan Lee said.

"Christ, you're one screwed-up serial killer," Kara said.

Stan Lee knew Kara wasn't real. He understood that when he talked to her, he was talking to himself. Likewise, when she talked to him, he was simply thinking. But he needed her. Without Kara, he would be all alone.

The stash of liquid Ketamine Stan Lee bought in Memphis was gone. And he was running out of money. Maybe he could slum it and use the drug in powdered form. Commonly known as K, or sometimes Special K, the white powder was a rapid-acting drug that was soluble in water and could be bought on any street corner for twenty bucks a vial—if, if—you knew where to look.

"I need another fix," Stan Lee said.

"No, you don't," Kara said.

Stan Lee ignored her and grabbed the map. They were no more than thirty miles outside Kansas City. He'd never been to KC, but he'd always heard what a dump it was. It should be perfect. Seedy neighborhoods with shady people standing around on street corners.

But powdered Ketamine wasn't what Stan Lee was looking for. He needed to score the Ketamine in liquid form, the kind that came straight from the manufacturer. At low doses, the liquid was perfect for taking the edge off and calming him down, which seemed to be more and more necessary lately.

"Too much will kill you," Kara said.

"I know what I'm doing."

Stan Lee grabbed Winston Young's cell phone and typed in *'emergency veterinary clinics.'* There were three. One was in a neighborhood called Greenway Fields. Sounded wealthy. Next, he typed in *'best neighborhoods in Kansas City.'* Greenway Fields was on the list.

Having robbed veterinary clinics in the past, there were a few things Stan Lee knew: First, emergency clinics were open 24 hours, so he wouldn't have to break in. He could just walk in. Second, veterinary clinics in better neighborhoods had notoriously bad security. And third, veterinary clinics stocked liquid Ketamine.

*   *   *

The Greenway Fields Emergency Veterinary Clinic was a long, low brown brick building with enough parking spaces to handle twenty cars. There were only four cars there. One most likely belonged to the vet. Another probably to the receptionist or assistant. The third was probably an animal owner.

Stan Lee sat in the fourth car, parked off to the side in the shadows, waiting for the owner of the third car to exit the building. Half an hour later he was still waiting.

"Call them," Kara said.

"And say what?" Stan Lee said.

"Tell them your dog is horribly sick, ask them if they can take you immediately."

Not a bad idea.

Stan Lee dialed the number for the clinic and a man picked up on the third ring. "Greenway Fields Emergency Clinic, can you hold?"

"No, I can't hold," Stan Lee snarled. "My dog is sick! Can you take her?"

"We're in the middle of a procedure, sir, the wait shouldn't be long."

"Are there other people waiting? If you're too busy tell me and—"

"No, sir, no one else is waiting," the man said. "Bring her in, the Doc will be available in just a few minutes." Then the line went dead.

"Am I smart or what?" Kara said.

Stan Lee did not respond. He hated being outthought.

Ten minutes passed and the front door of the clinic swung open, and a man and woman exited. The woman was clearly distraught, and the man was doing his best to comfort her.

After they drove away, Kara said: "Showtime, you ready?"

Stan Lee grabbed the gun off the seat, then got out of the car and headed for the building.

*   *   *

Dr. Leslie Dvorak placed the used syringe in the biohazard disposal container and the barbiturate anesthetic bottle in the metal locker and wiped away tears with her sleeve. Knowing the procedure was rapid, inducing a state of unconsciousness within seconds provided some comfort. But she also knew the impact of the animal's death on its owners was devastating. Her instructors in veterinary school said it would get easier. They were wrong.

Suddenly, the door burst open and her assistant, Michael, entered the room, followed by a man holding a handgun. "I'm sorry, he—"

Stan Lee smashed the side of the gun into the side of the assistant's head, and he dropped to the tiled floor, unconscious.

"Your Ketamine, where do you keep it?"

"We don't keep inventory on hand," Dvorak said.

"Well, that's too bad, because then you and he are dead," Stan Lee said taking a step forward and pointing the gun at the woman's face.

"Okay, okay," Dvorak stammered. "I'll show you."

Stan Lee motioned with the gun for the woman to move, and she led him to a locked cabinet on the far side of the room. "It's in here," she said nervously.

"Open it," Stan Lee commanded. Dvorak fumbled with her keys until eventually finding the right one, then slid it into the lock and opened the metal door.

Bingo.

"Please, take it, there's no reason to—"

Stan Lee pulled a plastic bag from his pocket and tossed it on the table. "Fill it up, and be quick."

Dvorak did as she was told, placing forty vials of liquid Ketamine into the bag.

"Syringes, too."

The woman threw a handful of syringes into the bag and held it out to Stan Lee, her hands shaking.

Stan Lee lifted the gun and pointed it directly at the woman's forehead. "Are you going to say anything?"

"No, no, I promise, I swear."

Stan Lee kept the gun pointed at the woman, his finger on the trigger but didn't fire.

"Do it, kill them," Kara said from the corner of the room. "They've seen your face."

"They save animals," Stan Lee said.

Dvorak looked around the room to see who the man was talking to.

"Who cares, Stan?" Kara asked. "They can describe you to the police. Do it!"

"No, it's not necessary," Stan Lee said, lowering the gun. "Don't call the cops. If you do, we'll know, and we *will* be back and we'll kill both of you."

* * *

"You should have killed them," Kara said when Stan Lee returned to the car.

"I couldn't," Stan Lee said as he reached in the bag and removed one of the vials, and opened it. "They help animals and we all know animals are better than people."

"She'll turn you in," Kara said.

No, she won't, Stan Lee thought.

"I don't get you," Kara said. "You drive back to kill the woman in the parking lot, but not the vet. You're out of your mind."

Stan Lee removed a needle from its plastic wrapper and did his best to ignore her.

"You're not going to do that here, are you?" Kara asked.

"Why not?"

"Because when the police get here you don't want them to find you passed out in the parking lot."

"I won't pass out," Stan Lee said.

"That's what they all say."

"Fine. We'll go." Stan Lee started the engine and pulled out of the parking lot. Five minutes later, he pulled the Camry to the curb on a dark residential side street. "This okay with you?"

There was no response.

Kara was gone.

Good, Stan Lee. He needed quiet.

Five minutes later he was unconscious, an elastic tourniquet around his bicep and the needle and syringe still in his arm.

Chapter Fifty-Three

FBI director Pipi Esperanza stood behind the podium strategically placed in front of the FBI Wall of Honor, waiting for the press to stop snapping photos. Eventually, Pipi cleared her throat into the microphone and the room quieted down.

"Good morning," Pipi began. "On behalf of every member of the FBI, it's both an honor and a moment of deep personal sadness to be here today to remember Special Agent Winston M. Young."

Pipi paused as a door opened and Newt and Maggie entered, taking their places along the sidewall of the room.

"I find that, in moments like these, there are no words that can be said to make a loss like this any easier. There is nothing more devastating to the FBI Family than the loss of an agent in the line of duty.

"Before walking across the graduation stage at the FBI Academy in Quantico, every special agent swears an oath to put service over self, and while I didn't have the privilege of knowing Winston the way many of you here did, it is clear to me that he honored that oath above and beyond the call of duty.

"Until now, the bureau has been tight-lipped regarding the circumstances surrounding Special Agent Young's untimely death. So, I'd like to take a minute to explain why his death has been treated with such secrecy.

"At my direction, Agent Young took on one of the hardest jobs in the FBI, participating in a covert undercover mission that placed him in grave danger. It was a mission that he willingly accepted and did not shy away from.

"As much as I would love to explain the specifics of Winston Young's death, I cannot."

A rumbling of groans came from the attendees, specifically the media, who had come just for the details Pipi was withholding.

"Now, many of you in the press will interpret this as evasion on the bureau's part, an attempt to avoid responsibility. I assure you, it is not. I am here to tell you that Special Agent Winston Young's death was the direct result of poor decision-making on my part, and I take full responsibility. His death was my fault, and mine alone."

"Did you know she was going to do this?" Maggie whispered to Newt.

Newt shrugged and didn't answer.

"Madam Director, can you please explain what the operation entailed, and why you are taking personal blame?" a reporter called out.

Pipi shook her head and stood her ground. "As much as I would like to share those details, I cannot do so at this time without jeopardizing the lives of other agents still in the field."

"If Special Agent Young's death was your fault, are you planning on resigning?"

Maggie leaned toward Newt and whispered, "You believe the balls on these people? Resigning is the last thing Pipi would ever do."

Pipi continued: "Serving as the director of the FBI has been one of the most prestigious jobs I could have ever dreamt of having. But it is a job that requires the highest levels of integrity and sound judgment. To those ends, I have failed, and yes, I will be stepping down."

In an instant, the event went from being a quiet and somber affair into sheer pandemonium.

* * *

"That was a nice honor for Winston Young," Newt said once he and Maggie had returned to his office.

"So, you really didn't know about this?" Maggie asked.

"No," Newt said. "I knew she was going to do something, but not that she was going to leave."

Pipi Esperanza had promised Newt she would handle the situation and, true to her word, she did. The circumstances around Winston Young's death would never see the light of day. Any blame would be placed on her, not Newt.

It was an enormous sacrifice on her part.

"Do you know what special assignment Winston Young was working on that got him killed?" Maggie asked.

Newt remained silent, unsure as to how much he wanted to involve her.

"There's something you're not telling me," Maggie said. "Well?"

"Winston Young was killed by Stan Lee Mungehr," Newt said. "That's what Pipi covered up. This was my fault, and she took the blame. She did it for me."

Chapter Fifty-Four

C had Chatterton was invited to the event honoring the in-the-line-of-duty heroism of FBI Special Agent Winston Young, but he was still reeling from the situation in Crimson Cove. Sheriff Clay Daniels IV had run into the blazing circus tent to save Chad's life, only to lose his own. So, rather than attend, he retreated to the isolation of the Ghost Division's basement office and buried himself in work.

"So, what did I miss?" he asked when Maggie walked in.

"Oh, nothing big, just Pipi Esperanza taking the blame for Winston Young's death and resigning as director," Maggie said as she put her laptop on the desk and sat down at the desk opposite Chad.

"What? You're kidding, right?" Chad said in disbelief.

"I wish."

"Wow, where does that put us and the Ghost Division?"

Maggie shrugged. "Newt says it's business as usual."

"So, we keep sifting through the files and see any patterns appear?"

"Yeah, well, speaking of patterns—I've got a favor to ask."

"Sure, shoot."

"First, I've got to read you in on something that must stay confidential, strictly between us," Maggie said. Chad nodded and waited for Maggie to continue. "It has to do with serial killer Stanton Lee Mungehr."

"I know about Mungehr," Chad said.

"What do you know?"

"Mungehr was caught and killed in a shoot-out in Oregon three months ago," Chad said.

Maggie shook her head. "That's the story, but it's not the truth."

"Okay."

"Mungehr was taken alive," Maggie said. "For the last few months we had been holding him in a cell in the basement of St. Elizabeth's hospital so Newt could study him."

"*Had* been holding him? Where is he now?"

"He escaped."

"Oh, no." Chad put his hand on his head. "Are you telling me—?"

Maggie held up her hand, cutting him off. "Wait. It gets worse. Winston Young was killed by Mungehr during the escape."

"Shit," Chad said.

Maggie nodded and let the implications settle in.

"Is that the *real* reason Pipi resigned?" Chad asked.

"Yes, she's covering for Newt."

Chad remained silent, thinking, then said, "So, what's the favor?"

"I think Stanton Lee Mungehr is going to go after Newt. I want you to run Newt's Predictive Data Algorithm program to look for any discernible patterns that might clue us in on Mungehr's movements."

"The Drugged Spider Program?" Chad said. "I thought that was a myth."

Maggie shook her head. "No, Newt used it when Mungehr was using Ketamine to predict where his next abduction would take place. In an area of ten square miles, he was off by one block. It works."

"When did Mungehr escape?"

"Three days ago."

"Well, he could be anywhere by now," Chad said.

"I don't think so," Maggie said, shaking her head. "I know this guy, he'll come back and go for Newt, I'm sure of it."

"Then Newt should get out of D.C., and so should you," Chad said. "He might come after you, too?"

"No one's coming after me," Maggie said. "Now, please, run the program."

"What if Mungehr's not using drugs?" Chad asked. "Then the program is useless."

"He'll be using," Maggie said. "He's not only a serial killer, he's an addict."

I'll need clearance to access the program and a password," Chad said.

"I got you clearance already, and the password is Spider-Boy."

* * *

Chad couldn't believe what he was seeing. The Predictive Data Algorithm Newt created was nothing short of genius. Should he have expected anything less? Newt *was* a genius. Chad had no idea the man could write such intricate code.

The program worked from the assumption that when subjected to drugs—such as cocaine, LSD, PCP, acid, marijuana, Ketamine, and even caffeine—a spider's behavior became erratic, but erratic in predictable ways. Rather than spinning a classic spiral-shaped web, spiders on drugs zig-zagged all over the place.

In the same way, serial killers usually started killing somewhere near home, then worked their way out in a somewhat predictable pattern. The pattern wasn't always obvious, but if you looked hard enough, it was usually there.

Newt compared the kill patterns of 371 known serial murderers to over six thousand webs spun by spiders under the influence of various drugs. Their patterns were almost identical. If you knew where the spider or the serial killer started, the program could predict where the next kill would take place with 88% accuracy.

Chad input every piece of available data and started the program. Three hours later he had the result.

*   *   *

"I have good news and bad news," Chad said to Maggie over the phone.

"Okay, good news first," Maggie said.

"You were right, Newt's program works. I've never seen anything like it, Newt is an absolute genius."

"I keep trying to tell you," Maggie said. "So, what's the bad news?"

"The bad news is, if Stanton Lee Mungehr isn't using drugs, there's virtually no way to know where he might be. But if he is, then he's most likely somewhere in D.C."

Chapter Fifty-Five

We need new plates," Stan Lee said as he navigated the heavy traffic on the Theodore Roosevelt Bridge across the Potomac River. It was the easiest way to reach the Foggy Bottom neighborhood and the western areas of downtown D.C.

"Over there," Kara said from the back seat, pointing to a Trader Joe's parking lot when they reached 25th Street Northwest. "Look, there's a silver Camry."

"It's not gray."

"It's close enough," Kara said.

"We need something to take the plates off with," Stan Lee said once he parked the car in the lot.

Kara shook her head in disgust. "Look in the bag, dipshit," she said, pointing to the front passenger seat.

Stan Lee reached over and opened the bag to see a small screwdriver. When had he bought that? Jesus, he *was* losing control.

"You bought it at the truck stop outside Charleston," Kara said.

"We went to Charleston, when did we do that?"

"You're losing it, Stan," Kara said. "Just get the plates."

Stan Lee got out of the car and walked to the silver Camry, then bent over and pretended to stop and tie his shoe. A minute later he had the plates. A minute after that, he was back on the road.

*   *   *

Stan Lee pulled into the parking garage across from Ford's Theater in the 900 block of F Street NW and looked at the sign with the parking rates. "That can't be right. Twenty-one dollars? That's ridiculous."

"Just pay it, for the love of God, and park the car," Kara said.

Stan Lee lowered the window and took a ticket from the machine and the gate raised.

"I'm thinking we should take the tour," Stan Lee said as he removed his prosthetics and applied a generous dollop of skin lotion, and massaged his aching stumps.

"Tour of what?" Kara asked.

"Ford's Theater, what else," Stan Lee said. "I've always wanted to go, and here we are. Besides, we have time."

"That's not the point," Kara snapped. "The fewer number of people we come in contact with, the better."

Stan Lee glanced at his watch to see it was only 6 p.m. He didn't want to get to the FBI building until it after dark. "I'm not sitting in the car for two hours. You want to sit here, be my guest, but I'm taking the tour."

Kara remained silent as Stan Lee put his prosthetics in place and pulled tight on the leather straps. "Are you coming?"

Kara did not respond.

"Fine, have it your way," Stan Lee said and exited the car. "But you're going to wish you'd come."

* * *

"Do you see what time it is?" Kara asked when Stan Lee returned to the car.

"Yeah, it's 8:10 p.m.," Stan Lee said.

"Exactly. So, what makes you think Drystad will still be in his office?"

"The man's a workaholic," Stan Lee said. "I'd be surprised if he left before midnight."

"You better be right."

Stan Lee didn't answer her. He started the car and wound his way through the garage toward the exit.

"It was a nice tour," Kara said finally. "Makes you appreciate the dedication John Wilkes Booth had, to jump off the balcony like that, break his leg, and still get away."

"I knew you'd come," Stan Lee said.

"Yeah, well, where you go, I go."

"I wish we could have toured the house across the street where Lincoln died, though," Stan Lee said as he turned on the car's headlights and pulled into traffic on F Street.

"It would be nice if we had Drystad's home address," Kara said.

"We don't," Stan Lee said.

"I *know* we don't," Kara said. "I'm merely saying it would be nice if we *did*."

Stan Lee didn't need to know where Newt Drystad lived. He knew where he worked. "According to the map, the Hoover Building is a few blocks away."

"Really? Then why didn't we just leave the car here and walk?" Kara asked.

She had a point.

*   *   *

Stan Lee drove to the J. Edgar Hoover building, circled the block, and immediately knew he'd made a mistake moving the car. There was no street parking available whatsoever.

For a moment he considered going back and re-parking the car in the garage he'd just left, near Ford's Theater, but then he found a garage directly adjacent to the FBI building.

Once he found a spot, he turned off the engine and immediately fished a vial of Ketamine from the bag. He had no intention of taking enough to pass out, he just needed a little bump to get him by.

"You do realize this is your third hit today, right?" Kara said.

"What are you, my mother?"

Stan Lee finished injecting the liquid into his vein, then leaned back in the seat. He placed his head on the headrest and shut his eyes, waiting for the drug to calm him.

"Want me to sing a song?" Kara asked.

Sure, Stan Lee thought.

"Ring around the rosie, a pocketful of posies, ashes, ashes, we all fall..."

Stan Lee didn't hear the end.

He'd already passed out.

*   *   *

Four hours after the throngs of reporters had cleared the FBI building at the conclusion of Pipi Esperanza's presser, Doyle Slade crossed Pennsylvania Avenue wearing the Hickey Freeman suit he'd stolen from a man he'd taken in Philadelphia two days earlier. It was important to fit in with others on the street. And though he considered most of the people who worked in Washington D.C. to be clowns, he was not wearing makeup.

Once on the other side of the street, he positioned himself between the FBI headquarters building and the parking structure next door. Slade knew Special Agent Margaret

McCord parked there because he'd watched her exit the FBI building the day before and get her car. He'd considered taking her then and there, between the two buildings, but the risk of others being around was too high. In the end, he decided the best course of action was to wait until the next day and take her *inside* the garage.

Slade glanced at his watch to see the time was 8:45 p.m.

Shouldn't be long now.

Chapter Fifty-Six

A few minutes after nine o'clock Maggie knocked on Newt's door and waited for him to tell her to enter. Even though they were a couple, they went out of their way to behave as if they weren't, especially inside the building.

A few seconds passed and... nothing. She knocked again. Another few seconds passed, and a sense of panic began to set in. Except for the Pentagon, and maybe Fort Knox, there was probably no place in the world more secure than the interior of the Hoover Building, but anything was possible.

Maggie pulled her phone from her purse and dialed Newt's number. On the third ring, the phone answered.

"Hey, what's up? Newt asked.

"What's up is, I've knocked on your door for over a minute. Are you in your office?"

"Sorry, come in," Newt said.

Maggie entered Newt's office to find him leaning back in his Herman Miller Aeron chair, his feet up on the foam foot pillow. "What's going on, are you okay?"

"Yeah, I'm fine," Newt said. "I'm having a hard time getting over the sacrifice Pipi made to protect me."

Maggie walked to Newt's side of the desk and kissed him on the forehead. "She did it because it was the best thing for everyone, including the bureau. It wasn't just for you."

"Still."

Maggie plopped down in a chair and said, "Listen, I need to tell you something that is probably going to piss you off."

"Okay."

"I read Chad in on the situation with Mungehr escaping, and that Mungehr was the one who killed Winston Young."

"How did he take it?"

"Wait, you're not mad? I thought you'd be furious."

"I knew you'd tell him, Mags," Newt said. "If I was afraid of him knowing, I wouldn't have shared the information with you."

Maggie remained silent.

The comment stung.

Newt had just implied he couldn't trust her with information, not a good thing for someone who wanted a career with the FBI.

"Seriously, it's okay," Newt said, reading the look on Maggie's face. "I *wanted* him to know."

"Why?"

"Because you're too close to everything that's been going on to be objective. Chad is a rational person and—wait, that's not how I meant to say that. All I'm saying is that we need him as part of the team, and that means sharing everything we know."

"Then why didn't you tell him yourself?" Maggie asked.

Newt remained silent.

Then Maggie understood: Telling Chad he needed his help would make Newt look like he needed him, and the last thing Newt wanted was for Chad to have the upper hand. In anything. But if it came from her?

The whole thing was passive-aggressive, sexist, and chauvinistic male bullshit. But Maggie knew Newt, and she loved him. He was the smartest person she'd ever met, and the idea Newt had flaws made him that more attractive.

"So, what did Chad say?" Newt asked without answering her question.

"He said that I'm right about Mungehr, that you should be worried about him coming back to D.C. to try and kill you, and that you're a bull-headed idiot for not realizing it." She was still feeling hurt, so she left out the part where Chad had said Newt was a genius.

"So, he ran the program?"

"Jesus, you knew he'd run it?"

"Of course. So...?"

Maggie pulled the Predictive Data Algorithm report from her purse and slid it across the desk. It took Newt less than a minute to review the entire six pages.

"So Mungehr's probably here already," Newt said.

"Probably."

"You going to walk me to my car?"

"Damn straight," Maggie said. "Starting now, you're not going anywhere without me being there."

*　　*　　*

Maggie and Newt pushed through the side door of the FBI building and started the football-field length walk to the parking structure next door. They were completely unaware that the sharply dressed man at the corner, assumedly waiting for the streetlight to change, was watching them.

"By the way, did Chad say anything about the code?" Newt asked as they walked past the man and toward the garage.

"What code?" Maggie said, playing dumb.

"What code do you think? I'm asking about the base code for PDA."

"Oh, the Predictive Data Algorithm program. Yes, he did."

"Well?"

"I think he said it was genius, written exactly the way he'd have done it," Maggie said. "Happy?"

Neither Newt nor Maggie noticed the man at the corner was twenty feet behind them walking in the same direction.

*   *   *

Slade watched the side door of the FBI building open and saw Special Agent Margaret McCord push through the door. Only she wasn't alone. There was a man with her. He was feeling strong and knew he could overpower the female agent. But the man? Probably not.

The man with her was tall, easily six feet, and he looked wiry, like the guys on his high school wrestling team. Maybe he should call off the attack and wait for a better opportunity.

Damn it anyhow.

And then he saw the man at the bus stop, passed out drunk on the bench. And the empty beer bottle.

Slade walked to the bench, grabbed the beer bottle, and waited for McCord and the man to pass by him. Several seconds later, he started walking after them toward the garage.

Once they entered the garage, Slade watched as the pair went to the elevator and pressed the down button. They didn't take the stairs. But Slade did.

Slade hurried, taking two stairs at a time, ensuring he would get to the bottom floor before they did. He made it just in time and took a position against the wall, next to the elevator doors.

A second later, the elevator doors slid open, and Maggie McCord stepped out, followed by the man. Slade stepped forward and smashed the beer bottle into the side of the man's head as hard as he could, sending him crashing headfirst to the floor.

"Hello, Maggie," Slade said.

Maggie had no idea who the man was, or why he'd just knocked Newt unconscious. All that mattered in that instant was to follow her training and neutralize the subject. She took a step back and simultaneously reached into her jacket and drew her Glock.

"Hands up now!" Maggie yelled, pointing the gun directly at the man's chest.

The man raised his hands, smiled, and took a step in Maggie's direction.

"Stop there and get on the ground!" Maggie screamed. "If you don't get on the ground now, I will shoot you."

Slade lowered his hands, then took another step in Maggie's direction.

Maggie pulled the trigger, the sound of the gunshot echoing off the walls of the garage. The bullet seemed to go straight through him. The man did not go down.

"I said, get on the ground!" Maggie yelled.

Slade took another step forward and Maggie pulled the trigger a second time. He was unaffected. Slade took another step in her direction, and she emptied the rest of the clip into him.

Bang.

Bang.

Bang.

Bang.

Bang.

Bang.

Click.

Click.

Click.

"Here, maybe this will help," Slade said, putting the index finger of each hand into the corners of his mouth and stretching his mouth open into an exaggerated, clown-like smile. "I was hoping you'd be in that cute outfit you were wearing at the circus."

Maggie realized it was Doyle Slade. She'd only seen the man in his clown makeup, so there was no way to recognize him.

Slade took a step toward Maggie and a wave of fear swept over her. Then, suddenly, Newt reached out and yanked hard on Slade's ankle, sending him crashing to the cement garage floor.

Before Slade could recover, Maggie was on top of him, doing her best to pin him down. But Slade was too strong. He threw Maggie off him and scrambled to his feet.

At that moment the elevator slid open, and all three of them turned to see Pipi Esperanza standing there.

Chapter Fifty-Seven

Stanton Lee Mungehr was in the driver's seat of the Camry, parked in the basement of the garage next to the FBI building, when the sound of gunfire stirred him from his Ketamine-induced state of unconsciousness. It took a few moments to realize what was happening at the opposite end of the garage.

There were three people:

The first was a woman he recognized: Special Agent Margaret McCord, holding a handgun in her outstretched hand.

The second person was a man in a suit, with a creepy smile on his face.

The third person was lying on the ground and appeared to be unconscious.

Stan Lee watched as the person on the ground appeared to regain consciousness and grabbed the man's leg and sent him onto the floor, where a scuffle ensued. Then the elevator door opened.

"What in the hell is going on?" Kara asked from the passenger seat.

Stan Lee shook his head and shrugged.

He had no idea.

All he could do was watch.

*　　*　　*

"Looks like we're having a party," Slade said, turning his full attention to Pipi. Maggie took the opportunity to help Newt to his feet and steady him as they watched Slade and Pipi face off against each other.

"A going away party," Pipi said. "For you."

Maggie and Newt watched as Slade and Pipi began circling each other, like prizefighters in a boxing ring, deciding how to engage in the fight.

Slade moved to his right, and Pipi took a step to her right to counter his movement, making the fight seem more like chess than boxing.

"I saw your press conference," Slade said. "You looked good up there, too good perhaps. Kind of unfair—a woman leaving her job because she can't hide the fact that she's not aging. That is the real reason you're stepping down, isn't it?"

"Astute observation," Pipi said. "For a clown."

Slade lunged forward and smashed his fist into Pipi Esperanza's face, the punch landing so hard that Pipi was knocked backward, but she was able to stay on her feet.

"Is that all you've got?" Pipi said, taking two quick steps forward and landing a hard right hook to Slade's chin, sending *him* staggering backward. In any fight between two living people, both would be bruised and bloody. Neither was.

"Let's do this," Slade snarled, stepping toward Pipi once again.

"You know how this ends, right?" Pipi said.

"The only way it can," Slade said.

Maggie and Newt stood there, watching as Slade and Pipi lunged forward wrapping their arms around each other, each with their hands on the back of the other's head, to ensure neither of them could pull away.

Then their mouths came together.

In seconds, the color in Pipi's face began to drain away, making her look gray and old. It appeared Slade was winning as Newt and Maggie looked at each other helplessly.

Moments later, the color started coming back to Pipi's face, and Slade began turning gray. It was like watching two TV sets, one with a color picture and the second in black and white—the color oscillating back and forth from one person to the other.

Finally, more and more color drained from Slade's face and hands while Pipi looked like she was glowing with energy. What little color Slade had left drained from him, making him completely transparent.

In the final seconds, before he vanished, Maggie thought she saw something in Slade's eyes.

It was fear.

A moment later, there was nothing left of him, and his empty suit dropped in a mound to the cement floor.

Maggie, Newt, and Pipi stood there, no one saying a word until Newt broke the silence. "What do you want us to do?" Newt said, blood still trickling down the side of his face.

"Call the police," Pipi said. "Tell them you were attacked by two assailants, but they got away."

"I discharged my service revolver," Maggie said.

"It was dark, and you missed," Pipi said. "I'll clear things up with the police tomorrow."

"What about you?" Newt asked.

"Me?" Pipi said as she bent down and grabbed Slade's suit and shoes from the ground and tucked them under her arm. "I was never here."

At the far end of the garage, a car turned on its headlights and the sound of an engine could be heard. "There's someone else here," Maggie said.

The car pulled out of its parking space and drove away.

"I'll get the CCTV footage from the parking garage," Pipi said. "Whoever it was, we'll deal with it in the morning."

*　　*　　*

Stan Lee's hands were shaking as he pulled out of the garage and made a right on Pennsylvania, trying to wrap his brain around what he'd just witnessed. There was only one possible answer:

Ghosts.

"Ghosts?" Kara said from the back seat of the car. "Not the ghost thing again."

Stan Lee reflected on the other time he'd seen ghosts, late at night at the Mulvaney Mansion in Charleston. He hadn't believed in ghosts until that moment, but what he'd witnessed shook him to his core. "Well, then you explain it," Stan Lee said to Kara's image in the rearview mirror.

Kara folded her arms and leaned back, then said, "So, where are we going?"

Stan Lee didn't know, so he said nothing. All he knew was his mission of getting revenge on Newt Drystad would have to wait.

Chapter Fifty-Eight

Newt and Maggie got in the elevator on the basement level of the FBI building and pressed the button for the seventh floor, still reeling from the events of the previous evening.

"Do you know if she was able to get the CCTV footage from the garage?" Maggie asked.

"Don't know," Newt answered.

The elevator doors slid open, and Newt went silent as Chad stepped in. "Jesus, what happened to you?" Chad asked when he saw Newt's bandaged head. "You look like you got hit by a bus."

"Not now," Maggie said.

"Okay," Chad said. "Anyone got an idea what Pipi wants?" Chad asked as the elevator continued upward.

Maggie and Newt remained silent.

Chad went silent, too.

Something big had obviously gone down, but Chad knew better than to press. They'd tell him when they were ready.

When they got to Pipi's office, they found the door open and Pipi busy behind her desk. "Come in, shut the door behind you," she said. "I thought it important we go over the events of last night and discuss the next steps."

"What happened last night?" Chad asked.

Pipi shot Newt a look and said, "You haven't briefed him yet?"

"We weren't sure how much detail you wanted us to go into," Maggie said. "We thought it'd be better if—"

"Last night, Newt and Maggie were attacked by Doyle Slade in the parking garage next door. I killed Slade. Now you're caught up."

"Doyle Slade? You mean, the clown from the circus who attacked Abigale Dietz?" Chad said.

"One and the same," Maggie said.

"Holy shit," Chad said looking in Pipi's direction. "And you killed him?"

"Killed isn't exactly the right term," Newt interjected. "More like she *ended* him."

"We're wasting time," Pipi said. "There are things that need to get done ASAP, starting with the status of the D.C. police. Maggie?"

"They seemed to buy the story, about getting mugged," Maggie said. "They thought the idea that I put nine bullets into the garage wall a bit reckless, but they seemed willing to let it go."

"The fact that we are the FBI didn't hurt," Newt said.

"Good," Pipi said.

"Would you mind if I asked the obvious?" Chad said.

"Which is what?" Pipi asked.

"Why am I part of this?" Chad asked

"Because you're a member of the Ghost Division, and we're dealing with ghosts," Pipi said.

"Don't get me wrong," Chad said. "I mean, I don't mind—it's kind of flattering, actually—but you've got everything covered already without me."

"I wish that were true," Pipi said, "but we don't."

Pipi turned her laptop around. "I got the CCTV footage from the garage last night. Remember the car that drove away? Well, look."

Newt, Maggie, and Chad watched as the grainy black and white image of the garage interior filled the screen, focused on the car as it drove off.

A man Newt and Maggie both recognized.

Newt leaned back in his chair and released a long breath.

"Holy—," Maggie said.

"What am I missing?" Chad said.

"It's Stanton Lee Mungehr," Newt said. "You were right, and I was wrong. I didn't think he would, but Mungehr came back here."

"We need to get this guy and we need to do it fast," Pipi said. "This is an all-hands-on-deck situation, and we can't bring anyone else in. The hands in this room are all we have, and you can't count on me, because I just resigned."

"Well, can you un-resign?" Chad said.

Pipi shook her head. "No. It's done. The integrity of the agency requires that I keep my word. Besides, the president called and made it clear he wants me out today. Better optics."

"So, in addition to chasing killer ghosts, the three of us also have to hunt down Stanton Lee Mungehr without any help," Maggie said.

"No, not the three of you, just the two of you," Pipi said, pointing at Maggie and Chad.

"What about me?" Newt said.

"You're going to be too busy getting up to speed on your new job," Pipi said.

"Oh, no, no, no," Newt said. "I can't—"

"Yes, you can," Pipi said. "I wrote the recommendation letter and sent it over this morning. The president has already agreed. It's you."

"Did you tell him about my condition and still needing to be on meds?" Newt asked.

"Yes, he knows," Pipi said. "He's more concerned with optics than ability. Appointing the youngest director of the FBI ever—a certified genius, no less—is a PR dream, which is precisely what they want."

"Wait," Maggie said. "I want to make sure I understand what's going on here. Pipi, are you saying—?"

"Yes," Pipi said. "Newt's going to need the two of you to carry the load of running the Ghost Division *and* catching Stanton Lee Mungehr, because he's going to be up to his ass in alligators as the next director of the FBI."

—End—

EPILOGUE

Two days after the circus fire...

Mohawk Joe sat in the darkness, listening to the waves crash on the rocks near the shore, feeling guilty that he'd chickened out on his promise to kill the clown. The truth was, he knew Slade was stronger than he was, and he didn't want to die. Again.

After the fire, he'd run off into the woods and watched as a line of Oregon Highway Patrol cruisers arrived, lights flashing and sirens blaring, followed by a fleet of ambulances. The EMTs raced around helping people who had smoke inhalation. Apparently, there was one fatality—a cop, he heard someone say.

As far as ghosts, the entire circus troupe had scattered.

They may have been dead, but they weren't stupid.

* * *

Four days after the circus fire...

Ulrich looked down at the motorcycle speedometer and smiled. He'd never driven so fast in his life, and never on a motorcycle. Feeling a bit guilty, he slowed the bike to 80 mph—running full throttle increased wear and tear on the engine. Then again, it wasn't his bike.

He was heading south on Route 1 along the ocean when he saw her. It was Antoinette, standing on the side of the road with her thumb out. Ulrich slowed the bike and pulled to the side of the road and turned off the engine.

"Nice bike," Antoinette said. "Did you steal it?"

"No, it's a loaner from a friend."

"You surprised to see me?" Antoinette asked.

"A bit," Ulrich said. "What about you, are you surprised to see me?"

"Not in the least," Antoinette said as she approached the bike and swung her leg over the seat behind Ulrich. "Like I told you, I believe in fate. Do you believe in fate now?"

"I guess I must," Ulrich said. "Where are we going?"

"I was planning on hitching my way to South Dakota," Antoinette said.

"What's in South Dakota?"

"There's a circus outside Sioux Falls," Antoinette said. "Small, but you never know—they might be looking for a couple of swingers."

*　　*　　*

Ten days after the circus fire...

The memorial service held at the Dietz Theater in Crimson Cove should have been a somber event, but it turned out to be anything but. Special Agent Maggie McCord volunteered to speak at the memorial service, but Chad insisted he do it since *he* was the person Clay had gone back into the tent to save.

In the middle of Chad's stirring tribute to the courageous sheriff, someone shouted, "It was Onyx! She's responsible for all this!"

When several other members of the Crimson Cove Merchant's Association chimed in, voicing their agreement, Maggie felt she had had to take action and nip the rumors in the bud.

Maggie walked to the stage and took the microphone from Chad's hand and said, "My name is Margaret McCord from the FBI. I am the special agent in charge of the circus fire investigation, and I can assure you—as covered in the coroner's report—Sheriff Clay Daniels' died of smoke inhalation. Onyx Webb has been officially cleared. She had nothing to do with it."

"So, you're admitting Onyx Webb *is* real?" a man shouted.

Having accidentally trapped herself, Maggie did what all good agents were trained to say when trapped: "We're from the FBI. We admit nothing."

*   *   *

Two weeks after the circus fire...

Pipi Esperanza sat on the veranda of the villa she'd rented in the small village of Cadaqués, located on Spain's easternmost point on the Costa Brava. She'd chosen it from a travel brochure because the pictures looked like something one would expect on a Greek island. Plus, the town had three other things going for it. For one thing, Salvadore Dalí had lived in Cadaqués. Second, Pipi was Hispanic and felt she would blend in easily. Most important, however, Cadaqués was a city with an older population—and lots of tourists.

Pipi pulled out her cell phone and typed in *Estadounidense*. It was something a neighbor had called her earlier that morning accompanied by what Pipi thought was a look of disdain. The definition came up. It said the word meant someone from the United States. At least it didn't mean, *ghost*.

*   *   *

Three weeks after the circus fire...

A large wooden chest washed ashore near the Chinook Winds Casino in Lincoln City, Oregon. When a local historian suggested the trunk might be a pirate chest, the casino saw an opportunity. An event was announced during which the mysterious chest would be opened. When the big day came, a thousand casino patrons looked on as a locksmith opened the chest. To everyone's disappointment—except for a black dress, a pair of red shoes, and a pack of French Sorbaines cigarettes— the chest was empty.

*   *   *

One month after the circus fire...

Carlos Rodriguez sat in the front seat of his car in the darkness, holding the 30-Day keychain he'd been given at his Gamblers Anonymous meeting the night before. It had been a long time since he'd sat at a poker table, and he was proud of the accomplishment.

He was also filled with anger.

Carlos knew he was a good card player, way better than average. What had he done to have deserved such bad breaks? If there was anything even close to karma, he was overdue for a big win. If he could get his hands on some cash, he could change his luck. There was only one place he could think of. Fifteen minutes of mental debate later, he tossed the keychain in the glove box and started the car.

Carlos guided his car into a parking space across the street from Noah's Grille and turned off the headlights. It was 12:45 a.m. and the place was dark, as he knew it would be. The only question was whether Ellen had changed the locks.

She hadn't. He was in. Luck was with him.

Now, for the safe.

54 left, 32 right, 1 left. It opened.

Carlos unzipped the blue bank bag and thumbed through the cash. There was at least $3,000, which was more than enough. He could get five hours of poker play, win, and return the cash to the safe with no one being the wiser.

*   *   *

Five hours later Carlos walked out of the Chinook Winds Casino with $26,400 in hundreds he'd won playing No-Limit Texas Hold 'Em in the high roller room. He checked his watch. He had to move.

Halfway back Carlos realized he'd made a mistake by not hitting the restroom before leaving the casino and pulled to the side of the road to relieve himself. Just as he was unzipping his pants, a car approached, but it didn't, instead pulling in directly behind his car.

It was a car he recognized.

Carlos watched as Mickey Spilatro walked stepped from the black Cadillac Esplanade and walked in his direction. "What, you thought you could win big, and nobody would call me?" Spilatro asked.

"Listen, Mick, I was—I was on my way to bring you the cash to make good on what I owe, I swear," Carlos stammered. "The cash is on the front seat, it's all yours."

"Damn straight it is," Spilatro said, pulling a gun from his pocket and pointing it at Carlos.

"Please, Mick, I promise—"

＊　＊　＊

Six weeks after the circus fire...

Noah was in the kitchen of the caretaker's house, making a sandwich when he heard a horn honk outside. When he opened the door, a white cube van was sitting in the clearing. "You Noah Ashley?" the driver asked, climbing out of the van.

"What's this about?" Noah said.

"Got a delivery for you."

"Who from?"

The driver glanced at the paperwork. "Doesn't say."

"What is it?"

The driver walked to the rear of the truck and opened the doors. Inside was Noah's Cherry red Harley Fat Boy. "I'll need you to sign for it."

Noah signed the paperwork and waited as the driver unloaded the bike. Then the driver handed Noah the keys and a carbon copy of the bill of lading. "Where did the bike come from?" Noah asked.

"I already told you, I don't know."

"I'm not asking *who* sent it, I'm asking *where* it was picked up from."

"Sioux Falls," the driver said. "Oh, I almost forgot, there was a note. Hang on." The driver retrieved the note from the cab and handed it to Noah. The note read:

Thanks for the wheels. You were right, the clutch slips from second. Take care of our girl.

As promised, Ulrich had returned the bike. Whatever else Noah thought of the man, it was a classy move. But he didn't like Ulrich's use of the term, *our girl.*

*   *   *

To help heal their strained relationship, Onyx surprised Noah with a three-night getaway at the Otter Rock Resort.

On the final night, Noah bought a six-pack of Rogue Dead Guy Ale from a local liquor store and took it down to the beach. Rogue was Clay's favorite. He should have made time to have a beer with his friend while he was still alive. Now it was too late.

Onyx offered to sit with him, but he waved her off, telling her he'd rather be alone. Like most men, he didn't want anyone to see him cry.

Get Entangled...

About the Authors

Diandra Archer is the pen name for professional speakers and best-selling authors, Richard Fenton and Andrea Waltz. Richard and Andrea have been entrepreneurs, writing and publishing non-fiction business books for over twenty years. Onyx Webb is their first fiction book series. They live in the swamps of Central Florida with their cat Storey, dog, Peppers, and an alligator in their back pond named Gary.

We'd love to hear from you.
Find us at:

Facebook: OnyxWebbSeries

Twitter: @OnyxWebb

Website: OnyxWebb.com

Visit our website and join our email list to receive news on the next book and other special updates and information.

Thank you so much for reading!

It's our goal to really bring Onyx Webb to life someday on the big or small screen... hello, Netflix and Hulu.

Your review of this book will go a long way to help spread the word and we'd be eternally grateful.

www.ingramcontent.com/pod-product-compliance
Lightning Source LLC
Chambersburg PA
CBHW070846250626
47159CB00003B/950